THE
TREASURES OF
MONTAUK COVE

A Montauk Mystery

THE TREASURES OF MONTAUK COVE

•

Diane Sawyer

AVALON BOOKS
NEW YORK

Published by Avalon Books,
an imprint of Thomas Bouregy & Co., Inc.
160 Madison Avenue, New York, NY 10016

Library of Congress Cataloging-in-Publication Data

Sawyer, Diane.
   The treasures of Montauk Cove / Diane Sawyer.
        p.   cm.
     ISBN 978-0-8034-7708-7
   1. Women photographers—Fiction.   2. Montauk
(N.Y.)—Fiction.   I. Title.
     PS3569.A8648T74 2010
     813'.54—dc22

                              2010022426

PRINTED IN THE UNITED STATES OF AMERICA
ON ACID-FREE PAPER
BY HADDON CRAFTSMEN, BLOOMSBURG, PENNSYLVANIA

As always, for my husband, Robert

Acknowledgments

I would like to offer special thanks to:

Kirk and Linda Sawyer and Barrie and Luis Buenaventura, for their encouragement, love, and enthusiasm.

Colin Sawyer, Cael Sawyer, and Sonia Buenaventura, for their unconditional love, wisdom beyond their years, and joyful attitude about life.

Grace Murdock and Peggy Nolan, gracious and talented St. Petersburg writers and exceptional friends, for their advice and continued interest in my work every step of the way from the first draft to the last.

My many family members and friends who encouraged me.

My classmates and friends from Greenport High School who welcomed me home to the reunion in 2007 with kindness, love, and encouragement.

The librarians and staff at the St. Petersburg Public Library, South Branch, for their help and friendship.

The incredible Avalon staff: Faith Black for her enthusiasm for my writing, her assistance with the manuscript, and her uncanny insightfulness which strengthened the storyline and characters. Chelsea Gilmore, for guiding me through the final stages of publication and always making me feel like a member of the Avalon team. Lia Brown and Jen Graham for their steadfast assistance with editing and production matters.

Chapter One

Lilli skipped a shell across the sparkling waters of Grayrocks Beach. Shielding her eyes from the late afternoon sun, she watched young families building sandcastles and collecting shells. She was glad to be back in Grayrocks, a small resort town on the eastern tip of Long Island. What a great place to immerse herself in her photography and forget her troubles.

Troubles? Handsome, sexy Zack Faraday was at the top of the list! He had broken her heart. Lilli picked up fistfuls of shells and hurled them into the water. *Stop thinking about him,* she told herself. *You are a photojournalist on assignment, writing an article about the history of Long Island's North Fork. Attend the convention on Long Island history, and stay focused on your work.*

Lilli ambled along, watching the whitecaps roll toward shore, then retreat, leaving a trail of shells and seaweed as the tide receded. She blinked. Something dark glistened in the sand a few steps ahead. Buried treasure? She chided herself for thinking like the Grayrocks locals. She'd heard many of them at the Corner Café speculating about stumbling upon the treasure of the infamous pirate Captain Kidd. He'd buried his fortune—worth about one million in today's dollars—in the late seventeenth century, possibly on Gardiners Island or Grayrocks Beach.

Lilli hurried over, dropped to her hands and knees, and scooped away handfuls of sand. She rocked back on her heels. A green wine bottle. Some treasure! Probably partiers' litter. Or perhaps last night's heavy storms roiled the water and tossed the bottle up on the sand.

Had someone left the bottle there intentionally? Zack would do something like that if he wanted to win her back. He knew she was

1

coming to Grayrocks and that she loved the beach. She wouldn't put it past him to leave the bottle with a note inside where she would find it. She stood up and scanned the beach huts overflowing with rental umbrellas, chairs, and floats. She would let him know he couldn't treat her shabbily and get away with it.

Lilli's gaze took in the picnic tables nestled among the trees that separated the beach from the neighborhood shops across the way on Bay Street. Was Zack around somewhere, waiting to surprise her? *Get a grip,* she told herself. *He's a busy New York City detective, solving cases, saving lives—when he's not romancing his old flame, the irresistible Isabella. Okay, stop obsessing!*

She picked up the bottle and held it up to the fading sunlight, hoping there might be a note inside. She sighed. It was full. Red wine, from what she could make out through the dark green glass. There was no label; the sandy surf must have washed it off. The cork seemed intact. With luck on her side, maybe salt water or oxygen hadn't seeped into the bottle and spoiled the wine. She looked around, searching for someone looking for something they had lost. No, nothing like that. Parents were rinsing out their kids' pails and shovels and packing up, probably heading home for supper.

Lilli didn't consider finding a wine bottle very surprising. The wine industry had become very popular in Grayrocks and the other towns that dotted the twenty-five-mile strip of Long Island's North Fork. Part of her research for the history article indicated that Long Island wine was a sixty-five-million-dollar industry that employed more than four thousand people. On her drive from New York City to Grayrocks, she'd noticed signs for vineyards and wineries in the soil-rich towns. Tourists came to the area by the busload for wine tours, wine tastings, and wine buying sprees.

As she slipped the wine bottle into her tote, an idea sprang to mind. She would share the bottle with her old friend Gram Jenkins at Baywatch Inn. Gram had invited her to stay at the inn while on assignment. Tomorrow and Saturday, the Convention on Long Island History was holding seminars and workshops in Grayrocks and other towns along the North Fork. Guest lecturers, experts in their field, had been pouring into town for days. Gram said every mouse hole in town displayed a NO VACANCY sign. The town council had approved tents in the parks and campgrounds, even at certain areas along the beaches, to accommodate the crowds.

Before heading back to the inn, Lilli decided to climb Lookout Bluff. On her last visit to Grayrocks, she had decided it offered the best panoramic view of the area, especially beautiful Grayrocks Bay. Now she hoped to see the bay as well as the tents and campers so that her article would be complete, showing all aspects of the conference and its environs. She struggled up the slippery, stony path. When she reached the tufts of grass on top, she went immediately to the pay-per-view telescope. Resting against it while she caught her breath, she gazed out over the water. Now what could those black dots rolling in the whitecaps be?

She slipped a quarter in the telescope's slot and peered into the distance eastward toward Shelter Island and Gardiners Island. Squinting, taming her mass of red corkscrew curls with a ponytail holder, she saw a dozen divers bobbing in the waves, their wet suits glistening in the fading light. A small fishing boat rocked nearby in the choppy water. Gripping the telescope's holding bar, she leaned close and looked into the lens. Blurred images jumped at her. She adjusted the setting. Whoa! The words DOUG'S DIVING SCHOOL stood out on the side of the boat.

Well, how about that? The one guy in the boat, probably Doug, his blond hair pulled into a ponytail, was looking back at her through his binoculars. He wore khaki shorts and a black T-shirt. Lilli noticed a green bottle poking out of a wooden box in his boat. It could be a soda bottle, or maybe a wine bottle. Could the bottle she had found belong to him? It could have fallen out of his boat and drifted ashore. She reached into her tote, pulled out the bottle, and waved it with exaggerated motions. Doug turned toward the divers. He must have told them something about a storm coming, because they all headed toward the boat at once.

Lilli decided that when her magazine assignment was finished, she might call Doug and set up some diving lessons. An avid swimmer and novice snorkeler, she had just finished a class in underwater photography. It would be fun to learn to dive before leaving Grayrocks. Maybe she'd check with Gram, who knew everyone, and see if Doug was a good choice.

Looking again at the divers, Lilli watched them climb into the boat. They didn't have cameras or fishing spears or anything else in their hands to indicate what they were doing. They must be simply learning how to dive. Well, it was a diving school, after all. Lilli knew she had a bad habit of finding intrigue wherever she went. It made her a good photojournalist, but it often got her into hot water. She'd lost count of how many times she'd been accused of sticking her nose in other people's business and stirring up trouble. She was working on overcoming those shortcomings. Last time she took stock, her success-failure rate was running close to fifty-fifty. Okay, more like forty-sixty. She hoped to improve those odds, but it was very hard work.

She looked down at her surroundings. To her left was Grayrocks Beach, now nearly deserted. To her right, beyond a jetty of large gray rocks, stretched Montauk Cove. The area included Clam Hollow Beach and the historic landmark Thirteen Steps, thirteen large flat rocks that descended from Bay Street to the beach. Long ago, the Montauk Indian chiefs used them for their ceremonies. A string of dugout caves lined the base of the bluffs. Archaeologists figured that the Montauks had created the caves for use as steam baths. Later, pirates and bootleggers hid their treasures in those very caves.

The extraordinary hustle and bustle at Montauk Cove intrigued Lilli. Usually the area attracted few visitors, but today many campers, most likely in town for the conference, were busily building fires and preparing supper. Others were traversing the new pedestrian wooden walkway to Bay Street and hauling supplies from their cars and vans back down to the beach. Many people had already pitched their tents near the caves. A sign warned campers that beyond this point the terrain was rugged and not suited for camping. Lilli shot a dozen or so photos and promised herself to take more tomorrow when the light was better.

Taking in all of her surroundings, Lilli was overcome with bittersweet memories. She and Zack had met a year ago here in Grayrocks. She had been on assignment on Labor Day weekend, and Zack, a New York City detective, had come to town to attend his cousin's wedding. Cupid's arrow quickly found its mark, but there was little time for romance to blossom. Here in Montauk Cove, she and handsome, heroic Zack Faraday had confronted a serial killer and barely escaped with their lives. After that harrowing experience, they had returned to their separate lives. It turned out they lived about forty minutes apart, Zack in his New York City apartment and she in a cottage in the village of Suffern, north of the city. They began dating. Before long, they were head over heels in love. Or so she thought. Tears stung her eyes. She missed Zack. She still loved him. She wished that Isabella, his old flame, hadn't come between them.

A cool breeze picked up and the September sky showed off a dazzling palette of warm colors, from pale pink to raspberry, then lipstick red and flame red. Pulling a sweater from her tote, Lilli remembered the saying "Red sky at night, sailors' delight. Red sky in the morning, sailors take warning." A good omen, she thought, tugging her arms into the sweater.

She scrambled down the bluff and crossed Bay Street. She walked past several shops and stopped to admire the display outside Nautical Treasures, where tourists liked to pose for photos. A fierce wooden pirate, leaning against the shop window, wore an eyepatch and colorful clothes, including a red hat, sash, and boots. His eye glinted. So did the golden cutlass he held high over his head.

"Hey, Silas," she called out as she stepped inside. The bell over the door jangled. She saw the wonderful familiar clutter of brand-new merchandise—mugs, place mats, cookbooks, you name it—mixed in with antiques and used merchandise with intriguing past lives. Everything had a nautical theme. Tourists complained they needed to find their sea legs before they could walk around the cramped shop.

"Lilli," said the tanned robust man, about fifty years old. He rushed from the back room, brushing sawdust from his jeans. The light glinted off his glasses, as he pushed them up into his silver-flecked hair. "Welcome back! Gram told me you were coming to town. You're covering the history convention, right?" He leaned sideways and peered past her to the door. "You're alone? No big-city detective?"

"Right both times." Avoiding any talk about Zack, Lilli rested her elbows on the counter next to a jumble of papers, notebooks, and folders. "What's all this?" she asked. "Are you still researching Grayrocks' past?" He amazed her with his quest for knowledge and his desire to share that knowledge with anyone who would listen, especially when the subject pertained to the sea.

"Sorry about the mess." Silas hastily slid two manila folders under a stack of papers. His hands trembled.

Lilli had never seen him so jittery and flustered. Where was his usual laid-back self? "I thought I'd stop by and say hello," Lilli said. "I'd like to find a birthday present for my father. He loved last year's gift."

"A barometer set into a whale carved from elm. I remember. One of a kind." Silas raised his arm and, with the sleeve of his denim shirt, wiped the perspiration from his brow.

He must be coming down with a cold, Lilli thought, pulling her sweater close.

"Take a look around," Silas said. "I'll just be a minute. I need to make a quick call." He stepped into his back room, where he created toys the old-fashioned way, with hammer, chisel, and gauge, for the busy Christmas season. He was well known and respected in Grayrocks as a master craftsman.

"There are some oak pieces with wonderful grain near the back wall," Silas called out. He leaned against his handcrafted bird's-eye maple workbench and worked his hands slowly back and forth along the front edge, as if to check for rough spots that needed sanding. Lilli remembered his telling her that it was his favorite creation. He glanced over his shoulder at her.

She looked away, then turned back just in time to see him reach under the workbench, fiddle with a handle or something, then open a drawer. He didn't put anything in the drawer or take anything out. He just stared down at the contents and then shut the drawer. "I've added some high-quality whaling items," he called over his shoulder. He sounded edgy, almost frightened. And he'd been so nervous when he slid those manila folders under the stack of papers. Something was definitely upsetting him. Could it be something in those folders?

Silas reached for the telephone on his workbench. His back was toward Lilli. Temptation beckoned. She knew she shouldn't give in to it, but old habits were hard to break. Okay, one quick peek, and she'd curb her curiosity. Keeping one eye on Silas, she reached across the counter to the pile of papers and slid out both folders. Scrawled across the top folder were the words *Hey, Tom, hope this helps. Silas.* The initials TJ were printed on the folder's subject tab.

She glanced at Silas, who was still talking away, and looked at the next folder. Side by side were two symbols, each about the size of her hand. They looked like wavy, zigzagging pitchforks, each with three prongs of varying lengths. Strange. What did they mean? Holding her breath, she reached down to open the folders.

Uh-oh. Silas was hanging up the phone. Heart pounding, Lilli quickly slid the folders back in place.

"Lucky you caught me in the shop today," Silas said, nervously polishing his glasses with his shirttail. "I'm closed tomorrow so I can attend the conference. My friend, Professor Thomas Reed, is one of the morning speakers. He was my professor of marine archaeology at New York University, and we stayed friends. He's a brain. I'm a collector."

"What will he be discussing?"

"Marine archaeology and shipwrecks, and he's on the Ships of Olden Days panel. Can't miss that."

"That's right up your alley," Lilli said and ambled toward the back wall. She figured the professor was the "Tom" referred to on the first folder. But why hide the folders? And why be so uneasy about it?

In the distance, police sirens wailed, interrupting Lilli's thoughts. The sirens grew louder. Lilli and Silas turned toward the front door. Several police cars, red lights flashing, whizzed past the shop. They sped past the Thirteen Steps, around the bend and out of sight. Brakes screeched. The sirens ceased.

"What do you suppose that's all about?" Lilli asked.

"Some campers are probably having a wild party and disturbing the peace," Silas said. "A chance for Hank and Grayrocks' finest to strut their stuff in front of tourists."

Lilli laughed. Everyone liked to poke fun at Hank Borden, the chief of police. He took his job seriously when there was an audience, especially if they came from "The City," meaning New York City, and acted superior to the locals.

"I see you still have your figureheads," Lilli said, admiring the three wooden figures, their paint faded and chipped. They had been bolted to ships' bows in years past.

Lilli leaned down, going eye to eye with the wooden eagle figure-head perched on a table in front of the rear window. Its wings were spread; its beak gripped a banner with the word LIBERTY carved in block letters.

Silas came and stood by her side. "I keep jacking up the price so no one will buy them," he said, running his fingers over the eagle's broken claw. "They aren't museum-quality pieces because of their condition, but they're like old friends."

"This is my favorite," Lilli said. She reached up and planted a kiss on the cheek of the wooden Indian chief with the magnificent feather headdress.

"It's probably a guy thing, but I prefer that one." Silas pointed to the carved buxom woman with red-painted lips. She wore a scoop-necked flowing dress with red, white, and blue stripes. "I call her 'Lady Liberty.'"

"You're so patriotic," Lilli teased. He left her alone, and she spent time searching for a gift for her father. Something dark darted past the window, startling her, breaking her concentration. She looked toward the window, but she couldn't see much in the murky light. Must have been a bird, she decided, and put it out of her mind.

"Oh, this is perfect," she finally said, choosing a mahogany box in the shape of a pirate's chest. It held two decks of cards. "Dad and Mom play rummy. They've had a running tally for thirty-five years. Mom's ahead, but Dad says that's because she's the scorekeeper."

As they chatted, Silas wrapped her gift in nautical blue paper imprinted with sailboats. Several times he checked his watch. Lilli got the hint. It was after 6:00.

"I'd better go," she said and swiped her credit card through the machine. A few minutes later when Silas walked her to the front door and hung up the CLOSED sign, she definitely knew it was time to leave.

Outside, she looked up and down the street, wondering whether she had time to visit several more shops. Too late. They were all closed. It was Thursday night in mid-September, and the only shops still open were on Front and Main streets. She decided to go straight to Gram's Baywatch Inn and prepare for tomorrow's work.

The lights went out in Silas' shop. She waited a few minutes near the bike rack where his red Schwinn was chained. She wanted to ask him for suggestions for a thank-you gift for Gram, but he never came out. He must have left by the back door. Maybe he walked somewhere. Maybe he wanted to avoid her. He sure was acting strange.

Lilli looked in the direction the police cars had gone. She heard men's shouts, and then the chief's voice hollered into a bullhorn. She thought about following her instincts and seeing if there was a story in the making over there near Montauk Cove, but she really needed to reread her notes and check her cameras. She patted her tote. And, of course, there was a bottle of wine waiting to be shared. Chin jutting forward and determination in her step, Lilli set out for Baywatch Inn.

Chapter Two

Beneath the darkening sky, Lilli walked briskly away from Silas' shop toward Baywatch Inn. So much for the "red sky at night" theory. A storm was brewing. She passed people carrying bags and packages struggling to stay ahead of the rain. Wind rustled through the elms. Branches creaked and swayed. Mists swirled across lawns. She became aware of footfalls behind her, approaching fast.

She glanced over her shoulder. Several people, some with umbrellas in their hands, scurried down side streets. Once again, she heard footsteps, but this time when she looked, no one was there. It must have been twigs whipping across the sidewalk, she reasoned. Still, her skin prickled. She grasped the wine bottle around its neck, ready to brandish it as a weapon.

A sneeze somewhere behind her pulled her up short. She spun around quickly, her grip tightening on the bottle. Something . . . no, someone—definitely the shape of a person—ducked behind a thick hedge. Now she was sure someone was trailing her. It wasn't her imagination.

Lilli walked more quickly. There, up ahead, the twenty-four room Baywatch Inn with its yellow clapboard exterior stood out from the others. Big fat raindrops pelted the sidewalk. She looked back one more time. The street was deserted. She strode up the crushed-shell path lined with marigolds and zinnias. She glanced at her Bronco parked in the side lot, and then stepped inside before the screen door slammed the backs of her legs. Whew! She was relieved to be indoors, out of the wind-whipped rain and safe.

She checked her watch. 6:30. Guests on the meal plan would have congregated on the glassed-in back porch at 5:30 for complimentary punch and hors d'oeuvres, and then gone to the dining room for dinner at 6:00. Everything went like clockwork at Baywatch Inn. Gram Jenkins would be in the lounge with Bud Conklin. He owned a photography shop in the heart of town. They acted like teenagers. Gram, who was in her sixties, called Bud her "boyfriend," although he was in his late fifties. He called her "Margaret," never "Gram." They always watched the 6:00 news. That was Gram's relaxing time, and she preferred to spend it in the lounge rather than in her apartment tucked away on the second floor. She liked to be close enough to the kitchen and dining room in case any emergency arose. She also liked to be available to guests who wanted advice about Grayrocks' nightlife.

Lilli plucked three wineglasses from a shelf above the wine cabinet in the kitchen alcove, grabbed a corkscrew, pulled the bottle of wine from her tote, and headed down the hallway toward the lounge. As she passed the dining room, she heard muffled conversations and savored the delicious aroma of tonight's special, the catch of the day sautéed in a lemon-butter sauce, sprinkled with almonds. She and Gram and Bud would enjoy the same delicious dinner, based on Gram's recipes, after the guests had scattered.

Perched on a couch with her legs crisscrossed, Gram waved Lilli into the lounge. "Wait until you hear this," Gram said, tossing her thick gray-flecked braid over her shoulder. Bud ducked just in time to avoid being swatted in the face and waved hello to Lilli.

"That conference you're going to?" Gram exclaimed. "One of the lecturers, an archaeology professor, was murdered. Stabbed with a knife!" Her eyes nearly popped out of her head. "At a deserted area of Montauk Cove where he was camping. Can you believe it? They just interrupted the regular news to report it."

Lilli's breath caught in her throat. "Not forty-five minutes ago, I was standing on Lookout Bluff looking down at the campsites along Montauk Cove." She set the glasses and bottle of wine on the coffee table. "Later, I heard sirens wailing and saw police cars rush toward the beach. Now I know why." She plunked herself down next to Gram, keeping her eyes glued to the TV screen.

"Maybe you were a witness," Bud said. "Did you see anyone

suspicious? Anyone with a knife? Anyone running away from the campsites?" His questions came fast, like minnows racing in the currents.

"I didn't see anything," Lilli said, but a feeling of dread crept into her thoughts. "Did you hear the professor's name?"

"No," Bud said. "I wasn't paying close attention."

"Me neither," Gram chimed in.

"Could it be a Dr. Thomas Reed?" Lilli asked.

Gram snapped her fingers. "Reed, that's it." A surprised look crossed her face. "How did you know his name?"

"I was in Silas' shop. He mentioned his friend, Dr. Reed, a guest lecturer. They're both interested in ships and—"

Before Lilli could say more, Skeet Nelson, the teenager who ran errands for Bud and helped Gram clean up after dinner, rushed into the lounge. "Hi," he said. He dropped his Grayrocks High gym bag, with WRESTLING TEAM emblazoned across it, and plopped down in the recliner. "Did you hear the news? A guy was killed down at the cove. Murder! Jeez! I came here from the big city to live in a small town and what happens? Murder!"

The TV crackled. "Another newsbreaking story," said the bubbly blond newswoman, Karlie King.

"Now what?" Bud grabbed the remote and turned up the volume.

"Another murder has occurred in Grayrocks," Karlie said somberly.

"Oh no," Lilli said. "Two murders?"

Karlie turned toward the camera. "The body of Silas Jones, the owner of Nautical Treasures, was found in the bushes behind his shop on Bay Street, near Montauk Cove."

"My God! I just left Silas' shop," Lilli exclaimed. A shiver ran up her spine. "I might have been standing out front while he was being murdered behind his shop."

"I can't believe it," Gram said. Her face turned pale. "He was such a gentle man. Who would do such a—"

"And now, on the scene at Montauk Cove, we have our reporter, Tim Burroughs," newswoman Karlie said, her voice high-pitched. "He has with him our chief of police, Hank Borden. Tim? Tim? Go ahead, Tim."

Blinking away raindrops, Tim stood near the dugout caves by the Thirteen Steps. By his side, holding a bullhorn, stood Hank, squinting into the camera.

"Thanks, Tim, for the chance to speak to the folks of Grayrocks," Hank said. "My officers and I are on the job. We'll have answers soon. Meanwhile, stay calm." He wiped away the raindrops that landed on his face. "Anyone with information should call the police station. That's it." He saluted with his bullhorn. "I have to get back to work."

"I'd better call," Lilli said as the telephone number flashed across the bottom of the screen.

"Let me handle this," Gram said. "Hank's a friend of mine, but sometimes his communication skills are downright crappy."

"I remember," Lilli said. They had had run-ins before. He thought of her more as an adversary, an investigative reporter, rather than a concerned citizen or guest.

"Every loony bird in Grayrocks will be calling," Gram said. "I'll try Hank's private number."

Gram dialed on the old-fashioned phone on the wall. "Hey, Hank. It's Gram. You remember Lilli Masters." She pulled the phone away from her ear and shot Lilli a knowing look. "Yes, I know you're in the middle of a police investigation. Give me some credit. I've been watching you on TV. Lilli was at Montauk Cove, near the campsites. And she was at Silas' shop. She may have been the last person to see him alive."

Gram paused, twisting the phone cord between her fingers. "Yes, Hank, I know she's an outsider, but she knows how things work here. She's trying to be helpful, not take over your job or get in your way. Be nice. She may be your best lead. A slice of my blueberry pie is riding on this."

Gram waved Lilli over to the phone.

"Make it fast," Hank greeted Lilli. "The gosh-darned rain is washing away the crime scene."

Lilli filled Hank in on everything she'd seen, including the two mysterious folders with the initials TJ and the strange design. She added, "Silas may have had the folders with him when he left his shop. I think he was going to give them to Dr. Reed, who was scheduled to speak at tomorrow's conference."

"Describe the design," Hank said, his voice calmer, almost solicitous, as if she held the key to the double murder.

"Lines, squiggles, like—"

"Put those lines and squiggles on paper," he said, not hiding his impatience. "I'll come over to pick up your drawings as soon as I can get away. We need to have a little chat. Don't leave town."

"Of course not. Besides, I'm here for the weekend conference."

Hank coughed his annoyance. "Don't get any ideas about writing this up with crazy drama-queen stuff and scaring people away. This is a good town with lots of good people. We need the tourist dollars."

"Don't worry. I'll be too busy writing about North Fork history to take on anything else." She knew that was what he wanted to hear. But here she was, right in the middle of the action. A really big scoop, the chance of a lifetime, was within reach. Could she pass that by and continue to call herself a writer? She would call her editor first thing in the morning and test the waters about an additional story.

"I may have you come to Silas's shop to look for those folders," Hank said. "We didn't find anything like that near his body." He barked an order at his men, and then came back to Lilli. "Did you see anything suspicious at the campsites along Montauk Cove?"

"No."

"Did anyone see you?"

"I don't think so."

"Did anyone follow you when you left Silas' shop?"

She hesitated. "Maybe. It was getting dark and windy. It's hard to say for sure."

As soon as Lilli hung up, she grabbed some paper and pencils from her tote. "Hank wants me to draw the design I saw on one of Silas' folders. See if you can help me figure out what it is." Everyone gathered around.

"No doubt about it," Gram said as Lilli finished sketching the last of the two sets of squiggly lines. "Those are flashes of lightning."

"Could be," Bud said, "but I'd guess pitchforks."

"Me too," Lilli said.

Bud turned the sketch. "Could be the silk sticking out of an ear of corn."

"Creative, but a bit farfetched," Gram said, nudging Bud in the ribs.

Skeet studied the design. "I'm thinking twigs or stick figures." His eyes twinkled. "Could be two skinny cheerleaders."

A knock came at the door and Gram was there in a flash. Lilli heard Gram's whispers and then her voice loud and clear. "Hey there, Hank. Nice to see you in such a pleasant mood. Come on into the lounge."

With fire in his eyes, Hank barged into the lounge, snorting like a bull and leaving a trail of sandy footprints.

"Lilli Masters," he said, tapping his fist into his open hand, "I'll come straight to the point." Droplets of water dripped from the brim of his hat onto his jacket. "Last year, you were a pain in the neck, doing all kinds of dangerous stuff for a story. Listen up, this is my town. The people in it are my responsibility. Don't even think about sleuthing and snooping. But"—his gruff voice turned suddenly gentle—"if you happen to come across something that will help my investigation, then by all means call me and spill your guts. That's the procedure you will follow. Am I clear on this?"

"Very clear."

"And here's something else to digest along with Gram's fried fish suppers. Last year that detective friend of yours, Zack Faraday, kept his eye on you and protected you. He was on vacation and had lots of time on his hands. Good for him. This year, he's not here. That makes you my responsibility. And I'm a busy man. If you hinder my investigation in any way . . . if I have to leave what I'm doing because of you, if . . . if . . . if . . . you can fill in the blanks, I'll have you banned from the history convention. Am I making myself clear?"

"Clear as the waters of Grayrocks Bay," Lilli said.

Hank cocked an eyebrow and weighed Lilli's words. "No need for sarcasm. Just a simple yes or no will do." He turned and left, huffing and snorting his way to the door, shaking his head and mumbling something about reporters and pests.

"Hank sure gets fired up when you're around," Gram said as soon as Hank left. "You two are like oil and water."

"I like to think we're working on our communication skills," Lilli said cheerily. "Now, what do you say we relax a few minutes with this bottle of wine I found on the beach."

"Good idea," Gram said.

"Could be pirate's blood," Skeet said with a big grin.

"I knew Silas." Bud choked up. "He was in my poker group. A glass of wine would go down well right now." He knelt down and peered at the wine bottle. "As a rule of thumb, if the wine is below the shoulder of the bottle it's probably not drinkable. We're in luck. This wine touches the upper shoulder."

"So this wine is good," Lilli said.

"I'd give it two thumbs up," Bud said.

Gram checked the cork. "Bud, care to do the honors?"

Bud smiled affectionately at Gram and removed the cork. "We're supposed to let it sit and breathe, but maybe tonight we could make an exception." He poured the wine.

"I'll get busy with the kitchen," Skeet said.

Lilli, Gram, and Bud clinked glasses. "Nice and easy now," Gram said with a twinkle in her eye. "In Grayrocks, we no longer rush and gulp our wine. It's a big production. We swirl the wine, we savor the bouquet, we take a sip and roll it around our tongue, we—"

"Let's just drink the wine," Bud said, and everyone laughed.

"This is the best I've ever tasted," Lilli said.

"Me too," Bud said.

"I wish I knew the name," Gram said. "I'd buy a case."

"There's a wine seminar tomorrow at the conference," Lilli said. "I'll take the bottle with me and find out the name. Let's leave a little wine in the bottle. Maybe one of the experts can taste and identify it."

"Spoilsport," Bud teased. "I hate to give up a single drop."

After a delicious supper, topped off with blueberry pie and herbal tea, Lilli went to her room and set out her notes and maps for the history convention. She was immersed in her work when her cell phone rang. She was too busy to check the caller ID. "Hello," she said.

"Hi, Lilli. It's Zack."

Suddenly she was no longer busy.

"I saw the news about the murders in Grayrocks," he said. "Are you okay?"

Lilli could hear the concern in his voice. All the same, she gritted her teeth. "How's Isabella?" she asked frostily.

"I'd like to tell you about that whole episode in person. I'm coming out there Monday. My captain gave me clearance to tell you what's going on."

Lilli guffawed. "Oh, please. You and Isabella. A police matter?"

"Yes, it is."

The tone of his voice told Lilli he was serious.

"Monday afternoon, okay?" Zack asked. "I want to set things straight. I've missed you."

Her emotions played a tug-of-war. She wanted to see him, but she wasn't going to knuckle under to his sweet talk. He would have to win her over. And he needed to suffer at least a little bit. "I'll be busy shaping up my notes on the conference, but I guess I can make time for you."

"I want things to be the way they were," Zack said.

"See you Monday," Lilli said and set her phone down.

For a time after she'd caught Zack with Isabella, she had refused to listen to his excuses. She'd spurned his calls, trashed his e-mails, ignored his text messages, and vowed never to see him again. She was beginning to thaw a little now.

Hmm. He sounded so sincere, so sexy, so . . . Maybe her habit of overreacting had gotten just a wee bit out of control.

Chapter Three

About an hour later, a soft tapping on Lilli's bedroom door broke her concentration. She zigzagged over the trail of notes. From the bureau to the desk, Long Island history lay scattered like a path to the door.

"Gram, what a nice surprise. Come on in."

"Don't mind if I do," Gram said. She stretched out on the bed and laced her fingers behind her head. "I won't pretend I stopped by to see if there's anything you need. I couldn't help but notice you weren't your usual chatty self at supper. There's a problem, isn't there?"

Lilli straddled the desk chair and faced Gram. She picked at the lint on her navy sweatpants. "It's Zack."

Gram snapped her fingers and sat up. "Man trouble. I knew it. Well, you've come to the expert. The rest of the country has Dear Abby. Around here, it's Dear Grammy. Now tell me what's going on."

"Zack is seeing Isabella, an old flame."

"Seeing her, like—"

"Kissing, holding hands in a romantic restaurant. I saw them. Zack saw me."

"Give me some details to work with. When, where—you're a journalist. You know the drill."

"Okay, here goes," Lilli said. "Two weeks ago I was at a photo-shoot of the romantic restaurants in New York City's SoHo district. Guess what?"

"I don't know," Gram said coyly. "You tell me."

Lilli balled her hands into fists. "I ran into Zack at a cozy booth for two. There he was, wining, dining, and kissing Isabella, a smoldering brunet."

"Your heart was breaking. What did you say?"

"I said, 'How could you?' "

"Not bad. And what did Zack say?"

"He said, 'If you would just let me explain.' He caught up with me as I stormed out of the restaurant. Now here's the zinger. He said, 'It's not what it looks like.' Yeah, right. The oldest line in the book. He could have at least tried for something more original."

Gram's eyes lit up. "So when he spoke to you after that, did he have an explanation?"

Lilli bit her lip. "I wouldn't listen. I saw enough to know there's another woman in his life."

"Okay, it's time to go to war." Gram pushed up her shirtsleeves. "Let me tell you what I did in a similar situation."

"Please, go ahead," Lilli said.

"As you know, I snagged Bud, a younger man, with my charms. We shared some good times dancing, biking, and playing bridge. Things were going great. Now here's the part you don't know. One day I saw a certain hot-to-trot widow hanging around Bud's photography shop."

Lilli squinted. "Hanging around, like . . ."

"Like leaning over the counter in her skimpy top. Batting those eyelashes clumped with mascara. Visiting his shop every day. Telling everybody her new hobby was photography."

"What did you do?" Lilli asked, resting her arms on the back of the chair.

"I'm a practical woman, but I have my flirty, romantic side too. I wore Bud's favorite outfit, fixed fried flounder just the way he likes it, rolled in cracker crumbs. I served him a double slice of my blueberry pie, washed down with his favorite Red Zinger tea. Then I looked him square in the eye and told him flat-out, 'It takes two to tango. Not three. If you want to keep on tangoing with me, drop her.' " Gram laughed. "I said 'her' real loud and Bud nearly choked on his Zinger tea. He insisted he wasn't the one doing the flirting."

"What happened to you-know-who?" Lilli asked, trying hard to imagine Gram caught up in romantic intrigue.

"Bud must have had a little chat with her. First thing you know, Bud gave me a present, for no real special reason. It was a CD of tango music. And Little Miss Hot-to-Trot must have taken up a new hobby. Painting this time, I assume, since she's been hanging around Ed's art supply shop ever since."

Lilli laughed. "You're good at this man-woman stuff, Gram."

"Learn from me, Lilli." Gram leaned forward and wagged her finger. "Start by thinking like the professional photographer that you are. Zoom in and get a clear snapshot of the scene. Think back to that restaurant where you saw Zack and . . . what was her name?"

"Isabella."

"What exactly did you see? Think. Did Zack take the lead? Was he kissing Isabella? Or was this Isabella, like Little Miss Hot-to-Trot, pushing herself on a man, in this case, Zack Faraday?"

Lilli squeezed her eyes shut and thought back to the restaurant. Her face flushed as Zack and Isabella came into focus. Her eyes sprung open. "Gram, my imagination was running wild."

"What else is new?" Gram asked with a shrug.

"I had things mixed up," Lilli said. "Isabella was all over Zack. Maybe it was surprise, not rapture, I saw on his face. How could I have jumped to such a conclusion? Why do I have such a problem with trust?"

"Trust Dear Grammy on this one, Lilli. You're a woman in love. This Isabella invaded your territory, tried to take your man. Kick back. Fight. Life is short. We've learned that from what just happened at Montauk Cove." She took a deep breath. "So what did I do? I went for flounder and blueberry pie. Those were the weapons in my arsenal. You'll have to figure out what weapons work for you."

Lilli ran Gram's advice through her mind. "Zack's coming here on Monday."

"That doesn't give you much time—only three days—to work out details, with your big assignment keeping you busy. Ask yourself, is he worth it?"

Lilli nodded. "Oh, absolutely. I'm head over heels in love with him. And I'm really, really ticked off at that Isabella. Who does she think she is?"

"That's the spirit," Gram said. "I'd better leave now. You need to make your plans, and then get some sleep."

"Thanks, Gram," Lilli said and felt as if a weight had been lifted from her shoulders. "I'll see you in the morning." Lilli didn't like to think that love was a game of strategy and that she had to be conniving to win over Zack. It wasn't her style. But Gram had certainly given her something to think about.

Lilli tossed and turned, uncertain as to what she wanted to say to Zack. Disturbing thoughts about the two murders crept into her mind. She couldn't settle down and fall asleep. She kicked off the blanket. The room felt stuffy. She got out of bed and cracked the window, hoping the fresh air would help her drift into sleep.

An hour passed. Lilli checked the time on the nightstand clock: 2:00. More time passed.

On the edge of sleep, Lilli thought she heard the crunch of footsteps on the crushed-shell parking lot beneath her window.

The growl of a dog jolted her upright in bed. Crouched low, she crept to the window and peeked over the sill. From her room on the second floor, she could see her Bronco in the dimly lit parking lot. Someone wearing a dark hooded sweatshirt was at the window on the passenger's side. She couldn't make out his face. He had some kind of tool in his hand. A dog barked, circled the man, and then lunged toward the man's feet. The man jumped back. A hammer or tool of some kind slipped from his hands. He was breaking into her Bronco!

Lilli grabbed a flashlight from her tote and hurried down the hall on tiptoe. She nearly reached the stairs when a shadowy figure came out of nowhere.

"Gram!" She cried with a jolt. "What are you doing here?"

"Sshhh. I live here, you know. The neighbor's dog, Blacky, woke me up. I saw somebody messing with your Bronco." She clutched a rolling pin in one hand and a broom in the other.

"Maybe we should call the police," Lilli said as they hurried down the stairs.

"I already phoned Hank," Gram said, her unbraided hair flowing down her back. "He wasn't any too happy about my three o'clock wake-up call." They reached the bottom of the stairs and crossed the foyer. "I'm not waiting for him. I don't like people skulking around my place, scaring my guests. It's bad for business."

"There's safety in numbers," Lilli said. "Let's go get him."

As Gram swung open the side door, a patrol car pulled in, its tires spitting oyster shells into the shrubbery.

"I've told Hank a million times not to do that," Gram muttered. "He's such a show-off!"

Caught in the car headlights, the burglar took off across the lawn, with Blacky barking at his heels.

Hank pushed himself out of the police car. "Stay here and don't touch anything," he said and chased after the man.

Lilli spotted a tool near her Bronco.

"That was to jimmy open your window," Gram said, nudging the shiny object with the toe of her slipper. "Hank will salivate at this kind of evidence."

Hank returned, huffing and puffing. "He's gone. I'll have forensics dust for prints."

"He was wearing gloves," Gram said. She turned to Lilli. "They don't call me eagle-eye for nothing."

"They should call you crazy," Hank said. "Coming out here, risking your neck. I don't know who's worse, you or Lilli. Let me and my officers handle intruders. Forensics doesn't just do fingerprints. Fibers, all kinds of clues can be left behind."

"Hey, give me some credit," Gram said. "I watch the CSI triple-perfecta: Las Vegas, Miami, the Big Apple. Can't get enough of those lab people toting flashlights and dropping those funny one-line zingers."

Hank stepped close to Lilli. "You seem to be up to your ears in this case. What do you suppose that guy wanted from your truck?"

"I don't know," Lilli said. "Anything of value is in my room."

"Anybody pay special attention to you since you arrived back here in Grayrocks?"

Lilli thought for a moment. "Just Doug from Doug's Diving School. I'd forgotten about that." She explained about the telescope and waving the wine bottle.

"I've never heard of Doug's Diving School," Gram said.

"Me neither," Hank said, "but I'll tell you what. You two get some rest. I'll send the tech team over to look for trace evidence, then I'll check out this Doug." He shook his head in disgust. "I hate it when tourists roar into town and stir up trouble."

"I didn't stir up trouble. Trouble found me."

"Either way, it hurts business. Folks around here are counting on money flowing from people at the conference. I'll be in touch," he said and stuffed himself back into the patrol car.

"Hank used to have the hots for me," Gram confided as Hank spun his tires, "but he saved face and bowed out when I took a liking to Bud. Since then, Hank kind of dances around me, not sure whether to make an exception and be nice to me, or push his weight around— and you see he's got plenty—like he does with everyone else." She chuckled. "Men are such a hoot."

She linked elbows with Lilli. "Let's go see what the Internet can tell us about Doug's Diving School. I've got a new computer with the works—copier, printer, scanner, twenty-two-inch screen, wireless mouse and keyboard—right in my own little kitchen, my command post. Every jazzy bell and whistle I need to run my business and social life."

Ten minutes later, Gram leaned back in her computer chair with contentment written all over her face. "Doug runs a diving school out of Riverhead. I don't know why he was here today. There are dozens of beaches closer to Riverhead."

"Maybe he and his students came here for the conference and decided to do some diving," Lilli said sleepily. But as she heard her own words, she knew she sounded naïve. Divers suddenly interested in the waters near where two murders occurred? There had to be more to it than that.

Chapter Four

The next morning, Lilli drove north on Main Street toward the community center. Her nerves were frayed from all that had happened since she'd arrived in town. Making a sharp turn onto Elm Street, she jerked forward and slammed her foot on the brakes, nearly rear-ending the car in front of her. As far as she could see, a long line of cars was traveling at a snail's pace. This wasn't typical traffic. Everyone in town must be headed to the conference.

She checked her watch: 8:30. The conference would begin in thirty minutes. She inched her Bronco forward and made a mental list of everything she wanted to accomplish.

One: gather ideas for the *Viewpoint* magazine article.

Two: check out the wine bottle she'd found.

Three: watch out for anyone acting suspicious who might be connected to the murders.

Okay, number three on her list was overtaking one and two. She was a freelance journalist. It was just a quick leap to becoming an investigative journalist. That really appealed to her. Write about North Fork history and at the same time investigate a double murder for a separate article. Multitasking at its very best. No journalist would trudge ahead doggedly on one assignment while a huge story was breaking all around her. She was really psyched. Her fingers were itching to snap photos and write text.

Uh-oh. She remembered the promise to herself not to cross the fine line between a photojournalist's professional curiosity and downright nosiness, especially when Hank was around. Promises were meant to be kept. Hmm. Why was that such a difficult concept to grasp when an important story was breaking?

24

Ahead, a long line of right-turn signals blinked.

Lilli's mind churned. Clues to both men's murders could pop up right here at the community center. What did she know for certain? Not much, but TJ, the initials on Silas' folder, seemed like a good clue. TJ could be a place. A thing. Someone at the conference. She had researched the speakers' names, but there was not a single TJ among them. TJ . . . TJ . . . what could it mean?

Beep! Beep! A truck at the intersection ahead on her right beeped and inched forward. The driver leaned out the window and signaled that he wanted to enter the road in front of her. He tipped his hat, a cowboy hat, and hooted, "Thank you, ma'am."

She waved him on. The clean and spiffy truck, overflowing with mums, asters, and dahlias, passed in front of her and turned into the line of traffic. She read the side panel: MATTHISON'S NURSERY, EAST MARION. She knew East Marion was a small town east of Grayrocks, where Gram and Bud liked to bike ride. The driver seemed to know people directing traffic, because they ushered him onto a special road marked VENDORS.

Those flowers sure looked gorgeous. What other varieties did he have? Maybe she would treat Gram to a special bouquet or maybe a shrub as a thank-you gift for welcoming her to the inn—and for her advice about Zack. Later, she would look for Matthison's Nursery and see what he would recommend.

She pulled onto the distinctive concrete drive imbedded with seashells that led to the brand-new Grayrocks Community Center in a parklike setting. The two-story white clapboard building with nautical blue awnings and trim really complemented the character of the seaside community.

Lilli squinted at the sunlight streaming through her windshield. Volunteers, wearing nautical blue T-shirts that read NORTH SHORE HISTORY CONFERENCE, greeted visitors. The comical scene printed on the shirts brought a smile to Lilli's lips. The scene showed barefoot kids in jeans and T-shirts standing on a dock. Wide-eyed and grinning, they untangled items caught on the bait hooks of their fishing poles. Lilli made out the Indian arrowheads, harpoons, whale teeth, bunches of grapes, and seaweed-draped pirate hats. There was even a touristy visor showing mermaids and mermen sunning themselves on rocks. As Gram would say, what a hoot!

When the teenage volunteer saw Lilli's press pass secured to her windshield visor, he smiled, his braces glistening in the morning sunlight, and waved her into the parking lot. A spry silver-bearded volunteer jogged ahead of Lilli's car and led her to the press parking area.

Lilli was not surprised by the joyful spirit that prevailed, even as the media described gory details of the murders hourly. This morning Gram had told her that the "Grayrockers"—that's what she called the people of Grayrocks—didn't want the murders to cast gloom over the conference. Grief was kept behind closed doors and everyone was working at maintaining an upbeat appearance in public.

They remembered the months of planning and work that went into the conference and the excitement that swept through town when their beloved Grayrocks was chosen as a conference site. The Grayrocks *Gazette* stated that conference organizers and family and friends of the victims had issued a statement: Mr. Silas Jones and Dr. Thomas Reed, who shared a vision where education made a difference in people's lives, would have wanted the conference to go forward as planned.

Gram had admitted that when the conference ended and visitors returned home, the sadness that the Grayrockers had put on hold would emerge and possibly overwhelm them. Gram had sniffled once or twice in telling Lilli this. Gram was compassionate, sensitive, and wise, Lilli thought. Other people that Lilli talked to, who were more cynical than Gram, thought that shopkeepers and others with commercial interests hyped the conference and downplayed the murders because they didn't want to scare people away and hurt business.

Lilli stepped out of her Bronco, lugging her tote bulging with cameras, supplies, and her press kit, packed with information about the seminars and workshops. Her head was spinning from all the Long Island history she had studied, especially her own research material that she'd left at the inn. Because the magazine assignment had come at the last minute, she hadn't finished reading everything. That would have to wait until later.

She was amazed at the crowds and huge number of vehicles.

Could Long Island history be this important to so many people? Or was it the free samples of wine and food?

Click! Click! Click! Lilli took photos with her panoramic lens to show the popularity of the event.

Click! Click! Click! She zoomed in to reveal the anticipation on people's faces.

Click! Click! Click! Here. There. Everywhere. Her camera lens found personal touches that would enliven her article. A jaunty straw hat. Bumper stickers that said I'D RATHER BE SAILING and TIME TO WINE DOWN. Sunglasses trimmed with sparkly metallic fish.

Finally the doors opened. Carried along in the crush of people, Lilli made it into the vestibule. She quickly read the bulletin boards that highlighted the events, and then headed to the wine seminar. She hoped someone could identify the wine she had found at the beach; she would like to buy more. She stepped inside room 106. Tables lining all four walls overflowed with displays from local wineries. She approached the distinguished-looking man in a tuxedo who appeared to be in charge. He was nervously patting his forehead with his handkerchief.

"Hello, Mr. Vincennes," Lilli said, reading his nametag. She squinted at the small print that gave his title, president of the North Fork Vintner's Association. "I'm not here as a member of the press. I'm a wine lover and I want to know about a certain wine."

"An oenophile," he said, more a question than a statement. He glanced at her T-shirt, jeans, and all-terrain sandals. "I see that wine lovers, like wine, come in many varieties."

She reached into her tote. "As one oenophile to another, I was hoping you could tell me about a bottle of wine I brought with me."

Mr. Vincennes sighed his annoyance and tilted his chin toward the ceiling. "Consultations are not permitted this morning."

"I'm sorry to hear that," she said and left the bottle in her tote.

Lips pursed, Mr. Vincennes continued staring at the ceiling. "Please come back at four o'clock. There will be a question and answer period regarding our local wines." He sighed again. "We will allow brief questions"—his nostrils flared—"about other wines as well."

"Mr. Vincennes," Lilli said, standing on tiptoe and looking directly into his eyes. "You should taste this wine now. It's the best my friends and I have ever drunk."

Crowds were elbowing their way into the room.

"I'm sorry I can't help you," Mr. Vincennes said, lowering his nose and looking around the room. "As you can see, we are a popular destination."

"Could you make one tiny little exception for me and taste my wine now?" Lilli asked. "It's very important."

"Absolutely not," he said firmly.

Darn, he was stubborn. "Okay, have it your way, Mr. Vincennes," Lilli said, disheartened. "I'll be back at four, with my questions and my bottle of wine." Turning away, she was jostled toward the door by people who were leaving, grumbling that wine samples wouldn't be available until the afternoon session.

Outside room 106, Lilli stopped to get her bearings. Small groups of people were milling around, mainly discussing their choices for the seminars. She saw a handful of gray-haired men in faded, rumpled clothes standing by a table where wine brochures were fanned out. These old-timers had leathery faces, eyes that perpetually squinted as if looking directly into harsh sunlight, and deeply ridged crows' feet. Lilli figured the men probably lived or worked on the waterfront. She envisioned including them in her article.

As the old-timers chatted away, enjoying each other's company—laughing, jabbing at each other playfully, patting each other on the back—they noticed the brochures. They picked them up and leafed through them. One of the men must have said something upsetting. Anger was suddenly written all over their faces. In what appeared to be a heated argument, each man furiously tapped the brochures with his index finger to make his point. One of the men, with a disgruntled look on his face, scribbled something in his brochure and waved the open page in the other men's faces.

Curious, Lilli came and stood by the end of the table and pretended interest in the brochures. The smell of fish stung her nostrils. The men glanced at her, then turned away and lowered their voices. Lilli held up her bottle of wine, hoping they might know something about it. Before she could ask a question, they hurried away into the scattering crowds. The disgruntled man crumpled up his brochure and tossed it into the trash. What could be written in those brochures that angered the men so? Trying to be as nonchalant as possible, she plucked the brochure from the trash and tucked it into her tote.

Her curiosity revved up a notch. She absolutely had to know what the man had written. In case it was really important, like—well she didn't know exactly what—she wanted privacy. She looked left, then right. All the rooms were busy with seminars. The rest rooms? None nearby. Any empty room? She saw a janitor leaving a supply closet carrying packages of paper towels. Whistling away, he flicked off the light switch and walked down the hallway.

Perfect! Lilli ducked inside the supply closet, flicked on the lights, and retrieved the brochure. She flicked through the pages. Two words, *liquid gold,* had been scribbled on the page, which featured a map of Long Island. No other words were written on any of the other pages. What did those words mean? What reference did they have to the conference? She dropped the brochure into her tote.

The door squeaked open. Lilli gasped.

"Hello?" It was the janitor. "I saw the light under the door. Can I help you find something? Towels? Soap?" He looked at her tote suspiciously as if she might be stealing supplies.

"I took a wrong turn," Lilli said, seeing the doubt in his eyes and knowing how lame her excuse sounded. "I'll just gather my things and be on my way."

"Okay, you do that, and I'll get back to work," he said sharply and closed the door.

Relieved that it was only the janitor and not someone who wanted to harm her, Lilli pressed her hands against the wall and took several deep breaths.

The door behind her opened again and, over her shoulder, Lilli saw a flash of navy blue as a man's arm wrapped around her. In a split second, he forcefully covered her mouth with his hand. He grappled her tote away from her and reached inside it. Lilli's heart raced. She struggled to break away, but his muscles were like steel. She turned her head, hoping to see his face. No luck. She jabbed her left elbow into his ribs. Her right hand flailed, then *crack!* Her Irish friendship ring struck his ring. A gold ring. Left hand. Making one last all-out effort to free herself, she squirmed and squirmed. She managed to tilt her head. She didn't see his face, but she got a good look at the ring. It had a crossed-swords design.

The man grabbed the wine bottle, pushed Lilli down, and ran. Gasping for breath, she struggled onto her knees and opened the door. She saw the man sprinting away. He wore jeans and a navy blue hooded sweatshirt.

Feeling frightened and vulnerable, Lilli reached for her cell phone and called Hank Borden, the chief of police. Forcing herself to remain calm and rational so that he wouldn't insist she leave the conference, she said, "Chief, it's Lilli."

"Make it quick," Hank said. "I'm in the middle of . . . never mind. What's up?"

"You wanted me to keep you in the loop."

"Okay, but speed it up."

She spoke rapidly. "I understand you're busy with two murders, and this may be very minor, but I wanted you to know that there was a bit of an incident involving me here at the conference."

"Uh-oh. Incident, you say? Were you hurt?"

"No, I'm fine."

"Was anyone hurt?"

"No."

"That's a relief. Give me the bottom line."

"Someone sneaked up on me, got me in a choke hold, and stole the wine bottle I found yesterday on the beach."

"Did you get a look at him?" Hank asked.

"No, but I'm thinking it could be the same man who followed me from Silas' shop. And maybe that's the same man who tried to break into my Bronco."

"Hold on there, Lilli. Now back up." Hank let out a long whistling breath. "Do you think the man was looking for that bottle of wine then? Do you think it's valuable?"

"I don't know, but I hope to find out. Anyway, he'll sure be in for a surprise when he finds it was nearly empty."

"You need to come down and file a report."

"Of course," Lilli said sweetly. "I'll come by later. Right now, I need to attend some seminars. You know, find out some wonderful historical things about Grayrocks and other towns on the North Fork and report it to thousands and thousands of readers who might—"

"That's enough bunkum. Just be careful. If there's any more trouble . . ."

"I understand, Chief. We're a team, doing what's best for the investigation."

"A team has only one leader. Got it?"

"Yes, sir."

Lilli hung up and immediately called her editor, Jan O'Rourke. Walking down the hallway, she quickly filled in Jan about the murders. "This story is going to crack wide open, and when it does I'll be here, with my eyes open wide for every detail," she said.

"Don't take any chances, promise?" Jan asked, and Lilli could hear her chewing on her nails.

"Promise," Lilli said, and the scene of the man grabbing her flashed through her mind. She saw the ring clearly. Gold, embedded with miniature pirate swords. The kind of jewelry Silas sold in his shop.

Her eyes widened in fear.

Chapter Five

$\mathbf{A}$pproaching room 131, Lilli saw a notice, edged in black, taped to the door. *We regret to inform you of the untimely passing of our guest speaker, Dr. Thomas Reed. Dr. Edward Winfield, professor of archaeology from Andrews University, has graciously agreed to conduct Dr. Reed's seminars.*

Lilli had met Dr. Winfield several months ago. Gram had introduced them at a Montauk Cove picnic. At the time, Dr. Winfield and several of his graduate students were excavating an area of the dugout caves. Lilli enjoyed all their tales about the pirates and bootleggers who had used the caves for nefarious purposes. She wished she could talk to Dr. Winfield right now. He might know something about the pitchfork-shaped symbols on Silas' folders. She remembered that Dr. Winfield had said that he often visited Silas' shop to share stories about Long Island's history.

Still wondering about the meaning of those symbols, Lilli stepped into room 131. In the semidarkness, she crept across a row of people and found a seat. The title of the film, *Ethical and Legal Issues of Shipwrecks,* flashed across the screen. The narrator announced in a deep baritone voice, "The map you see highlights an area of Long Island Sound frequently referred to as Wreck Valley. Through the years, hundreds, possibly thousands, of chartered vessels have sunk there."

Immediately the map of Long Island Sound sparkled with tiny red flashing lights, marking shipwrecks. Then a chart listed the name and type of each known vessel, the year it was lost, and the depth of water at the wreck site. Lilli was astounded by the sheer number and variety of vessels. Tankers, freighters, sailboats, steamboats, liners, cruisers, gunboats, destroyers, and yachts filled the chart. Some dated back to the 1700s. Others were quite recent.

Actors wearing period clothing read diaries retrieved from lifeboats and sunken ships. Other actors quoted eyewitness accounts given by people on shore and nearby boats who had watched in horror as ships besieged by flames, storms, or collisions sank beneath the waves. The film's soundtrack swelled as shipwreck survivors told wrenching tales of recent rescue attempts and the loss of loved ones.

Facing such a huge amount of material, Lilli narrowed the scope to ships lost near Grayrocks. She scribbled in her notepad, *The passenger ship* Commodore *was lost off Horton Point in 1866. The yacht,* Karen E, *off Greenport, in 1981. The tug,* Barataria, *near Southold, 1971.*

The film's narrator commented, "Hundreds of ships lost in Long Island waters have not yet been discovered. But with today's advances in techniques and equipment, they may soon be found. Let's take a look at the OE 6000, a system armed with sonar that can search one hundred square miles of ocean bottom per day."

The narrator paused as underwater scenes of wrecks came into view. While Lilli was scribbling about hulls nearly intact and other ships that looked like junkyards of rusting remains, the narrator continued, "Under the right circumstances, operators on the surface could detect items as small as an individual wine bottle."

At the mention of "wine bottle," Lilli jerked up her head and peered at the screen. Divers were bringing up single bottles and whole cases of wine from a shipwreck.

The narrator said, "Wine has been discovered in ships' pantries, in racks or cases, and even thrown far from the wreck. Wine in excellent condition retrieved from shipwrecks can be so profitable that it is frequently called 'liquid gold.' "

Liquid gold! Lilli's eyes grew wider. Those were the very words written in the brochure by that old-timer. And shortly after that, someone had knocked her down and stolen her wine bottle. Something bad was happening in Grayrocks, and it seemed somehow connected to wine bottles salvaged from the sea. She would get to the bottom of this. The person who could help her, Dr. Edward Winfield, was right here in this very room.

The narrator moved on. "In the old days after a shipwreck, salvers rushed to the shore with their horses and wagons. Paid by the owner, they carted away the tobacco, wine, spices, and anything else the ship had been carrying. However, a finders-keepers mentality often existed."

The narrator paused while a scene portrayed salvers waist-deep in churning water filled with splintered wood and tattered sails. They reached out for every carton, case, and box that floated by. The background music soared and the narrator said, "That was the old-fashioned way of doing things. Then in 1942, Jacques Cousteau invented the Aqua-lung, and salvers were able to dive beneath the seas to rescue cargo. Sophisticated equipment now exists relying on sonar, even robots, and we can now explore ever deeper regions of the sea. But harmony does not necessarily prevail.

"Today when it comes to salvaging valuables from shipwrecks, two opposing views exist. First, there are marine archaeologists. They believe that the found items should be conserved in a museum for present and future generations. Fortune hunters, on the other hand, insist that they are entitled to whatever they find since they take the risks of diving."

The screen went dark, the soundtrack faded away, and the lights came on. Dr. Winfield strode to the podium. Every step of the way, his shock of silver hair glistened under the lights. His rigorous good health gave testimony to his lifelong passion for the outdoors and years of physical labor at archaeological sites. Standing there like a block of granite, he welcomed everyone in his sonorous voice.

Taking the microphone in his big meaty hand, he looked across the sea of faces and said, "Let me begin with an apology. I cannot possibly hope to fill the shoes of Dr. Reed. He is . . . was . . . an archaeologist specializing in nautical issues. I have focused on land issues. I have read Dr. Reed's books and familiarized myself with his research, but I am not an expert in his specialized field. However, let me assure you that Dr. Reed and I have been united in our belief that the environment and our national heritage must be preserved. Let me now introduce Dr. Elena Ellison, a friend of Dr. Reed. She has a real fondness for this particular area of the North Fork, where her relatives still live and where she used to clam and fish and swim. She continues to visit as often as her work permits. Above all, she is a scientist who extends the hand of friendship to all environmentalists."

Men's voices, whistles, and shouts of "Bring her on!" broke through applause. Dr. Ellison walked up the steps to the stage. Her long skirt swirled over her boots as she sauntered toward Dr. Winfield. What a femme fatale, thought Lilli, as she watched Dr. Ellison slink with feline grace across the stage.

"Like Dr. Reed, I am a marine archaeologist," she said, "and I hope to include his point of view in my answers." Her breathless speech, more like a cheerleader after a pep rally than a femme fatale, was an unexpected surprise. As the knowledgeable Dr. Ellison continued speaking, Lilli realized that she showed a passion for the sea and the preservation of history. Her golly-gee-whiz style really won over the audience and stirred their emotions.

Dr. Ellison pressed the microphone into Dr. Winfield's hand and stepped aside.

Dr. Winfield continued, "As you can see, Dr. Ellison and I agree that sunken treasure is of historical significance, giving us an opportunity to study the past, and should be treated with respect. Taking an opposing point of view is Mr. Ronald Larson, a fortune hunter—"

"I prefer treasure hunter," said Mr. Larson, a feisty, muscular guy with short jet-black hair, who rushed onto the stage and wrested the microphone from Dr. Winfield, "but you can call me Ron." He swaggered toward the audience, a mix of boyish charm and guy-next-door demeanor. "Just to set the record straight, I don't have a degree in marine archaeology or any other kind of archaeology. I don't need that stuff for the sink-or-swim world of treasure hunting. What I do have is a slew of swimming medals and a degree in physical education."

He dropped to all fours and quickly completed several one-handed push-ups, then jumped to his feet. Applause quickly filled the room and Ron Larson flashed a dazzling smile. *What an exhibitionist,* Lilli thought, but he was winning over many in the audience.

Dr. Winfield took back the microphone and clutched it to his chest. "And now Ron, Dr. Ellison, and I will entertain questions from the audience."

Ron piped up, "And please make your questions entertaining."

Lilli noticed a blond man with a ponytail rush down the aisle and take a seat near the front. It was Doug from Doug's Diving School, the man she'd seen through the telescope at Montauk Cove. She was convinced he had a bottle of wine very much like hers, so she wanted to meet him. He had been so close to the caves and seemed interested in watching the coast with his binoculars. Maybe he knew something about the murders or her bottle of wine. But all that would have to wait. She turned her attention to the speakers.

The lively question-and-answer period moved along at a brisk pace. Doug and many others cheered and whistled each time Ron, the treasure hunter, got the upper hand. The cheering made Ron smirk and Dr. Winfield sneer. Dr. Ellison remained somewhat aloof during those exchanges. But as the questions became more personal, Dr. Ellison, who had a snappy personality and amusing anecdotes to relate, seemed to have more in common with Ron Larson than with Dr. Winfield. Ron and Elena—they addressed each other by first names—seemed very chummy. Dr. Winfield seemed the odd man out. What were they up to, Lilli wondered. The entire presentation seemed contrived, like they were trying to create drama and draw attention to the ownership of recovered cargo.

Lilli wanted to ask about liquid gold, like what made it so valuable and why didn't it spoil at the bottom of the sea, but she decided to wait until she could speak to Dr. Winfield alone. She also wanted to tell him that her bottle of wine had been stolen. Maybe even show him the brochure with the message "liquid gold" that had angered the men.

Lilli's attention was drawn to the podium. The debate had heated up and become very personal. Ron grabbed the microphone. "Pardon me for stating the obvious, but Dr. Winfield is an egghead who lives in the ivory tower of the academic world. He should come on board, get his feet wet, and visit the real world of supply and demand."

He sure did speak from the gut and tell it like it is, Lilli thought.

Dr. Winfield's face turned red. He looked like he was about to explode. "Marine archaeology is the flashy newcomer on the block," Dr. Winfield said. "Archaeology in caves and underground is still the age-old tried-and-true science. Let's not forget that Dr. Reed admitted that his specialty owed much to the pioneers who came before him—the archaeologists who worked the soil."

Back and forth Ron and Dr. Winfield went, arguing their opposing points of view with humor, anger, and sarcasm. The audience enjoyed every minute of it. So did Dr. Ellison. But Lilli believed that Dr. Winfield's skillful use of facts and figures made him the winner.

When the debate ended, Lilli approached the podium. Dr. Winfield saw her, maneuvered his way through the crowd, and drew her into a big bear hug. "You won that debate hands down," she said.

"Our bad-cop, me, and good-cop, Dr. Ellison, wasn't too over the top?" he asked, grinning broadly. "We hoped our routine would get Larson to show his true colors."

"It worked," Lilli said.

"Flattery will get you anywhere," he said jovially.

"I must speak to you. I need your help. I hate to sound dramatic, but—"

The public address system crackled. "Dr. Winfield, please return to the podium," came a shrill announcement.

"I hate to leave"—Dr. Winfield said, holding Lilli at arm's length—"but I'm a wanted man. How about meeting me at six at the Grayrocks Tavern? They're hosting a wine-tasting gala for speakers and their guests. The tavern itself is worth the effort. It has a history of shady bootleggers and sinister meetings, just the kind of place a journalist would appreciate. What do you say?"

The public address system squawked. "Dr. Winfield, please come immediately to the podium," cried the high-pitched voice.

Dr. Winfield pointed at Lilli as he backed away. "Six o'clock. Grayrocks Tavern."

"See you then," she called out as he elbowed his way through the crowd toward the podium.

Whew! Struggling toward the door, Lilli felt relieved that she could discuss her concerns with Dr. Winfield. But then doubts nagged at her. How well did she really know him? Gram's granddaughter had admitted that he could be self-serving, especially about his career. Gram had said that since his wife's death, he'd become moody and sometimes lashed out at people. Lilli had heard about the rivalry in the academic world and during the debate she had seen hints of it, especially between the two branches of archaeology. Did Dr. Winfield intend to capitalize on the death of Dr. Reed to advance his own career?

Lilli's cell phone pulsed. She checked the caller ID. It was Chief Borden. Had he cracked the case already? The words *journalistic scoop* raced through her mind as she returned his call. She chided herself. She could be just as self-serving in her career as Dr. Winfield might be in his.

"Chief Borden," she said amiably into the phone. "How may I help you?"

"Forensics finished at Silas' shop. I'd like you to come over here and see if everything looks the same as it did yesterday."

"Yes, sir," Lilli said. She looked over her shoulder. She thought she saw Dr. Winfield talking to Doug, the diving school instructor, but she couldn't be sure. She headed for the front entrance, wondering if they knew each other or if they were meeting now for the first time.

The sun was shining, a gentle breeze skimmed the leaves and flowers, and she had just been invited to a crime scene. What more could she, a freelance journalist on assignment, ask for?

Chapter Six

As she drove toward Nautical Treasures, Silas' shop, Lilli willed herself to remember every detail about yesterday's visit. Fragmented images—papers, folders, merchandise, toys, and tools—flashed haphazardly through her mind. Now she wished she'd paid more attention to her surroundings. She never imagined that her recollection of details would play a part in a murder investigation.

When Lilli arrived at Silas' shop, Hank opened the door to greet her. "Just pretend Walt and me aren't here," he said, nodding toward his officer, a wiry man of about forty. "Look around. See if anything looks different."

"I'll try my best," she said and set to work searching through the folders.

The ticking of the clock on the wall and Walt's snapping gum resounded in her ears. "Chief," she called over to him, "it's just as I suspected. The folders I told you about with the initials TJ and the weird squiggly designs are gone. I'm convinced Silas had them with him. It's not such a stretch to say he was probably murdered for those folders."

"Don't get carried away," Hank said. "You're not a witness to a murder, and you're certainly not a detective. Got it?"

"Sure," Lilli said sweetly, not wanting to be asked to leave the crime scene. She checked the front of the shop. "Nothing seems out of place," she said. As she headed toward the back, she stopped short. She couldn't believe her eyes. "All three of Silas' figureheads are gone!" she exclaimed. "They were right here yesterday."

Hank and Walt came to her side.

"One was an Indian, over six feet tall," Lilli said, holding her

39

hand high over her head to show the height. "The second was an ea-gle, life-size, sitting on that table right in front of us, with wings spread. And the third, Silas' favorite, wore a red, white, and blue-striped dress. He called her 'Lady Liberty.' "

"Keep looking," Hank said, hardly able to conceal his delight in Lilli's discovery. "Maybe something else will pop up. Meanwhile, I'll check this out with my team. Those figureheads didn't get up and walk or fly out of here." He made a call, telling someone, probably the officer on duty, about the missing figureheads. Hank referred to them as "this new development in the case."

"I can tell you one thing," Lilli said as soon as Hank signed off.

"Let's hear it," Hank said eagerly.

"Those figureheads were heavy. It would have taken at least two strong men to carry them away."

"Thanks for the tip," Hank said and shot Walt a glance that said *Don't you hate it when people tell us what we've already figured out?*

Lilli got the message. She walked through the shop again, looking left and right, up and down. She gave one final look at the back wall and the empty spaces where the figureheads had rested. She stopped abruptly.

"What is it?" Hank asked, not masking his enthusiasm.

"Something or someone darted past that window last night when Silas and I were discussing his figureheads. Someone might have been watching us. They might have been planning to kill Silas. This is giving me the creeps."

Walt's eyes opened wide. "If you had gone out the back door in-stead of the front—"

"Walt," Hank cut in, "get the crime techs here. Have them check for footprints outside the window and fingerprints on the windowsill. You know the drill."

"I'm on it," Walt said, grabbing his cell phone.

"Think hard, Lilli," Hank said. "Did you see anything else? Do you remember anything else?"

Lilli started again at the front door and retraced her steps through the shop. Hank kept his eyes on her the entire time, as if willing her to see something important to the case.

"Nothing. That's it," Lilli said apologetically.

"Okay," Hank said. "You can run along back to the conference."

"But—"

Hank held up his hand as if stopping traffic. "We'll take it from here."

Not wanting to cross Hank, her best connection to the murder investigation, Lilli decided to leave. She had her hand on the doorknob when Hank's cell phone beeped. She lingered, poking through her purse for her keys, hoping to gain a few moments to pick up a lead.

Hank listened to whoever had called, nodded a few times, and then turned to Walt. "Those figureheads were here at four this morning during the shift change. Then things went hinky. The new guy got an emergency call from his wife and rushed home. Says he was gone maybe a half hour—"

"He goofed," Walt cut in. "No surprise there."

Hank's cell beeped again.

"We're on our way," Hank said into his phone and snapped it closed.

"More news about our case?" Lilli asked.

"My case," Hank said. He turned to Walt. "I think Silas' figureheads just surfaced. Kids building a fort in Big Creek Woods behind the recycling center found them. One of the kids, Sweeney's boy Kyle, remembers seeing them in Silas' shop. Let's roll."

"I'll go too," Lilli said.

Hank gave her an exasperated look.

"You need me. I know what Silas' figureheads look like."

Hank sucked in his breath. "Yeah, like there's a hundred missing figureheads in Grayrocks."

Unwilling to give up, Lilli trotted behind Hank. "I'll follow in my Bronco."

Minutes later, Lilli was trying to keep up with the patrol car as Hank and Walt whipped toward the outskirts of town. She figured they planned to leave her far behind, but she pursued like a shark after a school of fish. After some harrowing twists and turns on Old Pond Road that kicked up swirls of dirt, sand, and leaves, they pulled up to the recycling center. Lilli slammed on her brakes and swerved into the shell-scattered area next to Hank.

A freckle-faced blond boy, wearing a T-shirt, jean shorts, and muddy sneakers, waved Hank toward the woods.

"Over here, Chief!" the boy shouted, tugging down his baseball cap.

"That's Kyle Sweeney," Hank said to Lilli as she came around to his side of the car. "Hey, I think you exceeded the speed limit back there. I could ticket you, but time's a-wasting." Judging from Walt's grin, this ride from hell might have been some kind of initiation ceremony they put journalists through.

"Kyle's the one who called us," Hank said. "He won that cell phone in some gosh-darned contest last month. Goes around with one of those do-hickeys in his ear, talking a blue streak. Thinks he's a big shot."

"He said he learned that from you, Chief," Walt said. He cleared his throat. "About cell phones being cool. Not about being a big shot."

Lilli suppressed a laugh. Walt liked to cut people down to size. Everyone, including Hank, was fair game. She wondered if her turn was coming soon and how funny it would be to be the object of his ridicule. Egged on by Walt, she sprinted by his side across the grass toward the woods. Lumbering behind, Hank wheezed like a train running out of steam. Lilli figured that Walt was using her to gang up on Hank, two to one. His half-smirk, half-smile told her he enjoyed getting the upper hand against Hank.

"This way!" came Kyle's voice from the thick groves of pine and spruce.

Lilli and Walt swatted away low-hanging branches and hurried along. Lilli didn't dare take her eyes off the ground. She was afraid that the logs and slick carpet of damp leaves would trip her. She had no time for a sprained ankle, especially now with a big story ready to crack wide open.

Finally they came to a small clearing. Kyle and three other boys stood there, leaning on their beat-up shovels. They protectively guarded the makings of a fort: an old canvas tent, a pirate flag, and a pile of tattered burlap bags that, according to the printed design, had once stored Long Island potatoes.

After Hank's hasty introductions, Kyle said, "We found the ship stuff over there." He pointed toward a log poking through leaves and ferns. "None of it was here yesterday. Somebody must have dumped it after we left."

"It's like a burial ground," Lilli said, stepping over the log and seeing the remains of Silas' three figureheads lying among the leaves.

Hank bent down for a closer look. "Now, why would somebody lop off their heads and hack their bodies apart?" he asked.

"I think we figured it out," Kyle said, pulling burrs from his socks. "Whoever hacked them up must have thought they were hollow."

"These days, everybody's a Sherlock Holmes," Hank said out of the side of his mouth.

"They were looking for something hidden inside," Kyle said, his eyes big as saucers. "Like a treasure map. That's our theory."

"Yeah," Larry said and popped his gum.

"You got that right," said redheaded Willy.

"We're right, don't you think so, Chief?" asked Joey, yanking up his jeans.

Kyle crossed his arms over his skinny chest. "Hey, Chief, do you have a better theory?"

"I do," Hank said, curling his lip. "And here it is. You boys should be in school."

"We got out early," Kyle said. "Our teachers went to the conference."

"But they gave us an assignment," Willy said, curling his lip.

"We have to do something educational," piped up Larry.

"Yeah, and write a report on it," chimed in Willy, with a scowl.

"What's educational about a fort?" Hank said, lifting a burlap bag with the toe of his shoe.

"It's not just any old fort," Kyle said. "These woods were important in Grayrocks' history. Lots of amazing things happened here."

"Yeah," Willy said. "Thomas Jefferson rode his horse through these woods."

"The Montauk Indians signed a treaty here." Joey stomped his feet as if to make his point. "Right here."

"That's great, boys," Hank cut in, his voice dripping with sarcasm. He turned to Walt. "Jeez, I'll be glad when this history conference is over. Then maybe we can get back to the present and quit thinking about the past."

He kicked a pile of leaves. "Okay, Walt, why don't you secure the area while I call this in. See if something got dropped in the leaves. Maybe a monogrammed lighter with clear fingerprints and a drop of blood, like on the TV shows. You know, clues coming at you left and right, and the case is solved in an hour. Forty-nine minutes if you don't count commercials."

"Sure thing, Boss," Walt said and stepped away, his eyes focused on the ground. "Lighter . . . blood . . . fingerprints coming up," he mumbled into his scrawny chest.

Hank snapped open his cell phone and punched in some numbers. "When the crime techs are done checking out the window at Silas' shop, send them out here to Big Creek Woods behind the recycling center. We got some possible evidence in Silas' murder." His face grimaced with exasperation while he listened to whoever was on the other end. "You'll see when you get here. Meanwhile, I wanted to give you a heads-up. Three heads-up to be exact."

Hank didn't laugh at his own little joke. Neither did Lilli. They looked at each other intently, but didn't say a word. She was thinking, *Trouble has really come to Grayrocks.* She knew from Hank's worried expression that his thoughts were similar to hers. This murder case was baffling. And very disturbing.

Chapter Seven

Returning to the conference, Lilli struggled through crowds gathered around exhibits from the Suffolk County Historical Museum, the Southold Indian Museum, and the East End Maritime Museum. Everyone was admiring crafts and items relating to Montauk culture, whaling history, and folklore. She snapped a photo of the biggest attraction, a thirty-foot whaleboat tipped on its side to display antique whaling tools and scrimshaw. Skeet Nelson, the teenager who did chores for Gram and Bud, came toward her with a notebook in his hand and a pencil tucked behind his ear.

"Hey, Skeet," she said. "How's it going?"

"I'm feeling lucky. I just bought four raffle tickets." He waved them at her. "How'd you make out with the wine bottle?"

"It's a long story. I'll tell you later at Gram's," she said, not wanting to take up his time with her scary experience. "What are you up to?"

"I'm looking for info for my senior history paper. Then I have to get back to classes."

"What's the topic?"

"Well, our choices were limited to things we could research here at the conference. Then we tie in that research with whatever we gathered from other sources. I went with Thomas Jefferson because there's so much stuff about him in books."

"Taking the easy route?" Lilli teased.

"The fast route," Skeet said. "My working title is 'Man of Many Talents.' You know, Jefferson the horticulturist. Jefferson the author. The inventor. The wine lover. I liked 'The Father of Archaeology' the best. Did you know Jefferson found an Indian burial mound on his Virginia estate? He developed excavation techniques."

"That's news to me," Lilli said.

"It was to me too. I'm on my way to the seminar about famous people who visited Long Island's North Fork."

"I take it Jefferson was one of them."

"Right. He seems like a cool guy, galloping around here on his horse." Skeet opened his notepad and ran his finger down the page. In a very professorial voice, he read, "On June 13, 1791, Thomas Jefferson, then secretary of state under President George Washington, rode horseback across Suffolk County."

That was the second time in the past thirty minutes Lilli had heard that tidbit about Jefferson. The boys who found Silas' figureheads mentioned it too. Maybe she needed to work the president into her article.

"I wish I could stay for some of the wine seminars," Skeet said, "but I could lose my chance at a scholarship if I cut classes. I was hoping to pick up info there about Jefferson too."

"I could do that for you," Lilli said.

"Really? That would be great."

"Give me some idea what you're looking for."

Skeet flipped through his notebook. "I came across Thomas Jefferson's place in wine history."

Lilli read his notes over his shoulder. *Thomas Jefferson, third president of the United States, was considered America's first distinguished viticulturist and the greatest patron of wine and grape growing in the country. He became wine advisor to Presidents Washington, Adams, Madison, and Monroe.*

"I'll see what I can dig up for you," Lilli said. She was happy to research anything to do with wine. Something might come up that would tell her about the bottle she'd found on the beach. It could happen. Some of her best stories came about by chance, by being in the right place at the right time.

"Thanks. See you later," Skeet said. He was about to take off when a cute teenage girl rushed to his side and linked arms with him.

"Oh, Lilli, this is my friend Maggie." He smiled. "Maggie's the star of the girls' track and field team."

"Hi," Maggie said, and then gazed up at Skeet all dreamy-eyed.

Ah, young love, Lilli thought as they took off. She turned the corner. There were cheers and laughter coming from the first room on her right. She heard a man's deep voice counting "ten . . . nine . . . eight," down to one, followed by bursts of applause. What was going on? The energy in the room drew her in like a magnet. She saw six artists holding up their sketchpads. People were mixed among the artists to watch them work and peer at their nametags. The artists were in some kind of contest racing the clock to create interpretations of words called out by the audience.

Lilli made her way past a petite blond—Mia, according to her nametag—and stood behind her. Mia wore huge chartreuse hoop earrings that swung back and forth. A paint-spattered tunic flowed over skinny black pants that touched the tops of her chartreuse sneakers.

"Suggestions?" the moderator asked, starting the next round.

A woman in the back row shouted out, "Long Island!"

"Long Island it is," the moderator announced.

The six artists threw themselves into their work, sketching furiously. According to a sign on the wall, they were students from the Art Academy in Mattituck, a nearby town.

"Sixty . . . fifty-nine . . . fifty-eight." As the moderator began the countdown, Lilli followed Mia's quick pencil strokes. Mia deftly sketched the outline of New York State. Then she placed a giant fish with its eye near New York City and its supersized two-pronged tail poking into the Atlantic Ocean. She detailed the fish's tail with baroque flourishes—lines, curves, and swirls—that resembled the ornate patterns on elegant dinner forks. With only five seconds remaining, Mia scrawled the title of her work, *Fishy Forks,* across the bottom of the page.

Lilli liked the work. The large elaborate tail called attention to the fishing industry on Long Island's North Fork, which extended past Grayrocks to Orient Point, and on the South Fork, which extended to Montauk Point.

"Time's up, pencils down," the moderator exclaimed. The artists held up their work and received cheers and applause along with several surprised "oohs" and "ahs."

The judges awarded third place to a sketch that showed Indian feathers and arrowheads scattered across block letters that spelled LONG ISLAND. Mia won second place. First place went to a young man with a Mohawk haircut, who sketched Long Island vertically, covered with fields of blossoms poking up from a vase. Instead of a two-pronged fish tail, his end of Long Island burst into two bouquets of flowers. Beneath the sketch, the artist had scrawled the title, *Flora.* In parenthesis he wrote, *The name that Henry Hudson gave to Long Island. It means flowers.*

"Next round!" the moderator called out, and the artists picked up their sketchpads. "Suggestions," he shouted.

"Liquid gold!" Lilli exclaimed.

"Liquid gold it is!" the moderator announced and began counting. Lilli was amazed at the results. Four of the six artists portrayed wine bottles and sunken ships in their sketches. She had never heard of liquid gold until today, but the expression apparently was well known around Grayrocks. Maybe she had overreacted when she'd found those two words written in a brochure. She definitely needed to rein in her habit of finding intrigue around every corner . . . and on every page.

When the event ended, Lilli chatted with the artists and photo-graphed them holding their sketches. She bought the three prize-winners' drawings of Long Island, rolled them up, snapped a ponytail holder around them, and set them in the bottom of her tote. Before leaving the room, she plucked her to-do notepad from her purse and jotted down, *Check on TJ for Skeet.* Skeet was such a great guy. She wouldn't leave until she found information for his senior paper.

Clicking her pen shut, Lilli stared at her notepad in disbelief. TJ, the very initials on Silas' missing folders, practically jumped off the page. TJ! Thomas Jefferson? It couldn't be. She must be losing her mind. What on earth could he have to do with the mur-der of Silas Jones or Dr. Thomas Reed? She added to her to-do list to find out what TJ was doing on the North Fork besides riding horseback. She wouldn't let her overactive imagination encourage her to jump to faulty conclusions and get pushy and nosy and turn people off. No way. She had turned over a new leaf. *Reason . . .*

logic . . . those were the words she would abide by now. But wow, what if . . .

Someone behind Lilli tapped her on the shoulder. Startled, she dropped her notepad and spun around. She found herself staring into ice-blue eyes. It was Doug from Doug's Diving School.

"Excuse me," he said.

"Just a minute." She bent down to retrieve her notepad, but Doug beat her to it.

"I think this is yours," he said, as he handed her the notepad.

"Thanks," she said and dropped it into her purse. She wondered if he had read over her shoulder what she had written. She was definitely going off the deep end, suspicious of everyone.

"I'm Doug. And you're—"

"Lilli. Lilli Masters."

They shook hands.

"I noticed you in there buying those sketches," Doug said. "And I believe that was you yesterday waving to me from Lookout Bluff." He looked left and then right. His face grew serious. "There is something we should discuss, something that might be of interest to both of us."

"What might that be?" Lilli asked, glad there were plenty of people around. She wanted to find out what he knew about the murders and the wine, but she didn't want to be alone with him. After all, he could be involved. Anything was possible. He could—

"How about if we discuss this over a cup of coffee?" Doug asked. "The Terrace Café is right outside. They serve a great brew."

"Sounds good to me," Lilli said, looking out the window and seeing crowds of people.

Doug steered her out the door toward the terrace overlooking beautiful flowering gardens. He plunked down opposite her at a table for two and waved over a waitress. After they ordered coffee, he said, "Let me come straight to the point."

"By all means," she said eagerly.

"You bought three sketches. I'd like to buy the fish one for my niece. She's crazy about fish. I'll pay you double what you paid. What do you say?"

Lilli was immediately suspicious. Doug was fidgeting with the sugar packets. He couldn't look her straight in the eye. "What's your niece's name?" she asked.

"Uh . . . that would be Mary." He stumbled over the two syllables.

Lilli doubted that Doug even had a niece. He probably made up that story just to get the sketch. "I can't part with it," she said. She couldn't wait to get back to Gram's and examine it. There must be something there that she hadn't noticed, something important. But she had no idea what. Maybe Bud, Gram, and Skeet could help her figure it out. They were locals. The artist was local. Doug was from a nearby town. It must have meaning to them that she couldn't decipher.

The waitress set down their coffee mugs along with two compote dishes filled with a creamy yellow pudding. "Compliments of the chef, this is *samp*. That's short for *sappaen* pudding, a Montauk Indian treat made with corn," she said and hurried to the next table.

Lilli tasted the samp. It reminded her of Gram's delicious corn custard casserole. She gripped her mug with both hands and rested her elbows on the table. She grew impatient as Doug took his time savoring the samp and sipping his coffee.

"You brought me here to talk about that bottle of wine, didn't you?" Lilli said through the steam rising from her mug.

Doug nodded.

"You had a bottle just like it on your boat," she said. She wasn't certain they were identical, but she wanted to test Doug's reaction. "I saw it through the telescope."

"You're wrong," Doug protested.

"Come on. I saw something green in a cooler on your boat."

"You're right about the color, but it wasn't wine. It was soda. I don't drink and dive," he said.

Lilli chuckled despite herself. She figured Doug was amusing her with a line he'd used many times. "You mentioned there was something of interest to both of us. I'd like to hear about it."

"First, you need to let me see your bottle of wine."

"It's gone. My friends and I drank it."

"Where did you get it?"

"Hold on. You said there was something that would be of interest to both of us. So far, all you're doing is asking me questions."

"Before I tell you anything, I need to know where that bottle came from." He reached across the table and gripped her hand.

"Let go," she said. She pulled her hand free and stood up to leave.

"If I were you, I'd sit back down," he said, and his face turned cruel. "Now."

Chapter Eight

I'll sit back down when you agree to answer my questions," Lilli snapped. "And if you put your hand on me again, I'll scream for help."

"Okay," Doug said. "Sorry. I overreacted. There's a lot of stress in my life right now."

"That was a wine bottle in your boat, am I right?"

He nodded, and she sat down.

"Was it similar to the one I had in my hand?"

Doug leaned forward. "From what I could see through my binoculars, I'd say so. They have the same distinctive shoulders and neck," he said, pulling a pen from his pocket. He sketched a wine bottle on his napkin and tapped it where the shoulder of the bottle sloped away from the neck. "Where did you find yours?"

"Washed up on the beach below Lookout Bluff," Lilli admitted, realizing that the bottles were identical. "What about yours?"

He whispered, "In a dugout cave at Montauk Cove."

"Near where Dr. Reed's body was discovered?"

"I don't know anything about that body or any other body," Doug said defensively.

"I'm curious," she said. "Which cave?"

He averted his eyes. "I don't know."

"We need to be honest with each other." She cut him a sharp look.

"The cave furthest from the wooden steps, closest to the water."

So it is the cave nearest the campsite where Dr. Reed was murdered, she thought.

"We've got company," he said. "It's the Bond brothers, Frank and Carl, and they don't look happy." He crumpled the sketch and dropped it under the table. "This could turn nasty."

52

Lilli looked up in time to see two guys, mid-thirties, approaching the table. They resembled each other with their piercing dark eyes, hawk nose, and pronounced cheekbones, but marked differences set them apart. The taller one had shoulder-length dark, curly hair and a two-day stubble. The other was clean-shaven, face and head. They were very tan, rugged, outdoor types, like Doug. She remembered seeing them in the audience during Dr. Winfield's debate with Ron Larson. They had sat next to Doug. They cheered raucously for Ron each time he spoke in favor of treasure hunters keeping the cargo they had found.

"We need to talk to you, Doug," the dark-haired brother said, then nodded to Lilli, "when you're done hitting on the pretty lady."

"No problem, Frank. I'm done," Doug said, standing up. He shrugged at Frank and said, "I must be losing my charm. She won't have anything to do with me. Seems I'm not classy enough for her." He tossed a few bills on the table and said, "Okay, Miss Stuck-Up, if you decide to come down off that high horse, you know where to find me."

Lilli figured that Doug was willing to continue their conversation in private, but he didn't want the men to know who she was, so she played along. "If you'd like to quit acting like a Neanderthal and apologize, call me."

As soon as the words left her mouth, doubt set in. Was Doug protecting her or just hoarding his inside track? For now, she would trust Doug.

Lilli overheard the clean-shaven brother, Carl she assumed, refer to her as a "snooty broad."

As the men turned away, Lilli furtively fished a business card out of her purse. Keeping her eye on the men, she passed it to Doug.

"Later," Doug said, quickly stuffing the card in his jeans pocket. He left with the men. Actually, it was more like they hustled Doug along. He looked like someone about to walk the plank.

Lilli plucked her digital camera from her tote and quickly checked the zoom lens. "Hey guys, wait a minute," she called out and heard her own nervous laugh. "You forgot something real important."

Doug and the brothers stopped and turned toward her.

"You forgot to smile!" She snapped another photo.

The brothers glared at her.

"Thanks!" she called out, pretending to ignore their menacing looks and put her camera away. She was curious about who they were. She wished she'd thought to notice if either was wearing a ring with crossed pirate swords. Each brother was tall and athletic enough to have been the guy who wrenched the wine bottle from her. She checked the image. Too bad. It was fuzzy. She thought she'd found the thief, but she couldn't see if either brother was wearing a ring.

Lilli lingered in the Terrace Café and jotted in her notepad, *Talk to Doug. Find out more about the wine bottles.* She picked up the crumpled sketch from under the table and tucked it in her notepad. She added to her list, *Research wine bottle shapes.* With every passing minute, her list grew more tentacles, like an octopus groping into the hiding places under the sea.

Chapter Nine

The next few hours set Lilli at a dizzying pace, packed with seminars and workshops. So much to look at; so much to learn. For the moment, thoughts of the murders slipped away. She liked best the ship-in-a-bottle workshop, where the demonstrations were filled with humorous anecdotes that would certainly delight *Viewpoint* readers. It delighted her too for personal reasons. It reminded her of Zack. He had one in his apartment that he and his uncle had made when Zack was a young boy. On and on she went, taking notes and photos, not editing her thoughts, not even stopping to consider how she would tie everything together. Finally, needing a breath of fresh air and a chance to clear her mind, she stepped outside.

Nearby were displays from North Fork nurseries and florists. Interspersed among them were booths that exhibited lawn decorations, gardening tools, decorative fencing, whimsical birdhouses, and so much more. A short distance away she saw a sign that read MATTHISON'S NURSERY, definitely the largest nursery display among the dozen or so represented. Here was her chance to choose a pretty shrub for Gram's yard or a potted plant for Gram's patio.

She sauntered over and saw the man who had been driving the Matthison Nursery truck earlier. He was answering a young couple's questions about shrubs. He sure looked like a cowboy with his hat, gloves, boots, and jeans. The nametag pinned to his denim shirt read CHUCK MATTHISON. Waiting until he was free, Lilli admired the hanging baskets and walked among the potted shrubs. The standout was sedum with deep pink flowers. Among the flowers, blue paradise phlox caught her eye.

She glanced at Chuck, who, from what she could make out,

seemed to have captivated the couple with advice and anecdotes.
Probably in his mid-thirties, he was average in height and looks, but
he had a very engaging way of holding people's attention—including
hers. Knowledgeable and personable, he would make a nice addition to the personal interviews she hoped to sprinkle throughout her
article.

"May I help you, ma'am?" he asked and tipped his hat as the
young couple strolled away. He didn't seem to recognize her from
this morning at the intersection.

Lilli tapped her fingers on her press credentials. "I'm writing a
magazine article about the North Fork's history. Maybe something
like how landscaping has changed over the years. Anything you'd like
to tell me that would interest my readers?"

"Well." He removed one of his gloves and wiped the perspiration
from his brow. "That depends."

"On what?"

He squinted at her press credentials. "On you, Lilli Masters." His
smile was warm and friendly. "I'm sure I can spin a few yarns and
relay some interesting local stuff . . . if you'll have a drink with me
later."

Lilli smiled and shook her head. "Does that line work most of the
time?"

"Hardly ever," he said with a shrug and a smile, "but I keep trying.
Come with me and we'll talk." Lilli followed him to a wheelbarrow
overflowing with containers of orange and rust coleus, and he began
setting them on a table. "I'm third-generation Matthison in this town,"
he said. "I spent some time in Wyoming on a ranch. I really liked
those big skies and wide-open spaces, but I'm home to stay now. You
want history, you said? Well, my grandfather designed the Grayrocks
Tavern. It's the most unusual building for miles around. Have you
seen it?"

"No, not yet."

"Don't miss it. It's the work of a creative genius. The local library
has lots of material about my grandfather and his architectural creation. His detractors—people with small minds and narrow views—
call him a misfit. He was a misunderstood man, born way before his

time. My father, who inherited the tavern, was a builder. He loved the natural landscape, just as my grandfather did."

"And you are carrying on in their tradition," Lilli said, impressed by his passion for his family and their talents.

"I'm trying. Landscape design is my first love."

Lilli looked up at the sound of loud voices. It was several of the men she'd seen earlier heatedly discussing liquid gold. Now they seemed to be debating something—the price, she figured—with a vendor who was exhibiting sundials and other lawn ornaments. His sign, handwritten in large block letters, read SHIP TO SHORE. Lilli thought that many of the ornaments, such as cannons, winches, chains, anchors, and harpoons—some items polished, others painted, and many left in a natural weathered state—would seem more at home on a ship than on a front lawn or in a garden.

"Chuck, do you happen to know those men?" Lilli asked.

Chuck looked their way and shielded his eyes against the sunlight. "I don't think so. Well, not by name. But I've probably seen those old salts hanging out at the fish camps around here. Mostly they sell bait and amuse tourists with their tall tales. You know, about the enormous fish they just caught but doesn't seem to be anywhere in sight."

"Sounds interesting. I was thinking of interviewing them."

"Don't waste your time," Chuck said. "I've been told you really can't believe much of what they say, especially about where the fish are biting."

Lilli was disappointed. So much for learning anything about their connection to liquid gold. She couldn't chat with Chuck any longer. She needed time to go over her notes before the next seminar. "I need to get back to work," she said. The shrub for Gram would have to wait too.

"What about that drink?" he asked, somewhat shyly, while he set out snapdragons.

She picked up one of his business cards and dropped it into her tote. "I'd like that. I'll be in town until Monday. Okay if I call you?"

"My pleasure, ma'am," he said and brushed away the loose potting soil that had spilled across the table.

"Oh, one more thing. I'd like to pick out some plants or a shrub for a friend of mine and could use your help. Maybe you know her? Gram Jenkins."

"Sure do. Everybody knows her."

"What would you recommend?"

"Something to fit her personality." He winked. "Wildflowers? Seriously, I've seen her raised patio in the back. Potted plants on the steps would be nice."

"Thanks," Lilli said, liking his choice, and waved good-bye.

She wandered away from the nursery area searching for a quiet spot to work on her notes. But displays of kitchenware with nautical themes hand-painted by local artists captured her attention for almost an hour. Finally she settled on a bench beneath a shady maple tree and jotted down the questions she wanted to ask the wine specialists at the 4:00 seminar.

"Penny for your thoughts," a man's voice said.

Startled, Lilli looked up and saw Chuck Matthison standing in front of her. He had a very serious expression on his face.

"Just some notes," she said.

He sat down next to her. "We're both busy so I'll come straight to the point," he said, gripping and releasing his fingers again and again. "I followed you here to have a serious talk."

So that explained his somber expression.

"You're going to hear things about my family, some of it rumors, some outright lies and very hurtful to my family's memory," he said. "I don't know you well, but you seem like a decent person. I'm asking you for a favor." His piercing gaze held her attention.

"I'm listening."

"Write about my family's contributions to Grayrocks. Don't print lies, rumors, and the crazy stuff about a Matthison Curse."

"What curse is that?"

"Crazy stuff. That the tavern is haunted by the spirits of Montauk Indians. A place where the Matthison men die young, because of my grandfather's supposed poor judgment."

"What do—"

"I'd like to talk to you more, Lilli, but I can't neglect my customers." He jerked his thumb over his shoulder toward his nursery display. "I have to go." He stood up and repositioned his hat.

Lilli thought he seemed very vulnerable.

"I'd like us to have that drink we talked about," he said. He seemed to have a hard time saying all this, as if he were by nature shy and reserved.

"I have your number. I promise I'll call," Lilli said, and in the blink of an eye he was gone, striding back to his nursery exhibit. Mystery. Melancholy. Chuck Matthison had cornered the market on both. She wanted to talk to him again and find out what made him tick. A mysterious man appealed to her as a writer . . . and as a woman.

Lilli whipped out her cell phone and tapped in numbers. "Gram? It's Lilli. You know everybody for miles around. What can you tell me about Chuck Matthison and his family?"

"Those Matthisons," Gram mused. "A bad strain there. They die young. Chuck's grandfather had a heart attack in the tavern's wine cellar when he was in his forties. Chuck's father was killed in a freak accident, an electrical fire in the basement of the tavern, when he was in his early forties. Some people say it's because of the Matthison Curse."

"I was hoping you knew about that. I'm all ears."

"Folks around here say Chuck was frightened by it," Gram said. "It predicted he would die in the tavern wine cellar while still a young man. Just like his grandfather and father."

"But that hasn't happened."

"No. It's common knowledge that to escape the Matthison Curse, Chuck stays away from the place. You know, afraid of fulfilling his destiny, stuff like that. He spends most of his time alone in his big house in East Marion, near his nursery. But he comes to Grayrocks every now and then. Way I hear it, he walks the beach at night near the tavern. Comes out of nowhere like a ghost and scares people. He left town for a while. Went to Wyoming to escape what he called 'a small town's small minds.' Anyway, that's the local scuttlebutt running along the Grayrocks' grapevine. Chuck has his own explanation."

"I'd sure like to hear it."

"He claims people who were jealous of—here comes some highfalutin' words—jealous of his grandfather's artistic vision brought about his untimely death. He says they started rumors that his grandfather had built the tavern on sacred Montauk burial grounds. As the story goes, this outraged the Montauk spirits and they sought revenge. They come back every generation to kill off a Matthison male."

"What about his father's death?" Lilli asked.

"Chuck has his own interpretation for that too. He claims that electricians working at the tavern were jealous of his father's wealth. They murdered him and stole money and jewelry from his safe."

Lilli was intrigued. "What do you think about the Matthison Curse?"

"Just a bunch of hooey from guides who want to drum up business for Ghost Tours in Grayrocks. The tavern isn't built on sacred burial grounds, but it makes for a good ghost story. Ghosts. Revenge. Baloney."

Still curious, Lilli said, "I'm guessing Chuck's not married."

"That's right. You have your eye on him? Let me give you some advice. You hit the jackpot with Zack Faraday, that handsome detective of yours from New York City. Zack's nice, funny, and crazy about you. Stay away from Chuck Matthison. You don't need weird in your life. You still there, Lilli? You're awful quiet. You listening to my advice?"

"I am, Gram, but some strange noise is distracting me. I'll call back later."

The *thwomp thwomp thwomp* noises grew louder. Lilli looked up and saw Mia, the sketch artist, hurrying toward her carrying a long tube, the kind used for mailing maps and artwork. *Thwomp thwomp thwomp*, Mia's chartreuse sneakers struck the wooden deck. Her earrings swung wildly with each stride.

"There you are," Mia said, gulping a breath. "I've been looking for you everywhere."

"Sit down," Lilli said, making room for her on the bench. "What's wrong, Mia? You seem upset."

Gulping another breath, Mia plunked down. "I need my *Fishy Forks* sketch. You can have your money back."

"Of course you can have it, but tell me what's wrong."

"Please. There's no time to discuss this."

Lilli could see the fear in her face. "Give me a clue what this is about," Lilli said firmly.

Mia looked over her shoulder and then back at Lilli. "Someone made me an offer I can't refuse. It's the chance of a lifetime, the lucky break I've been waiting for." Her words tumbled out.

"Tell you what," Lilli said. "You wait right here, and I'll bring you the sketch."

"Thanks," Mia said and breathed a huge sigh of relief.

"Just give me five minutes," Lilli said and took off with her tote slapping against her leg. She went straight to the media room and got in line for the copy machine. Three long, slow minutes later, it was her turn. Making sure no one saw the fish sketch, she made two copies of it. Moving on to the fax machine, she sent a copy to Gram at the Baywatch Inn. Then she pulled out her cell phone and punched in numbers.

"Hi, Gram. It's me, Lilli, again. I'm in a rush. Please help me out. Look at the sketch of a fish in the tray of your fax machine. See if you can figure why two people are desperate to buy it from me. Please don't show it to anyone. I'll see you soon. Thanks."

"Don't hang up," Gram said. "I've spotted some guys driving back and forth in front of the inn. Casing the joint, I'd say. I called Hank. He's checking it out. Be careful, Lilli. You may have been seen at Montauk Cove or at Silas' about the time those murders occurred. Maybe you saw something you shouldn't have. It could be you they're after. Watch your back."

"I will. Thanks, Gram. Wait, don't hang up. Those two guys could be the Bond brothers, Frank and Carl. They seem like serious troublemakers. I saw them hassle Doug—you know, the owner of Doug's Diving School."

"I'll call Hank and tell him. Woo-eee! He loves it when Grayrockers cooperate. But, oh my, he dances a jig if a visitor comes forward with useful information. You know Hank. He has a low opinion of outsiders. Not that you're an outsider in my book, but—"

"A jig, huh?" Lilli said. "I'd sure like to see that."

"Keep coming up with clues and tips for Hank and you'll hear fiddlers fiddling a mighty-fine tune."

Lilli hurried back to Mia, who was pacing back and forth and checking her watch. "As promised," Lilli said and handed Mia the original sketch. She nervously touched the bottom of her tote to make sure the rolled-up copies were safe.

"This really means a lot to me," Mia said as she rolled the sketch and slid it into the tube.

"Please tell me what's going on," Lilli said.

"I can't," Mia said, gripping the tube so tightly her fingernails cut into it.

"You really should," Lilli said. "Two murders happened in Grayrocks yesterday. The killing spree might not be over."

Mia's eyes went big and round. "I promised I wouldn't say anything."

"Who did you promise?" Lilli asked. She expected Mia to name Doug or the roughneck Bond brothers.

Mia waved away her question. "I've said too much already."

"Just tell me what's so important about this sketch," Lilli said.

Mia shook her head. "I don't know. I wish I'd never sketched it. I thought it was a fun piece. Now suddenly everything's turned so serious."

Mia stood up. "Please promise you won't follow me. You could get me into big trouble."

"I promise," Lilli said begrudgingly.

Mia tucked the tube under her arm and headed toward the parking lot.

Lilli quickly pulled her binoculars from her tote and stood up. This wasn't being nosy. This was being a good investigative reporter tracking down a story. In two seconds, she had Mia's chartreuse earrings and sneakers in her sights. She saw Mia dart through the parking lot and stop at a black Lexus SUV, parked beneath a maple tree. Mia handed over the tube to the driver, a man wearing sunglasses, and immediately left. Lilli squinted. She couldn't get a good look at the man because his face was hidden by the leafy branches. She could see only the first letter, L, of his license plate.

The door to the Lexus SUV opened. The man stepped out and caught up to Mia. Lilli still couldn't get a good look at his face. She thought Mia might be in danger, that the man was about to grab her and drag her back to the Lexus. Lilli pulled out her cell phone to call the police.

While punching in the numbers, she caught glimpses of the man and Mia walking between cars. He didn't force her. She seemed to be going along willingly. Lilli held off punching in the final numbers and studied the man. Tall. Salt-and-pepper hair. Broad shoulders. Gray T-shirt. Black jeans. No one she'd seen before. He moved gracefully, like a panther. He could be a dancer. No, too beefy.

Lilli adjusted the focus. Mia and the man shook hands and went their separate ways, apparently parting amicably. Lilli closed her cell phone. This seemed like a personal matter, not police business. Lilli jotted in her notepad, *Check out Mia's family, neighbors, and adult male friends at art school.*

She turned the page. *Ask Hank to check out mystery man's black Lexus SUV. L begins license plate. Late model. Dent in right rear fender. Admit right up front this is a hunch.* She had the habit of gathering facts even when she wasn't sure if she could use them. Thanks to Zack Faraday, she had acquired a taste for detective work.

Lilli put away her binoculars. She sat down on the bench and tried to make sense of what had happened since the murders at Montauk Cove. All this talk about curses, revenge, and early deaths at the tavern made her feel uneasy, as if the worst was not yet over. What would come along next? But Lilli had little time to wonder about anything. It was time for the wine seminar.

Chapter Ten

Lilli rounded the corner toward room 106 and ran into people approaching from all angles. What a commotion! They rushed. They waved friends onward. They shouldered and elbowed their way toward the room. Carried along with the flow, Lilli caught pieces of conversations. Everything was about wine. The age of wine. The aroma—spicy, fruity, on and on. Bottles. Labels. Reputation. Price.

She overheard conspiratorial whispers. "The free wine will flow in ten minutes." "You get what you pay for." "There ain't no such thing as free lunch—or free wine."

Squeezing into the room, Lilli turned toward the sound of ear-piercing blasts. Ah, there was the source. A workman blowing a whistle and carrying a stepladder made his way through the crowds to the center of the room. He set the ladder down next to Mr. Vincennes, the president of the vintner's association, who was struggling to maintain order. Gripping a microphone in his pale fingers, Mr. Vincennes climbed midway up the ladder and looked down imperiously at the crowd.

"Ladies and gentlemen," he began above the din. "Due to the larger than expected crowds, we have decided not to field questions from a central location. To foster a more intimate encounter, our experts have stationed themselves at tables around the room. At my suggestion"—he puffed up his chest until Lilli thought the buttons on his shirt would pop—"banners posted along the walls above our experts indicate their special fields of expertise. For instance," he said and paused dramatically. Then while pointing here and there, he rattled off a list of topics. "History of wines. Wine as an investment.

Apéritif wines. Holiday wines." On and on he went until Lilli's head swam with details.

Finally Mr. Vincennes said, "Please line up at a table, and experts will answer your questions. To be fair to all, we will observe a three-minute time limit per person." He looked down, and his nose twitched with displeasure. "Wine samples will be available momentarily. German, French, and local wines here." He pointed left. "Italian, Chilean, and Portuguese there." He pointed right. "Here comes what you've been waiting for. Our wine tasting."

Cheers filled the room.

Mr. Vincennes narrowed his eyes as he began to descend down the ladder. "We respectfully ask you to please limit yourselves. Thank you." His words were drowned out by the sounds of happy voices.

Lilli headed toward the table beneath the banner FAMOUS NAMES IN WINE HISTORY. A petite silver-haired woman seated at the table fidgeted with the timer.

"My name is Lucy Cradshaw. How may I help you?" She set the timer at three minutes.

"I'm helping a friend research Thomas Jefferson's place in wine history," Lilli said. "We know that Jefferson was a connoisseur of wines and a wine advisor to four presidents. Is there anything else you can tell me?"

"Of course, dear," Mrs. Cradshaw said. "During his stay in France, he experimented with grape growing at his Paris garden on the Champs-Elysées. His home was called the Hôtel de Langeac," she said, her merry eyes twinkling.

"I was hoping you could tell me more about Thomas Jefferson's wine in America," Lilli said politely.

"My favorite tidbit," Mrs. Cradshaw said, a smile lighting up her heart-shaped face, "is that there is great speculation that bottles may still be floating around with Thomas Jefferson's initials on them."

Lilli's breath caught in her throat. Bottles floating around! Could the bottle she found have belonged to Thomas Jefferson? What a crazy idea! But it could explain why a man stole it and why Doug wanted it. The label had washed off, so there were no initials, but still . . . No, this was a really crazy idea! How could his wine have ended up on a Grayrocks beach? "Please tell me more," Lilli said.

Mrs. Cradshaw flipped through pages of a spiral notebook stuffed with articles, handwritten notes, and e-mails. "Ah, here we are," she said, pointing at a newspaper clipping. "In 1985, a wine connoisseur paid $156,450 for a single bottle of Jefferson's Laffite Rothschild 1787. In 1997, a bottle of Jefferson's 1800 Madeira sold for $23,000."

"How did Jefferson's wine turn up centuries after his death?" Lilli asked.

"There's a logical answer," Mrs. Cradshaw said. "He had a large supply of wine and he was a generous man."

"Could you elaborate?" Lilli asked, pulling a notepad from her tote.

"Certainly," Mrs. Cradshaw said. "When Mr. Jefferson was the ambassador to France, he visited many wine regions. He collected and sent the best wines home to America. When the French Revolution erupted in 1789, he returned home and took more than three hundred bottles of wine with him. He served the wines at his home in Monticello and sent some to President Washington, including Hermitage Rhones, Medoc Bordeaux, and others," Mrs. Cradshaw rattled off and Lilli scribbled away, spelling the French words as best she could.

Mrs. Cradshaw continued, "Later, during Jefferson's own presidency, his wine was served at the White House. He frequently gave wine to his friends as gifts. Apparently, many bottles were passed from one generation to the next. Every now and then, a bottle shows up and is met with great fanfare in the wine world."

She leaned forward and whispered, "Some are sold on the black market at sky-high prices. Super-rich people, who wish to remain anonymous, hire agents to purchase the wine so they can impress their wealthy friends, who hire agents too. You know, keeping up with the Joneses by showing off their wine cellars. Wouldn't you love to be invited to one of those dinner parties?"

"You said his wine bottles might still be floating around," Lilli commented, trying not to sound overly eager. "Did you mean literally floating around in the ocean?"

"It's just a figure of speech," Mrs. Cradshaw said, "but it is possible. His wines traveled by ship from France to America. Maybe a few got tossed overboard during a storm." Her timid laugh crinkled her nose. "Maybe there was a party on deck. Oh, I'm talking like a crazy person. Wine bottles eventually sink."

Rrrriiinnnggg! The timer went off.

"Can you tell me anything else?" Lilli asked hurriedly.

"Yes, dear," Mrs. Cradshaw said. "Mr. Jefferson preferred wine to whiskey. He drank three glasses of wine a day and considered it a healthy drink. He was a very intelligent man." She winked. "We could learn a lot from his example."

A ruddy-faced man standing behind Lilli tapped her on the shoulder. "Your three minutes are up."

Lilli thanked Mrs. Cradshaw and reluctantly moved on. She jotted in her notepad, *Research TJ's wines,* then proceeded to a table beneath the banner WINE BY REGION AND BOTTLE. This time the expert was none other than Mr. Vincennes himself.

"Mr. Vincennes, how nice to see you again," Lilli said.

He tugged at his jacket sleeves, and then set the timer. "Ah, if I remember correctly, you have in your possession a particular wine you are curious about."

Lilli didn't wish to waste her precious three minutes explaining that the wine had been stolen. "I'm actually intrigued by a particular green bottle. Would you happen to have pictures or descriptions of the various shapes of wine bottles?"

He plucked a book from the pile in front of him that threatened to topple over at any moment. "You have come to the right place. Now let me see. Green glass, you said?" He turned several pages. "Red or white wine?"

"Red."

He whipped through more pages. "Country of origin?"

"France, I believe."

Pages flipped by.

"Cork or cap?"

"Cork."

More pages flew.

"Long cork or cork stopper?"

"Long cork."

"Now we have something to work with," Mr. Vincennes said, looking extremely pleased. He turned several pages and pointed dramatically at pictures of four wine bottles all in a line.

Lilli leaned closer. Number three looked very much like the bottle she had found on the beach and the bottle Doug had sketched at the Terrace Café. But was it identical? She couldn't be sure.

"Could you be thinking of the Burgundy?" Mr. Vincennes asked, tapping his finger beneath the first bottle. "Note the sloping shoulders and the distinctive fat girth."

"Possibly," Lilli said.

"Perhaps the Rhone, with the angular sloping shoulders," he said. "It's not as fat as the Burgundy. And see here? It frequently has a coat of arms at the neck."

Lilli shook her head. "There was no coat of arms. What can you tell me about the next one?" she asked, eager to hear about the third bottle.

"Ah, the Bordeaux," Mr. Vincennes said, pursing his lips. "That often comes in dark green bottles with straight sides and tall shoulders. Is this the one you had in mind?"

"I'm not sure," Lilli said. "These shoulders seem a tad tall." She was disappointed. She had hoped that one bottle would stand out from the others and she would leave the seminar knowing the name of her stolen wine.

"That leaves the Alsace," Mr. Vincennes said, running his finger beneath the fourth bottle. "It comes in a tall, slender bottle, with a very gentle slope to the shoulders."

"No," Lilli said. "Too big a slope."

Rrriiinnnggg!

"Time's up," Mr. Vincennes said, not hiding his pleasure at dismissing her. "I suspect your memory may be playing tricks on you."

As she crossed the room, Lilli looked over her shoulder. The crowds were thinning and small sample cups and empty bottles filled the trash containers. She saw Mr. Vincennes speaking to someone on his cell phone. He looked surprised at what he was hearing. When she turned back, Doug was standing right in front of her.

"Lilli, I was hoping to find you here," he said. His face was flushed, as if he'd been running.

"Where are those roughneck Bond brothers?" she asked, curious about them since they had practically dragged Doug away.

"I have no idea. I don't know them well. We're in the same business."

"The diving business," Lilli said.

"Right. I need to talk to you, but this isn't a good time." He looked around warily. "Will you be here tomorrow?"

"Yes."

A flash went off.

"A newspaper photographer?" Lilli asked.

"I hope not," Doug said. He seemed upset that he might have been caught on film.

Lilli looked up and saw Mr. Vincennes watching them. Had he taken their photo? Had someone else? Or had the photo been of someone or something else?

"I'll look for you tomorrow," Doug said, peering in the direction where the flash had gone off.

"I'll count on it," she said cheerfully. He was her most promising lead about the wine bottle.

Doug hurried off and Lilli walked past several tables. She stopped when she saw the banner LIQUID GOLD. The expert, wearing thick glasses with black rims, his hair parted on the side, was probably in his early forties. He looked like a cross between a bookworm and a Geek Squad guy at a computer store. The line was ten-people long and would mean at least a twenty-minute wait. She picked up a brochure from his table and began reading it while she stood in line.

His name was Mark Mastriano. He was a well-respected wine buyer who chose wines for many of the North Fork's finest restaurants. He was quoted in an interview for *Wine News* magazine: "I view wine as an investment, and so do my clients. My representatives find it, usually at the bottom of the sea, and deliver it to me. My clients buy it, store it, and sell it for profit. Thanks to new technology, divers can now explore deep regions of the sea, which are free from life forms that gobble up wood and corks."

Lilli flipped through the brochure and saw in bold letters THREE FAMOUS SHIPWRECKS SHOW ADVANCES IN SALVAGING LIQUID GOLD. She scanned the information.

One: The White Star luxury steamer, the RMS Republic, *sunk in 1909, was discovered with thousands of bottles of wine on board, at a depth of two hundred forty feet in forty-degree waters. Three hundred bottles were recovered, but Christie's auction house found none in condition to be auctioned off.*

Two: In 1912, the Titanic *sunk to a depth of 12,400 feet. From the twelve-thousand-bottle cellar, three hundred wines were recovered with their corks intact, but most had spoiled.*

Three: In 1997, twenty-five hundred bottles of Heidsieck Monopole 1907 Champagne, destined for the tsar of Russia, were salvaged from the Swedish merchant ship Jonkoping, *sunk off the coast of Finland in thirty-five-degree water by a German U-boat during World War I. Private clients bought most of the salvaged wine, which was in perfect condition with corks intact. Twelve of the bottles sold for a total of $61,700 at auction by Christie's.*

Lilli was disappointed. She had been hoping that Thomas Jefferson would have been mentioned. That would add fuel to her hunch that she had found a bottle of Jefferson's wine on the beach. She jotted down in her notepad, *TJ wine—any possibility of a shipwreck?*

Several people dropped out of line. Lilli was next.

"Mr. Mastriano," she said, noticing his pale complexion under the harsh lights.

He smiled, showing small teeth as white as those in the ads for tooth-brightening products. "I saw you studying the brochure, uh, Miss . . ."

"Call me Lilli."

"And you may call me Mark." He peered at her through thick glasses that magnified his squinty eyes. "You seemed to enjoy my brochure. May I ask what caught your attention?"

"Shipwrecks. Wine. A good story. I'm a writer and . . . a history buff," she fibbed. "Presidents are my forté. Thomas Jefferson, our third president, is my favorite."

"And what does President Jefferson have to do with liquid gold?" he asked, as the pinched lines between his eyes grew deeper.

"I was hoping you could tell me," she said, again taking her notepad from her purse.

"Then I have to disappoint you. To my knowledge, no one has ever discovered Jefferson's wines aboard a shipwreck, nor have they been listed on the manifest of any sunken ship. End of story. Sorry."

Lilli felt the presence of someone on either side of her. It was those nasty Bond brothers, divers who had hustled Doug away from the Terrace Café.

"Have you seen Doug?" the shorter brother asked her. Perspiration glistened on his shaved head. His gruff manner turned Lilli off.

"No, I haven't," she fibbed.

"If you see him, tell him me and my brother, Frank, were looking for him," he said. They left before Lilli could say anything. Good riddance, she thought, sensing trouble.

Rrriiinnnggg! The timer went off, and Mr. Mastriano began speaking to the next person in line.

Lilli headed for the door. She needed to return to the inn and get ready for the gala with Dr. Winfield at the tavern. Out of the corner of her eye she saw the Bond brothers in the hallway talking to two of the men she'd seen earlier arguing about liquid gold. "Old salts" from fishing camps, Chuck Matthison had called the men. Her pulse raced. What were they talking to the Bond brothers about? The Bond brothers were divers, and the old salts were fishermen. Pretending to read her notes, Lilli watched the four men.

It looked like some kind of standoff. Tempers flared. The old salts shook their fists at the Bond brothers. Their faces, red as boiled lobsters, were mere inches apart. The old salts pushed the Bond brothers up against the wall.

"Security!" someone near the men yelled.

The Bond brothers ran into the crowd. A security guard looked around, didn't see any disturbance, and left. The other two men, the old salts, headed toward Lilli. She gulped, but they passed by her without a word and went straight to Mark Mastriano. No one was waiting in his line.

Turning her back to them, Lilli pulled out a pocket mirror and tissue and pretended to dislodge a speck of dirt from her eye. The men looked intense as they questioned Mark. Three minutes passed, and the timer rang. The men took brochures and left, passing right by her again. Lilli breathed a sigh of relief. Obviously they hadn't recognized her from this morning.

Lilli slid her mirror into her purse and strode to Mark's table. "I hate to be nosy, but may I ask what those men wanted to know?" She smiled, hoping to win him over. "Specific information sure helps to sell articles to magazines."

Mark's squinty eyes bored right through Lilli. "Why don't you tell me what's really going on here," he said.

"What do you mean?" she asked, genuinely surprised.

"Just like you, those two men were asking about Thomas Jefferson and shipwrecks. Care to let me in on what all of you are up to?"

Lilli thought fast. "I don't know about them," she said, "but I'm helping a high school kid write a paper about Thomas Jefferson."

"I'm not buying it," he said sulkily. "I saw you using the old mirror-over-the-shoulder trick. You were spying on them or me."

Lilli blinked her right eye rapidly. "It wasn't a trick," she fibbed. "My eye is killing me."

"The eye problem must be spreading," he said. "A minute ago, you were dabbing your left eye with a tissue."

"You are very observant," she said, "but I think you might be confused. It was definitely my right eye." She blinked a few more times. "I have to go," she said, "and put drops in my eye."

He gave her a long slow look. "Those men asked if anyone else had been inquiring about Thomas Jefferson."

"What did you tell them?" Lilli asked, checking over her shoulder to see if they were nearby.

"I told them no. They seemed relieved."

"Why did you lie to them?"

"There's two of them. Only one of you." He smiled, and Lilli thought his smile seemed more like a leer. "That's not a fair fight. I figured you needed me on your side."

"Did you happen to catch their names?" she asked.

"I did, but I'm having some sudden memory loss." He spread out his scrawny fingers and leaned across the table. "Why don't you join me at the gala tonight at the tavern? It starts at six. By then, I might remember their names."

"Sorry. I'm meeting a friend there."

His thin lips formed a hard straight line. "Get rid of him and be my guest. I have connections at the tavern. I'm the wine buyer for the best restaurants on the North Fork, including the tavern."

"Thanks, but I promised my friend—"

"I could give you a private tour of the tavern's wine cellar, just the two of us. It's the best-stocked wine cellar on the entire North Fork. I keep it up to my high standards."

"No, thank you," she said firmly.

"I'll see you there then. Maybe we can talk."

"Don't get your hopes up," she said and walked away. He was so transparent. He wasn't interested in her. He was curious about all the sudden interest in Thomas Jefferson and liquid gold. She didn't know what to make of this Mark Mastriano. The smart thing for her to do would be to talk to him, try to charm out of him what he knew about the men, the liquid gold, and Thomas Jefferson. If only he didn't give her the creeps.

Chapter Eleven

Lilli arrived several minutes early at the Grayrocks Tavern to meet Dr. Winfield for the gala. She snapped a half-dozen photos of the dramatic but somewhat foreboding two-story structure that overlooked the bay. Built to resemble a fortress, it was very different from every other building in the area. Chuck Matthison, the architect's grandson, had implied that some people considered it a "misfit." Different and unusual, even mysterious, she thought, but misfit seemed unfair.

Lilli climbed the steps and zoomed in for a shot of a plaque that read, GRAYROCKS TAVERN, 1939. BUILT FROM THE RUGGED LOCAL STONES THAT GAVE GRAYROCKS ITS NAME. Before entering, she touched the cool dark facade and felt its energy seep into her fingertips.

Photos of the tavern in various stages of construction dotted the walls of the reception area. But other photos taken the year before the tavern was built really caught her attention. The horrific damage created by the Great Hurricane of 1938 was astounding. Nicknamed "the Long Island Express," it was the most powerful storm to strike the Northeast ever recorded.

The text accompanying the photographs stated that the mighty hurricane made landfall near the Hamptons on the South Fork, roared across the island, and ripped apart the coastline, creating the Shinnecock Inlet.

An article from the Grayrocks *Gazette* featured an interview with tavern architect Samuel Matthison. When asked about the inspiration for his creation, the reclusive Grayrocks resident said, "After surviving the Great Hurricane, which took more than six hundred lives, I experienced a strange dream. A cubist-shaped being with mammoth fists of granite burst from the earth like a craggy warrior-god intent on blocking the fury of wind and wave."

What a dramatic description, Lilli thought. She read on. Mr. Matthison died in 1940 at the age of forty-five, shortly after the tavern was completed. The official cause of death was listed as a heart attack, but his widow insisted there were "mysterious circumstances and that a thorough investigation was never done."

Lilli's pulse quickened. Mysterious circumstances . . . hmm. The architect's widow could have been suggesting the possibility of murder.

Lilli decided that the Matthison family might make an interesting subject for a future article. Even though Gram called Chuck weird, she considered him affable. He was very willing to talk about his family. He could be a good source of personal anecdotes. Maybe she could dig into the "mysterious circumstances." She tucked a brochure about the tavern in her purse and headed toward the sounds of happy voices and laid-back jazz that echoed off the stone walls in the main room. She craned her neck looking for Dr. Winfield.

Catching sight of herself in a mirror, she smoothed her dark green scoop-neck dress and wondered if it was the right choice for this event. It was slinkier than the dresses she usually wore. Zack's eyes had nearly popped out of his head when she'd worn it on their first date in New York City, nearly a year ago. She sighed wistfully. She missed him. She couldn't wait for Monday to see him again. This time, she would control her emotions and listen to his explanation about Isabella. Zack Faraday, the love of her life, was still on her mind when Mr. Vincennes approached. He had exchanged his tuxedo for a beautifully tailored gray suit.

"Miss Masters, we meet again," he said. His lapel pin stated MAN-AGER.

"Yes," she said. "And I see you are a man of many talents. Manager here, president of the vintner's association at the conference."

Mr. Vincennes adjusted his elegant tie. "Dr. Winfield sends his regrets. He's on the telephone. He said he would join you very soon. Meanwhile"—Mr. Vincennes extended his hand toward the tables filled with wine and hors d'oeuvres—"please enjoy our gala buffet. We have planned an intimate gathering, a welcome contrast, I imagine, from the crowded, noisy wine tasting this afternoon at the community center, where we first met."

He leaned toward her and said in a low voice, "Sorry if I came across somewhat abrupt earlier today, but mingling with the commonfolk at a conference makes my blood boil. Now that I'm with the crème de la crème, the honored guests and speakers, and someone as lovely as you, I can be myself."

Lovely? He sure had changed his opinion of her.

He smiled, obviously happy to be in these surroundings with people he deemed worthy of his attention. "The sommeliers are at your service, hoping to reveal the heart and soul of wine. Local wines only, of course," he said with a touch of pride. "And here," he said, handing her the sheet of paper he'd been holding, "is a checklist to record your preferences. The bottom part is also your ticket for a door prize. The winner will be announced in one half hour."

"Thank you," Lilli said, folding the serrated bottom section of the paper and tucking it into her purse. As she wandered toward the buffet, she passed a splendid library, all dark polished wood that glistened in the lamplight of matching Tiffany lamps set on reading tables. She stepped inside and was delighted to find that the shelves were stocked with books about Long Island history, everything from the days of the Montauk Indians to shipbuilding, fishing, whaling, and farming. She was running her fingertips along the books about shipwrecks when she heard the murmur of low voices coming from somewhere beyond the shadows at the rear of the library. She heard a man's distinctive voice. She caught a few words about docks and wine bottles. And then, a woman's tinkling laughter.

Curious, Lilli walked in that direction, across the Persian carpet that swallowed every sound. What a surprise to come upon an intimate alcove, separated from the library by a dramatic black beaded curtain that swayed gently with the air currents and glistened like jewels. And who should be in the alcove but the two archaeologists, Dr. Edward Winfield and Dr. Elena Ellison. They were so engrossed in each other's words and glances that they didn't even notice her. Lilli backed away into the shadows. Her imagination prickled, and she wondered what they were discussing. Convincing herself that she was tracking a story, not eavesdropping, she strained to hear what they were saying. But they stood up, ready to leave. She backed away.

Leaving the library, Lilli wandered for several minutes, listening to sommeliers from Greenport's Ternhaven Cellars and Mattituck's Sherwood House Vineyards discuss their wines. There was no jostling to get to the front of the line as had occurred at the wine tasting earlier in the day. Here, in this intriguing place, crystal goblets sparkled on the crisp linen tablecloths. Now, the sommeliers' questions flowed along with the wine. "Do you taste a hint of cinnamon? Of blackberries?" "Is the color appealing?" "Merlot for you, miss?" "Chardonnay?"

Lilli chatted with the sommelier from Pugliesi's Vineyards in Cutchogue. With his guidance, she chose a Merlot and then headed toward the cheese display surrounded by gourmet crackers and dazzling china. Someone bumped into her, knocking the goblet from her hand. She reached down, lost her balance, and fell to the floor. The goblet crashed and shattered into glittering pieces. She was lucky to avoid getting cut.

"I'm so sorry. Please let me help you," came a man's deep voice from above. At the same time she saw a waiter's distinctive trousers hurrying toward her. When she looked up, it wasn't the waiter who held out his hand. It was the man she'd seen earlier with Mia in the community center parking lot. A very distraught Mia who had given her *Fishy Forks* sketch to him and didn't seem happy about it. Lilli couldn't believe her good fortune. Here was her chance to find out what that was all about.

"I see from your nametag that you are Lilli Masters." The man flashed a charming smile. His hair was dark, his eyes darker, glistening in his tanned face. "I've been looking forward to meeting you." He quickly selected two glasses of Merlot, and handed one to her. "I noticed that you like Merlot too," he said and clinked the rim of his glass against hers. "My students told me that you bought all three winning sketches from the first round of competition. Mia said you saved the day and sold her sketch back to her. Thanks for being so understanding."

He wrapped his arm around her waist and, before Lilli could object, he whisked her away to a quiet corner of the room. "There, that's better," he said, releasing his firm grip. "Now, Lilli Masters, photojournalist extraordinaire, we can talk. My name is Miko Andropolis."

"Miko Andropolis," she repeated, letting the syllables roll across her tongue. "Greek heritage, I assume?"

He nodded. "My father and grandfather were sponge divers in Tarpon Springs, Florida. I grew up around the gulf waters."

"What brought you to Long Island?" she asked.

"I was in Chicago, where I have a studio. Along came the chance to teach here on the North Fork. Water, water, everywhere," he said, extending his hand toward the windows overlooking the bay. "I was a visiting instructor at the Mattituck Art School for the summer semester. I'm staying on until my replacement arrives. I was hoping to discuss my students' sketches with you."

Now we're getting somewhere, thought Lilli.

"It seems there was a misunderstanding," Miko said. "Mia might have implied that I wanted only her sketch. Actually, I'd like to buy the other two winning sketches as well. I have a buyer who wants all three for the cover of *Artz* magazine. It's a chance to show off my students' talent and give the school some well-deserved praise."

Lilli had heard of the edgy magazine, popular with young, emerging artists. Why would Mia be upset if her work was chosen for the cover? Surely, that was a huge honor. "You must be proud of their work . . . and your influence," she said, hoping to hear more.

He smiled. "In my brief time here, I've encouraged my students to inject humor into their work. Mia learned very quickly. She has the talent to really go places. But I'm afraid that her artistic temperament might get in the way." He shrugged his broad shoulders, adjusting his denim jacket. "Do you still have the other two sketches?"

"Sure." Mia's tearful face flashed before her eyes. "I'm so curious. Do you mind interpreting the sketches for me?"

"I'd like that very much, but in quieter surroundings," he said. "How about dinner at my place tomorrow evening, say eight o'clock? You could bring along the other two sketches. I live on the bay in Mattituck, a great place for photographs." He held out his business card. Aquamarine, like the water, she thought.

"The map on the back will show you the way," he said.

She had been studying him as he talked. He was older and rougher around the edges than the men she had dated. He wasn't handsome like Zack, but he exuded a sexiness and self-confidence that she found appealing. She wasn't naïve. She had learned in self-defense courses the risks of a first date in a secluded place with someone she hardly knew. She would let Gram know her plans and give her Miko's address. "Tomorrow at eight," she said, exchanging business cards with him.

"That couple is leaving," he said, pointing across the hallway with his wineglass. "Let's grab their table in the alcove."

"I'd like to hear more about your work," Lilli said, when they were seated.

"The long version or the short?" he asked.

"Sorry, but it will have to be short," she said. "I'm expecting someone."

He looked disappointed. "Okay, short it is. For years I'd been working solely with metal, based on my years of experience in car chop shops. I guess you could say I'm more a blowtorch than a paintbrush type of guy. Anyway, I wanted something fresher and lighter than my usual industrial look. So I figured a change of scene would be good. The Mattituck Art School was a good fit for me. The area has been a real shot in the arm to my work, but the teaching takes up too much of my time. When a replacement teacher is found, I hope to finish all the projects I've got in the works and add more. Right now I'm working on objets trouvés, found objects, and combining them with the metal."

"What objects have you found?" she asked, impressed by his French pronunciation.

"Just what you'd expect in this area," he said. "Shells, crab traps, anchors, metal chains."

She noticed his tanned face and the calluses on his hands. "My instincts were right," she said. "I figured you worked outdoors."

"Right. How did you know?"

"A journalist's instincts," she said and then laughed. "Your tanned face was a dead giveaway."

Lilli caught sight of Dr. Winfield and waved him over. "Miko and I have met several times," he said frostily as the two men shook hands.

"We have a mutual acquaintance," Miko said. "Her name is Dr. Elena Ellison. Maybe you heard her speak at the conference."

"I did," Lilli said. "She was very impressive."

Miko chuckled. "She's been like that for as long as I've known her. We were childhood friends in Tarpon Springs. Our families went to the same church. We've stayed in touch through the years. Our parents thought that someday—well, you know how parents are."

Dr. Winfield cleared his throat. "Lilli, I'm sorry I took so long in catching up to you at this gala. Time got away from me."

Just then, Dr. Ellison strode into the room. Heads turned as she passed by. Winding her way toward Dr. Winfield, she gave Lilli a quick glance, then kissed Miko on the cheek. She whispered something in Dr. Winfield's ear, and his expression turned serious. She passed him a note and quickly departed, leaving an aura of mystery in her path. Lilli wondered if they were in a relationship or if this brief encounter was somehow related to their work at the conference.

Ring! Ring! Ring!

"Your attention, please!" Mr. Vincennes, the manager, called out, silencing the magnificent silver dinner bell with his hand. "We will now call the winning number for the door prize. Four dozen bottles of wine, one from each of the wineries represented here this evening." Amid applause and then hushed anticipation, he reached his hand into a crystal bowl and plucked one ticket. "The lucky winner is number seventy-two," he said, beaming.

"Yahoo!" shouted a male voice.

Lilli looked toward the door and saw one of those nasty Bond brothers.

"Your name, sir?" Mr. Vincennes asked.

"Lucky winner," he said with a sly grin.

"Bravo, Mr. Lucky Winner. And now, Mark Mastriano, the North Fork's most knowledgeable wine connoisseur, will lead you to the wine cellar, his showpiece. There you will be treated to an amazing tour and collect your prize."

Without another word, Mr. Lucky Winner followed Mark Mastriano.

"I must go," Miko said. "Until tomorrow." He hurried after the two men. Lilli wondered why Miko was in such a rush to follow them. Was there some connection between Miko and the man who won the door prize? With Dr. Winfield at her side, she watched their retreating path but lost sight of them in the crowd.

Chapter Twelve

Lilli left the tavern and drove toward the Baywatch Inn. She felt frustrated. There hadn't been much of an opportunity to discuss the mysterious pitchfork symbols on Silas' folders or anything else with Dr. Winfield. He'd acted fidgety, anxious to leave her. As she drove, questions tumbled through her mind about everything that had happened since she'd arrived in Grayrocks. It was as if many rivers converged, sometimes wandered away on a separate course, but eventually headed toward the same big murky ocean. If only she could sort all this out.

Her questions constantly returned to Silas and those chopped-up figureheads. If Silas had hidden a treasure map and the thieves hadn't found it, where was it now? Or were they looking for something else? Maybe she should look too, starting with a treasure map. Where would she begin her search? Silas' shop. But where in his shop? It was crammed full. There had to be at least a thousand items, countless maps and papers.

Lilli braked at the stop sign. Her eyes popped wide. She knew exactly where to look! Why hadn't she figured it out before, when she was back in Silas' shop? She pulled into the Baywatch Inn parking lot, grabbed her cell phone, and called the police department. She definitely intended to keep her promise to let Hank know anything pertinent to the investigation. "I'd like to speak to Chief Borden," she told the officer on duty.

"Is this an emergency?" asked the officer.

"Yes . . . sort of . . . it could be," she said impatiently.

"Have you or anyone else been injured?"

"No." Her fingers tapped the steering wheel a mile a minute.

"Has a crime been committed?"

"Not really." She clenched her teeth.

"The chief is at a budget meeting," the officer said.

"I must speak to him."

"He left instructions not to be disturbed. Dial extension 1000 and leave him a message or, if you'd rather, I can put you through to an officer who will help you."

Lilli didn't know anyone else in the department except Hank's sidekick, Walt. And she didn't know Walt well enough to confide in him. Gram had called him a slippery eel that wriggled in and out of situations, hoping to look good and take over Hank's job when Hank retired. Gram was a good judge of character.

She'd go with Gram's judgment. "Thanks. I'll leave a message," Lilli said. She called Hank's extension and got his voice mail. She quickly hung up without saying a word. Forget compliantly following the officer's suggestions. This was the time to be pushy. Under certain circumstances *pushy* could mean "effective." She knew a way to get straight through to Hank. She punched in numbers.

"Gram, I'm in your parking lot. This is an emergency." She saw the curtains move and Gram's worried face press against the window. "I need Hank's private number. . . . Yes, I know he gave it to you in strict confidence. . . . I don't mean to get you in hot water, but this is about Silas. . . . Thanks, Gram. You're the best! I'll make the call from my Bronco. . . . I don't want anyone in the inn to overhear me."

Gram rattled off Hank's number.

Lilli called. "Chief, it's Lilli. We—"

"How did you get this number? Do you have any idea what time it is?"

"It's nine o'clock Friday night, and you definitely want to hear this."

Hank harrumphed. "It better be good."

"It is. I don't know what the murderers were searching for in Silas' shop, but I think I know where Silas kept what it was they were looking for. I'm at Gram's. Could you meet me at Silas' shop?"

"I'll pick you up at Gram's in ten minutes. Don't go anywhere until I get there," he sputtered, "and don't spread this around. If your idea doesn't pan out, I don't want my photo with egg on my face spread on the front page of the *Gazette*."

"Who will be coming with you?" Lilli asked, ignoring Hank's bluster. She hoped it wouldn't be Walt. His sarcastic comments and negative attitude would ruin anyone's brilliant idea.

"I'm coming alone," Hank said. "I can't spare an officer for what may turn out to be zilch, zip, zero. I'll give you five minutes in Silas' shop. Five. Not a minute more."

"Thanks, Chief. You won't regret this."

"I already do," he said and hung up.

Lilli climbed out of her Bronco and strode into the Baywatch Inn, wishing Hank had more confidence in her. Passing the reception desk, where Skeet dozed over his calculus homework, she took the stairs two at a time.

"What's going on, Lilli?" trailed Gram's voice down the hallway from her kitchen.

"I'm going on a treasure hunt," Lilli called back, peeling out of her slinky dress. "When I get back"—she kicked off her sandals—"I'll explain."

"You're not going to do something dangerous, are you?" Gram asked, standing in the doorway, wearing her black spandex workout clothes. Pairs of neon yellow weights circled her wrists.

"No way," Lilli said, stepping into her navy blue sweatpants. "Hank is in on this with me." She tugged down her sweatshirt.

"In on what?" Gram asked, practicing her bicep curls.

"Tell you later," Lilli said, tying her sneaker laces. She tucked a flashlight in the waist of her pants. She pulled a pair of fresh latex gloves from the cleaning supplies kept under the bathroom sink and tucked them in her waist pack next to her staples: credit card, press pass, notepad, and pen. She needed to be prepared for any emergency. Hank might not bring such tools of the trade for her.

"Latex gloves, like on *CSI*," Gram said and cocked an eyebrow. "I sure wish I could come with you."

"Not this time," Lilli said. She tugged down her baseball cap and breezed past Gram.

Minutes later, an unfamiliar car with tinted windows pulled up to Gram's inn. The window on the passenger side rolled down. "Get

in," Hank said. As soon as she hooked her seat belt, he pulled out of
the driveway. "We'll go slow and easy. No need to alert all of Grayrocks what we're up to. Now tell me what you know and what you
think you know," he said.

As they drove toward Silas' shop, Lilli explained her theory and
Hank listened. The gusting wind blew twigs and leaves along the
street and sidewalks. There were few parked cars and little traffic.

"You just drove past Silas' shop," Lilli said.

"I know. I was casing the place. I don't expect trouble, but you
never know."

Lilli was impressed with Hank's concern for safety. She was glad
she had called him, even though she was following a hunch, not a
sure thing. What was the worst that could happen? She wouldn't be
able to find the treasure map or whatever Silas had hidden, and she
would lose all credibility with Hank. Possibly he might bar her from
all aspects of the investigation. The stakes were high for her. For
him too. Anything they found that would help solve the murders
would restore Grayrocks' reputation as a peaceful vacation town, a
favorite among tourists, and his reputation as the protector of the
people.

"Look over there," Lilli said, pointing toward the street to her left.
"That man hurrying along the sidewalk. I can't make out who he is.
Can you?"

Hank slowed, peering at the shadowy figure. "No."

"He's wearing a cowboy hat. Could it be Chuck Matthison, or are
cowboy hats in style in Grayrocks?"

"Baseball caps, cowboy hats, touristy fishing hats with lures,
straw hats"—he tapped his chief's hat—"we got more style of hats
in Grayrocks than there are stones on the beach. But let's keep our
eyes peeled. If we see a cowboy hat again, I'll cancel this idea. We're
not taking any chances during my watch."

Lilli looked over her shoulder. Whoever the man was, he turned
down an alley that headed toward the bay and disappeared into the
darkness. "He's gone," she said.

"Good." Hank turned off the headlights, coasted into a driveway,
and parked. "This is a friend's house," he said. "We'll walk from here.
I don't want to park on the street. Someone might recognize my car

and stop by to talk. Everybody becomes a nervous talker when a murder occurs." He slapped the palm of his hand against his forehead. "Theories you wouldn't believe. Well, maybe someone like you would."

Lilli didn't ask what he meant by that. She knew better.

In silence, they walked side by side along the deserted sidewalk. Silas' shop was just ahead. Lilli was glad that the streetlights gave some light, because the swirling mists hindered her vision. The shop was pitch black.

"Come on," Hank said, taking her protectively by the hand, and they crossed the street. They ducked beneath the neon yellow crime-scene tape that read DO NOT CROSS. Standing in the deep shadows of the shrubs by the back door, Lilli turned to Hank. "Time for latex gloves?" she asked.

"Yes," he said, and they each snapped on a pair.

She hesitated, realizing she stood inches from where Silas' body had been found. A sickening feeling came over her. She wanted to leave, but she couldn't. Not now. Not this close to possibly finding out why poor Silas was murdered. And just possibly, who did it.

Hank pulled a key from his pocket and tried it. "Come on, baby," he said and jiggled the key this way and that.

"Wrong key?" Lilli whispered.

"It happens," Hank said.

"Do you happen to have a credit card with you? If not, I have mine."

"Of course," he said. "Why?"

"You'll see," she said, and he passed her his credit card. "I saw this in a movie," she whispered, and Hank groaned.

She slid his credit card into the crack between the door and the frame. She worked it up and down.

Click.

"Success," she said, and Hank groaned again as he returned his credit card to his wallet.

Hank cracked the door open and slipped silently inside. Lilli followed on his heels.

Headlights flashed by the front window, briefly bathing the front room and workroom in light. The door between the two rooms was open, facing into the workroom where Lilli stood, just as it had been when she'd visited Silas minutes before he was murdered.

Hank pushed the door between the rooms until it was opened only a crack, then flicked on his flashlight. "Go for it," he said. "My watch is ticking."

Lilli quickly made her way to Silas' workbench and flicked on her flashlight. The bird's-eye maple wood glistened under the beam of light.

A tapping at the front window gave her a start. She flicked off her flashlight.

At the same moment, Hank doused his light and said, "Lilli, don't move."

The tapping came again. Lilli's pulse quickened. She peered into the darkness. A car drove slowly by, its headlights illuminating the front room. In their beam, the curved blade of a cutlass, gripped by a pirate, part of Silas' popular outdoor display, tapped against the windowpane. She blew out her breath. No one was out there after all.

"It's just an old pirate Silas found at a garage sale," Hank said, sounding relieved. "The wind must have blown it against the window."

Swallowing several deep breaths, Lilli flicked on her flashlight again and stood in front of the workbench. She tugged at the only drawer, the very drawer she had seen Silas open. It didn't budge. She tried again. No luck.

"You've got three minutes," Hank said, tapping his watch.

Lilli's fingertips ran along the front panel. She fiddled here and there, seeking a release button or sliding bolt, a catch or latch. Something . . . anything. She tried again and again.

"Two minutes," Hank said, and she heard the disappointment in his voice.

Exasperated, she dropped to her hands and knees, rolled onto her back, and shined her flashlight at the underside of the workbench. The distinctive bird's-eye maple design appeared front and center on the underside of the drawer.

"One minute."

The bird's eye. So obvious! And she had almost missed it. She reached up and pressed her fingertip into the dark mysterious center of the bird's eye.

Click!

Lilli reached up again and tugged gently on the drawer. With a whisper, it slid open.

"Time's up," Hank said.

Lilli clambered up. "Over here, Hank." She shined the flashlight into the drawer. Papers. At first glance, nothing unusual. No treasure map.

"Scoop up everything," Hank said enthusiastically and then glanced at the door.

"Okay," she said, setting her flashlight on the workbench and gathering the papers.

Hank shut the drawer.

Something slid from the papers Lilli was holding and landed on the floor. The beam of Hank's flashlight revealed a small notebook. Lilli picked it up. It was about the size of her hand. SILAS JONES was printed in block letters on the cover.

"You were right after all," Hank exclaimed.

Lilli was thrilled to win him over, at least for the moment. All would depend on what was contained in the notebook.

"Clever carpenter, that Silas," Hank said. "Creating a special drawer in his workbench."

"Very clever," Lilli added. "His notebook was under his watchful eyes in the very place where he spent most of his time."

The front door rattled. "Ssshhh," Hank whispered. He killed the flashlight beam. "Get behind that door and stay there until I see who it is."

Lilli spun around. She tucked the handful of papers and the notebook inside her sweatshirt and tucked her sweatshirt into her sweatpants. She crept behind the door that separated the workroom from the front room and squeezed into the corner. She gripped the doorknob with her left hand, keeping her right hand free.

The front door creaked open. Lilli's heart skipped a beat.

"Who's in there?" came a man's voice.

Lilli didn't move a muscle. She peered through the crack between the door and the front room. Darkness. Suddenly a flashlight beam shot across the floor of the front room.

"I know you're in here," the voice said menacingly.

Walt? It was Walt, Hank's right-hand man. What was he doing here alone, and why hadn't he identified himself? Hank hadn't said a word or made a move. Surely he would have recognized Walt's voice. Why didn't Hank say something? Was he still in the shop?

Walt walked across the front room, coming closer to Lilli, stuck his head through the doorway and flashed his light about. Lilli squeezed even tighter behind the door. Walt had just stepped back into the main room when a phone rang. Lilli heard Hank gasp somewhere on the other side of the door. She said a silent prayer of thanks that he was still nearby.

"I told you not to call me at this number," Walt said. "Hank's at a meeting. Trimming fat from the budget. Guess we both know where he should start." He laughed a croaking laugh. "The beer gut for starters." A pause. "I'm in Silas' shop. Thought I saw something. Just shadows I guess." Another laugh. "I'll do some more private investigating soon as I can."

The front door opened and closed.

Silence.

"That low-down sniveling snake," Hank hissed, as he made his way toward Lilli.

Lilli stepped from behind the door. "Why didn't you confront him?" Her breath rushed past her trembling lips.

"Keep your friends close and your enemies closer," Hank said. "Walt's getting too big for his britches. He wants the glory of solving this case all by himself. That's a bad plan. I don't want him to know we found something hidden in this shop. Agreed?"

"My lips are sealed," Lilli said.

"Good. This little expedition will remain a secret until I know what's in that notebook, and until I find out who Walt was talking to and if he's involved in anything connected with the murders. Let's go before Walt decides to come back."

Lilli grabbed her flashlight from the bench where she'd left it.

They made their way to the back door and slipped outside. Lilli shut the door behind her and inched along the wall behind Hank, cradling the stack of papers in her sweatshirt as if it were a baby wrapped in swaddling. Hank peered around the corner.

"All clear," he said, and they ran all the way to his car.

Hank started the engine. "I don't think it's a good idea to take Silas' papers to the police station. Not yet. If this is a hoax or some kind of cruel joke, I'll never hear the end of it. And I'm not sure if another officer is working with Walt. This is a real can of worms."

"You have your reputation to think of," Lilli commented. "Let's go to the Baywatch Inn. Gram and Bud are your friends. They are tried-and-true Grayrockers. They will do what's best."

"You could be right," he said. "We could do that."

"What are we waiting for?" Lilli asked. She was delighted to have gained Hank's trust. She was thrilled to be involved in a covert mission.

Chapter Thirteen

G o on ahead, Lilli. I'll catch up," Hank said as he pulled up in front of the Baywatch Inn. "I want to get this car out of sight and make sure no one followed us. Now listen up. With Gram and Bud, don't spill any more beans than you have to."

"Right, Chief." Lilli turned and bounded up the steps of the inn.

In a split second, Gram opened the door and Bud pulled Lilli inside.

"You look like you walked the plank and saw a dozen sharks circling," Gram said.

"Treasure," Lilli said, pointing at her sweatshirt. Hank's listen-up warning flew out the window. She whispered, "Could be papers that got Silas and Dr. Reed murdered. Silas hid them in a secret drawer."

"Her imagination's on overload," Gram said out of the corner of her mouth to Bud.

"We've been worried sick about you," Bud said, tugging down the brim of his baseball cap. "I was minding my own business playing Yahtzee on my front porch, when Gram, I mean Margaret, came charging across my front lawn like a flash. I jumped to my feet. She knows that spandex outfit drives me crazy. She—"

Gram touched Bud's arm. "Let's keep some secrets, Bud."

"Right. Anyway, Margaret told me to get over here pronto, that you were out of control, on some kind of treasure hunt. I know that meant you were keeping secrets from her. Bad idea, Lilli."

"Hank is with me," Lilli said. "I can't say much. I'll let him do the talking. He's in charge."

Gram's eyebrows shot up. "Did you hit your head, girl? When did you go all submissive?"

"Since the moment I decided to give up my bad habits of being pushy and taking control of everything, including police business."

"Bud, get the thermometer and see if she has a fever," Gram said with a chuckle. "Now follow me." Gram led the way up the stairs to her apartment. "And let's see what your papers can tell us. Skeet," she called over her shoulder, "buzz me for any reason. Use the code, just like we discussed."

"One if by land, two if by sea?" Skeet said with a grin, then put on his game face. "Sorry, Gram, I've been doing research about Colonial America for a history paper. I'll stick to the plan." He pointed at the special phone that connected directly to Gram's private apartment. "One buzz, a guest is checking in. Two buzzes—" He massaged his temples. "Two buzzes. Let me think. Could it be—"

"Quit messing with me, Skeet." Gram wagged her finger. "Two buzzes, trouble!"

"Right," Skeet said. "And three buzzes, cheese it, the cops!"

"Chief Borden will be here soon," Lilli said. "Does he need a special code all his own?"

Skeet opened his mouth to speak when the door slammed open and Hank strode across the floor. "Skeet, step outside for a minute." Hank waited until the door closed. "Bud, Gram, you are sworn to secrecy," he said. "What's said here, stays here."

"Do we get badges or anything?" Gram asked. "Okay, okay. I know when it's time to get serious. Come on, let's go."

Gram tugged at Lilli. Lilli's sweatshirt popped out, and the papers she'd concealed fluttered to the steps. The notebook landed with a dull thud.

Bud reached for the papers.

"Let me do that," Lilli said, gently nudging him aside. "I'm wearing gloves. We don't want to compromise the fingerprints."

"Compromise the fingerprints?" Gram shook her head. "Watch out, Crime Scene Team, you've got competition."

"We say 'tech team,' " Hank added.

Lilli was hardly listening to Hank. She was intent on reading the first page she'd picked up. The old-fashioned penmanship, filled with curlicues and flourishes, reminded her of Colonial documents she'd seen under glass in museums and on the History Channel.

"Wow!" Lilli said and turned to face Bud, Gram, and Hank. They had been reading over her shoulder. Their eyes mirrored the awe and wonder surging through her.

Chapter Fourteen

Plans flew from their lips as Lilli, Gram, and Bud rushed up the last few stairs to Gram's apartment. "Lilli, wait up," Hank said, as he lumbered behind.

"Go on with all your plans," he said, with a serious expression on his face. "I'll follow what's going on, but my suspicions about Walt can't wait. I need to make several calls about him right now. Last thing I need with a murderer on the loose is for an officer to be running his own little investigation behind my back. He could get fellow officers killed. Citizens too." His eyes narrowed. "Even those of you right here at Gram's. Now go on, and get cracking with those papers."

"Whatever you say, Chief," Lilli said, and rushed into Gram's kitchen.

Everyone's nonstop energy turned into action.

Lilli swiped the kitchen table with a dishtowel, set down the notebook, and spread out the pages. Bud whirled from window to window, closing the curtains. He flicked on the computer and opened a Web browser. Gram tore through the cleaning supplies under the sink, tossing aside spray bottles, dishwasher soap, and sponges, until she found a fresh box of latex gloves. Lilli grabbed two cameras from her tote and set them on the table.

Hank plunked down in the corner where he could see and hear everything that was about to unfold. He pulled out his cell phone and began making calls. He waved his hands and nodded his head, encouraging everyone to continue with what they were doing.

"Catch!" Gram tossed Bud a pair of latex gloves.

On went Gram's and Bud's gloves.

Lilli zoomed in on the table with her large camera, snapping photos. She switched to her thumb-sized camera and clicked away, copying every word.

"Can you believe this?" Bud peered at the pages.

"Correspondence between Thomas Jefferson and George Washington," Lilli said, and her voice quivered with excitement.

Hank jumped to his feet, accidentally knocking over his chair. "Thomas Jefferson and George Washington!" he exclaimed, setting his chair in place. "I probably couldn't name twenty presidents." He slapped his thigh. "But I sure as shootin' know those two guys."

"Let's start reading," Gram said, nudging her glasses onto the bridge of her nose.

"Go for it," Hank encouraged, then sat down, somewhat embarrassed by his spontaneous outburst of enthusiasm.

"I've got the first page," Lilli said. "Let's split up the rest."

"How about we mix it up," Gram said, choosing her three pages at random.

"Very democratic, Margaret," Bud said. "Washington and Jefferson would have approved."

They studied their pages and soon were chatting away. Then they got down to business.

"President Washington wrote to Thomas Jefferson," Lilli said solemnly, " 'Sir, no doubt His Royal Majesty Louis XVI enjoys your diplomacy, but I have more urgent need of you here.' "

Gram jumped in. "Jefferson replied:

Sir, I regret that I must delay my departure as Monsieur de Lafayette needs help drafting a Declaration of Rights for the French people. My rendezvous this evening with members of the Patriot Party may lead to the establishment of a constitution based on progressive principles, amenable to the National Assembly. I remain optimistic about a peaceful settlement even with the debilitating fiscal crisis and swirling rumors of bread riots."

"This is better than a history book!" Hank exclaimed from the sidelines, his phone clasped to his ear.

"Jefferson sure stood his ground," Bud interjected.

"So did Washington," Lilli said. "He wrote back, 'Alas, I must insist you return to America.'"

Bud waved one of his pages. "In a nutshell, Jefferson said 'not without my wine.'"

"That was cute, Bud," Gram said. "Care to elaborate?"

"Sure thing. Jefferson mentions that he left Le Havre, France, on September 28, with two ships, each carrying three hundred bottles of wine in wooden crates. They sailed toward America."

Lilli's eyebrows shot up. "Two ships? History books mention only one."

Hank slapped his knee with his hand. "Mark my words, history books will be rewritten."

"Any of you ever hear about a collier?" Bud asked.

"No," said Gram.

"Me neither," Lilli added.

"Nope," Hank chimed in.

Bud held one of his pages. "Jefferson says here that a generous benefactor gave him a ship, a British collier, named *Victory*." He turned to Gram's computer.

"Collier, collier, where art thou?" he asked as his fingers pounded the keys. "Aha! A collier is a sturdy and reliable two-masted ship with square sails. It was meant to carry bulk cargo."

Bud clicked the mouse furiously. "Whoa! Colliers were prestigious. Captain Cook sailed around the world in a collier. Captain Bligh's *Bounty* was a collier. During the American Revolution, British General Cornwallis sailed to Virginia with a fleet of colliers and his army of ten thousand men. Hey, they fought against us!"

Bud raised his fist in a victory salute. "But even with their mighty colliers, the Brits couldn't beat us!"

"Bud, you're adorable when you get all fired up about ships," Gram said. "Try and contain yourself, okay?"

"Yes, dear," Bud said and crossed his arms over his chest.

"Jefferson fired this back," Gram said. "'Sir, I am sailing forthwith to America aboard the *Clermont*. Rigging problems have delayed *Victory*'s departure, but I am assured she will follow later in the day. Wish us God Speed.'"

Lilli said, "Here's Washington's reply eight weeks later from New York City:

Sir, I welcome you home to Virginia with unfortunate news. Two trustworthy men on horseback from Long Island reported to me that your collier, Victory, was blown off course by a fierce storm. Victory's captain approached the New York coastline apparently hoping for safe harbor. Eyewitnesses on land and on a nearby ship stated that Victory first disappeared in the fog, then caught fire, and finally sank. Accounts varied, but Victory's final resting place was somewhere in the waters between Montauk Point and the village of Grayrocks. With deep regret I must inform you that the eleven crew members were lost at sea. May their souls rest in peace with our Divine Maker."

"Grayrocks!" Gram interjected. "Two famous presidents were talking about my Grayrocks!"

"Grayrocks!" Hank jumped to his feet and, much to Lilli's amazement, danced a quick jig, and then plunked down on his chair. "Keep reading," he said, flush-faced from jigging.

Gram whispered to Lilli, "I told you he'd dance a jig if an outsider helped him. Go, girl!"

Bud continued reading. "Here's a follow-up letter from President Washington. After some small talk he says:

Rumors have circulated that salvers retrieved two hundred fifty bottles of your wine, and they intend to keep them. This salvers' incident must not distract us and exhaust our energies. I am consumed with organizing the government here in New York City, discussing possible dates to move to Philadelphia, and formalizing plans for a presidential house. With your new responsibilities as Secretary of State, you would be prudent to drop the matter. As a cautionary note, let us remember that a confrontation with the salvers, should it reach the populace, might open festering wounds. Resentment against the British and their colliers continues to run deep among the American people."

Lilli tapped her finger against her chin. "So maybe Jefferson and Washington intentionally remained silent about the shipwreck and salvage efforts. That could explain why history books didn't pick up that Jefferson had sailed home with two ships."

"Could be," Gram said. "And part of me is feeling remorse. If they had spoken up, Grayrocks would be mentioned in history books. We'd be famous!"

"Look on the bright side," Bud said. "At least we have the peace and quiet of living in a small town." He tipped his baseball cap to the left. "Thank you, George." To the right. "Thank you, Thomas."

Lilli turned to her last page. "Jefferson replied to Washington, 'With a reluctant heart, I will abide by your wishes regarding the salvers. However, I deeply regret the loss of my precious wine.'" She looked up. "He signed off with *Your humble and obedient servant*. That's it. We've read all the correspondence."

Bud and Gram slid their pages across the table.

Lilli began collecting and stacking everything.

"These gosh-darned calls can wait," Hank said, snapping shut his phone. He dragged his chair over to the table and plunked himself down. "Let's find out what's in Silas' notebook. Then I need to call my supervisor and tell him exactly what we found. We'll follow his orders to the letter. Let's all be clear on that."

"Lilli, you do the honors," Gram encouraged. In one smooth motion, she went to the counter, cut slices of blueberry pie, and set them on the table. She slid the largest slice in front of Hank.

"Go for it, Lilli," Hank said and leaned forward, ready to devour every word of the notebook along with his slice of pie.

Lilli turned to the first page. It was so quiet that she felt she could hear a flake of piecrust drop to the floor. A rush of excitement matched her curiosity as Silas' familiar penmanship, marked with wavy crossings of *T*'s, curvy *M*'s, and loopy *I*'s, flowed across the lines. But when she glanced at the first few lines, a feeling of dread came over her.

Chapter Fifteen

Gram, Bud, and Hank sat at the kitchen table and listened intently as Lilli read from Silas' notebook.

"To the person who finds this Jefferson-Washington Correspondence (JWC) and my notebook, I beg you, heed my wishes, the wishes of a man in grave danger. Please turn over the JWC and notebook to my friend Dr. Thomas Reed, a professor of marine archaeology at Long Island University. If you can't reach him, please deliver them personally to Dr. Edward Winfield, professor of archaeology at Andrews University. Dr. Winfield doesn't know that the JWC and notebook exist, but he will do what is best. If you are unable to contact either professor, Margaret "Gram" Jenkins who lives here in Grayrocks is trustworthy. Everyone considers her the heart and soul of Grayrocks. She will help you do the right thing."

"Me?" Gram asked and clasped both hands over her heart. "I am the guardian of history?" She closed her eyes and folded her hands in prayer. "Silas Jones, if you're looking down from heaven, all I can say is wow, thanks, buddy-boy!"

"Time is slipping away," Lilli said. "Shall we continue?"

Everyone nodded and Lilli read again from Silas' notebook.

"Under no circumstances should this material be given to the police. I have received anonymous threatening calls to turn over the JWC. One of the callers hinted that certain officers are involved and will make my life a living hell. I wish the caller

had named names, but no such luck. Whoever you are, if you have any concern for Grayrocks and United States history, please abide by my request. No police!"

"Poor Silas," Hank said. "Some creeps scared him so much he was afraid to come to me for help. I'm going to find out who did this and see that justice is served. I owe Silas that. He was a homegrown history buff, a man who loved the sea, a real credit to Grayrocks."

"We know one officer who's a rotten apple," Lilli commented.

"That would be Walt," Hank said.

"You don't know the half of it," Gram added. "Walt wants to be named chief of police when you retire. Solving two murders could make him a serious candidate. Maybe even force you into early retirement."

"That two-faced—" Hank punched his fist into his hand. "But now's not the time. Let's get back to Silas' notebook."

Lilli turned the page and read.

"I want Dr. Reed to know that I discovered the JWC in the false bottom of an old trunk trimmed with copper strips bearing the imprint of anchors. I bought it at a garage sale in Cutchogue, hoping to restore and resell it as a toy chest. Since then my life has turned upside down. I believe someone hacked into my computer or Dr. Reed's and read our e-mails. I'm sure they searched my shop because one morning when I opened up, things were not in their usual order. Scrape marks on the floor tell me the trunk had been dragged toward the door. Scratches, probably from some tool, indicate that someone had tampered with the false bottom. I still receive terrifying calls."

"The contents of that trunk set off two murders," Bud said sadly.

"If only Silas had called me," Hank said, and remorse clung to his every word.

"This is giving me the willies," Gram cut in, setting out a plate of crackers, cheese cubes, and grapes, "but I have to know what happens next. Keep going."

Lilli continued reading.

"Those calls convinced me it was time to move the JWC from the safe in my apartment to the workbench in my shop, where I had devised a secret place that would elude even an expert thief."

Lilli glanced at Hank and he winked. She continued.

"For everyone's safety and the security of the correspondence, I decided to stop all communication until Dr. Reed returns from his Galapagos Islands expedition. I promised I would keep these papers confidential. I haven't broken my word. When Dr. Reed arrives at the conference on Long Island history this weekend, we'll make decisions."

Bud sat back in his chair, his face pinched with sadness. "Silas wrote this, just days before he died. He subbed in my men's Wednesday night poker game. I'll say this for Silas, he played his cards and his personal life close to the vest. If he'd confided in us, things might have turned out differently." He removed his cap and examined the brim before replacing it on his graying head. "Sorry. I got carried away. Keep reading, Lilli."

Gram's telephone rang. "Two rings," Gram said. "That's Skeet telling me there's trouble." Before she could cross the room, the phone rang three times. "Now he's telling me the police are here. Well, which is it? Trouble or the police?" She thought for a split second. "Skeet is a clever kid. He's letting me know exactly what kind of trouble has come to my inn. Douse the lights and keep quiet," she whispered.

"Gram?" Walt's smart-alecky voice traveled up the stairs.

With a sneer on his face, Hank nudged Gram and whispered, "That gosh-darned Walt is everywhere."

"I'll get rid of him," Gram whispered and popped a grape in her mouth. She strode to the landing and stood there in the dim light with her hands planted on her hips.

"Walt, what brings you here at this hour?" Gram made a big show of yawning, and Lilli smiled at her theatrics.

"I see Lilli Masters' Bronco parked in the lot," Walt said. "Is she here?"

"I don't keep tabs on my guests," Gram said peevishly.

"Tell her someone broke into Silas' shop and left the back door unlocked. A passerby saw a redhead running away from there. Tell Lilli to come down to the station in the morning and have a little chat with me."

"Thank you, Walt. Now, if you don't mind, I need my beauty sleep."

Lilli heard Walt snort a series of chuckles. Then he said, "Hey, Skeet, let's hope that beauty sleep works miracles." More chuckles, and then the door to the Baywatch Inn rattled shut.

"Beauty sleep?" Skeet hollered up the stairs. "Gram, you set yourself up for that one!"

"He's just fishing," Lilli said and chastised herself for forgetting to lock Silas' door behind her. "He made up that part about a redhead. I wore a baseball cap to conceal my hair."

She picked up Silas' notebook and hurriedly read.

"These creeps don't want the correspondence for its historical value. I'm certain they hope to find information pointing to the whereabouts of Thomas Jefferson's wine so they can sell it and make a fortune. I'll wait until Dr. Reed arrives. He's smart. He knows many professional people. He will know how to proceed."

Gram handed Lilli a glass of water. Lilli sipped before continuing to read Silas' words out loud.

"I must admit, as soon as I found the correspondence and before I contacted Dr. Reed, I began tracking down Thomas Jefferson's wine. Over a few beers, I posed this hypothetical question to my dock buddies: If a ship loaded with wine sank during a storm somewhere between Montauk Point and Grayrocks hundreds of years ago, where would you now expect to find the sunken wine bottles?"

"Uh-oh," Gram interjected. "Rumors might have spread along the docks about that hypothetical wine." She nudged the snack food closer to Bud. "Sorry, Lilli. Keep going."

Lilli continued reading.

"They believe, based on weather conditions, currents, and sea-men's sixth sense, that the wine would probably be found snagged on the third fork, off Montauk Point. However, my feeling is that they are mistaken about the third fork's location. My research—based on archaeological, maritime, and geological studies along with scant information about salvage efforts on Long Island in 1789—suggests that the third fork lies close to Grayrocks. That is where I predict Jefferson's wine will be found."

"Hot dog!" Gram exclaimed.

"Third fork?" Lilli peered over the notebook. "What is Silas talking about?"

Gram shrugged. "These ole eyes have only seen two forks out there as long as I've been around."

"I once heard something about a third fork at a fish camp near Mattituck," Hank said. "It was my day off. Those old fishermen selling me bait were swapping stories about a third fork. Seems every old-timer in every bait camp on both forks has a theory about where it's located. At the time I didn't pay it no never mind."

"Several of those leathery old-timers are at the conference," Lilli said. "Could be a third fork figures into all of this somehow."

"I'll Google it later," Bud said, scooping up a handful of grapes. "Those bait guys are very protective of 'their' bay. They don't want anybody poking and prodding around there without good reason. They don't want the fish to die out the way the oysters did. Fish are their livelihood. Sorry about the soapbox tirade. Keep going, Lilli. Does Silas say anything else about Grayrocks?"

Lilli read, " 'Rumors have persisted that most of the salvaged wine was stored somewhere in Grayrocks, but I have no confirmation about that.' "

"Cases of Jefferson's wine could be sitting right here in Grayrocks?" Bud speculated. "That would put us on the map."

"Last time I looked," Gram said and shot Bud an impish grin, "we were already on the map."

"So if Silas is right," Lilli said, "the two hundred fifty bottles of salvaged wine could be hidden here in Grayrocks and the remaining fifty bottles might still lie sunken somewhere in the waters off Gray-rocks." She cocked her eyebrow. "Maybe only forty-nine bottles if the one we drank was a Jefferson bottle."

"Oh my," Gram said. "Wouldn't that be something? All these possibilities are making my heart skip a beat."

"And I thought it was my charm," Bud said.

"I hate to ruin this romantic moment," Lilli said, "but, Bud, what can the computer tell us about this mysterious third fork?"

Chapter Sixteen

Bud set to work at his computer and researched furiously. Hank called his supervisor and reported everything that was happening and said he would call back when he had more details. Lilli and Gram nibbled on cheese and reviewed every word of the presidential correspondence and Silas' notebook.

"Hey, everybody. Come here. I got two hits!" Bud exclaimed, leaning back in his chair at the computer. "First up, a Long Island history site."

Hank said into his phone, "I'll get right back to you." He hurried over, along with Gram and Lilli, and studied the words on the monitor.

According to some geologists, the last glacier to arrive on Long Island deposited a ridge of debris beneath the Montauk Peninsula. The ridge may have been a third fork of land, extending from East Hampton on the South Fork into the Atlantic Ocean toward Montauk Point.

"Look at the illustration," Bud said, clicking the mouse. "It shows Long Island with three forks."

"The colors make the theory easier to comprehend," Lilli said. The illustrator had tinted the land beige, the water pale blue, and the third fork a vivid aqua to highlight its submerged location.

"So, the land formed three forks and one was submerged," Hank said, thinking out loud.

"Darn," Lilli said. "If this site is correct, the third fork is nowhere near Grayrocks."

"Let's take a look at the other site," Bud said and clicked the mouse. "Here we are." He pointed at the screen. "Some guy calling himself 'Beach Bum' has a Web site about Long Island geography."

They read in silence for several minutes as Bud scrolled through the information. Suddenly he jerked his hand from the mouse. "Whoa! Beach Bum claims the third fork parallels the North Fork, not the South Fork."

"Good. Beach Bum and Silas agree," Lilli said.

Bud ran his fingertip along the monitor. "Beach Bum nitpicks. He says the North Fork juts out between two bodies of water, the sound and the bay. His theory is that the third fork could lie submerged in either the sound or the bay." Bud cracked his knuckles. "Sound . . . bay. Either way, it's the North Fork."

"Just like Silas said," Hank added.

"So the third fork is close enough to Grayrocks to put our town's name in history books," Gram said. "I'd prefer the bay, because I can see it and walk to it barefoot. I have to put on shoes and ride my bike to the sound."

Lilli peered over Bud's shoulder at the monitor. "What's Beach Bum's evidence and source?"

"He doesn't say," Bud said. "He asks anyone with information to e-mail him, especially anyone who can improve upon his sketches."

"What sketches?" Lilli and Gram asked at the same time.

Bud scrolled further. "Oops!" He said sheepishly. "I didn't go far enough. His sketches show both possible locations of the third fork." He clicked ENLARGE, and the sketches filled the monitor.

"Wow!" Lilli exclaimed. "They look like the squiggly drawings on Silas' folder."

"They sure do," Gram said. "We thought they might be lightning flashes or pitchforks. Who would have expected forks? Land forks."

Lilli blinked hard. "I may be reaching, but all those flourishes, squiggles, and zigzags? They sure look like the shoreline's juts, coves, and hooks on Mia's *Fishy Forks* sketch."

"We've been so busy," Gram said, "I'd forgotten about that cute *Fishy Forks* fax you sent me. When it flipped into my fax tray, I didn't see anything unusual. Maybe we should take another look."

Bud turned away from the computer to face Gram and Lilli. "I seem to be out of the loop," he said.

"Me too," Hank admitted. "What are you gals talking about?"

"This," Gram said, pulling the *Fishy Forks* fax from a cabinet drawer.

Everyone studied the sketch. Lilli saw exactly what she'd seen when Mia completed the sketch. An outline of Long Island, shaped like a giant fish with a huge two-pronged tail that poked into the Atlantic Ocean.

"Mia told me she had focused on Long Island's fishing industry," Lilli said. "I see that. But could there be more?"

"Hmm," Bud said, examining Mia's sketch with the magnifying glass Gram kept near her telephone book. "All this talk about forks could be swaying my opinion, but look here." He ran his finger along Mia's sketch of the North Fork from where it began at Riverhead, passing by Grayrocks, to where it ended at Orient Point.

"I don't see anything special," said Lilli.

"Me neither," added Gram.

"That makes three of us," Hank chimed in.

Bud tapped the map near Riverhead. "Seems to me that Mia put a very big curlicue near Riverhead and then dragged the curlicue's snaky tail into the bay. She has placed a large loop-de-loop near Grayrocks. In an artsy way, Mia's sketch matches Silas' theory. Eureka! The snaky tail is the third fork."

"I agree," Lilli said, her eyes glistening with excitement. How incredible! The forklike sketches on Silas' folder and Mia's sketch all seemed like parts of one big treasure map pointing to the location of Thomas Jefferson's wine. "But something is bothering me. Is the third-fork theory such common knowledge that Mia would automatically put it in her sketch?"

Bud tapped his fingers on Mia's sketch. "Maybe Silas discussed this with Mia and his idea was on her mind."

"Or maybe Mia came upon the information some other way," Lilli said.

"I got more detectives here than down at the station," Hank said.

Gram raised her eyebrows. "One big curlicue with a curvy tail, and we're saying it's the submerged third fork? We're like an octopus, reaching in all directions."

"Maybe not," Bud said. "I found the third fork very easily on the Internet. Granted, everyone except Silas, Beach Bum, and Mia claim it's near the South Fork and out in open waters. Could be this whole concept of a third fork is well-known in certain circles, say, like marine archaeologists and marine artists."

"And old-time fishermen at bait camps?" Hank added.

"And student sketch artists?" Gram asked skeptically.

"I wonder—" Lilli said, her sentence trailing off as she reached into her tote. She pulled out the other two winning sketches from the art students and unrolled them. As she plunked them on the table, Bud anchored the corners with salt-and-pepper shakers.

Lilli leaned over the sketches. "Is it possible that Miko, Mia's art teacher, wanted to keep all three winning sketches because he doesn't want people diving in that area, because—"

"Because he suspects Jefferson's wine is there," Gram reasoned.

"Let's see if these two sketch artists put a third fork in their work," Bud said, turning the light brighter over the kitchen table.

They studied both sketches of Long Island.

"No water, no fork on that one," Gram said.

"Not on this one either," Bud said, and Lilli agreed.

Lilli furrowed her brow. "I'd say Miko offered to buy back all three sketches so as not to call attention to just one. I'm having dinner with him tomorrow night. He offered to discuss the sketches with me. I'll see what he has to say."

"Be careful," Hank said. "What do we know about that guy? He's not from around these parts."

"Neither am I," Lilli said.

"Point well-taken," Hank said.

"Turn on the charm, Lilli. Ask Margaret for advice," Bud said, and Gram nudged him with her elbow.

"What do I know about such stuff?" Gram asked, peering over her spectacles at Bud.

"Don't kid yourself, Margaret. There's still plenty of tread left on your tires."

Gram chuckled and helped herself to a cracker and cheese. "You sure have a way with words, Bud."

"What should we do about Beach Bum?" Lilli asked.

"He could be a nutcase," Gram said.

"He could be legit," Bud said. "His Web site is professional looking."

"Let's e-mail him," Lilli said. "What have we got to lose?"

"Plenty," Hank said forcefully. "There's a murderer out there somewhere."

"I think we should get Dr. Winfield over here right now and give him everything before we go any further," Gram said. "That's what Silas wanted. We need to respect his last wishes. I feel obligated since he mentioned me in his notebook."

Hank curled his lip. "I'm not so sure I trust Dr. Winfield. He's always digging in those caves and carting stuff away. He acts like he owns this town. That's exactly what I told my supervisor. He's giving me lots of wiggle room on this case." He exhaled his satisfaction. "My supervisor and his crew will keep tabs on everything going on here. He wants me to turn over the correspondence and Silas' notebook to him tonight."

"What's our role in all of this?" Gram asked eagerly.

"His orders are that we should play along, you know, stick to what's in Silas' notebook. Let Dr. Winfield think the police were not called in, that Lilli did this on her own." He turned to Lilli. "How do you like them apples?"

"They suit me just fine," she said cheerfully.

Gram piped up. "And naturally part of your supervisor's plan is that Lilli came here with the correspondence and notebook, and we helped her."

"Were you eavesdropping?" Hank asked. "Yes, that's how they want it to play out. Okay, let's get down to business. Gram, Bud, make two copies of everything, one for you and one for Dr. Winfield. Let's hope he doesn't get suspicious when he sees he has photocopies. Lilli, call Dr. Winfield and tell him you found the documents. Lay it on thick how you went behind my back. But let's not make a habit of this. If he doesn't know the police are involved, he may tip his hand. Who knows? He could be a good guy. Lilli, can you handle this assignment?"

Lilli was too thrilled to answer.

"Lilli Masters, have I lost my hearing or are you speechless?" Hank asked.

But Lilli ignored him. She was already searching in her tote for Dr. Winfield's phone number.

Chapter Seventeen

Lilli picked up her cell phone and punched in numbers.

"Dr. Winfield here," he said brusquely.

"Hi. This is Lilli Masters."

"Could you call back in an hour or so? Sorry, Lilli, but this conference has me busier than—"

"You need to come to Gram's right away," Lilli cut in. "Come alone and don't tell anyone where you're going."

"What's this about?"

"There's no time to explain." She heard a woman's voice in the background. "It's really important."

"I'm sort of in the middle of things here."

Lilli heard classical music and the muffled clinking of dishes. "Silas left some papers that you need to see."

"Can't this wait?"

"They could be very important to your career."

"I'll be there in ten minutes," he said.

"Come alone," Lilli reminded him and closed her phone. She turned toward Hank, Gram, and Bud. "Dr. Winfield has company. A woman."

"He's been playing the field," Gram said. "He went crazy with grief when his wife died, then—"

"Then he started chasing women," Bud finished her sentence. "And from what I've seen when he's in town, he has a real eye for beauty. He favors the exotic type. Odd how a man can change when his better half dies. He's almost like a different person."

"Good work, Lilli," Hank said. "I think he bought it. I'll stay out of sight in the bedroom while you hand over everything to him." He shook his head. "This is a whole new way of doing police work."

Bud patted Hank on the shoulder. "But if it works and you solve this case, all of Grayrocks will be proud of you. I know I will. And I'm betting so will everyone in this room."

"I like what I'm hearing," Gram said, beaming with pride. "Bud, you sound so civic-minded, so heroic."

A half hour later, a very happy Dr. Winfield left Gram's kitchen with the presidential correspondence and Silas' notebook locked in his briefcase. Before descending the stairs to the foyer, he leaned against the banister. "The three of you did the right thing. I thank you and so will legions of history buffs."

He descended the stairs rapidly and called over his shoulder, "It's late but I'd better start contacting people." He hit the foyer running and called back, "I'll see you tomorrow at the conference." He opened the front door. "Ships of Olden Days is first thing in the morning."

The door closed behind Dr. Winfield. Lilli almost expected him to shout some final news through the keyhole.

"There should be a tail on him, thanks to my supervisor," Hank said, "but let's see what we can see."

Lilli inched back the curtain and peeked out the window. In the dim light coming from the perimeter of the parking lot, she saw Dr. Winfield heading toward his car. Dr. Winfield opened the door and got in. In the few brief seconds that the interior of the car was illuminated, Lilli glimpsed someone in the passenger seat. A woman. Long curly dark hair. The exotic type, Lilli thought. Dr. Elena Ellison fit that description to a tee.

The car pulled away. An ominous feeling prickled the skin on the back of Lilli's neck. Dr. Winfield hadn't come alone to Gram's as she had asked. Could he be trusted to preserve the historic correspondence as Silas believed that he would? Or was he more interested in using Silas' notebook to locate Jefferson's wine and sell it on the black market?

Lilli was glad she had trusted Hank. Right now, Hank seemed a better choice than Dr. Winfield.

Chapter Eighteen

Before leaving Gram's apartment, Hank said, "Listen up, Lilli. Your sleuthing techniques led you to Silas' secret hiding place and that's great. When this is all over, you'll have your fifteen minutes of fame. Meanwhile, don't go playing detective. Get back to your job and let me do mine. And let Dr. Winfield do his. Does this sound reasonable?"

"Yes," Lilli said. "But sometimes our jobs overlap. You're investigating two murders. I'm reporting on those murders, the conference, and human interest stories about Grayrocks. You don't want me to curtail that, do you?"

Hank cocked an eyebrow. "Well, I guess I could cut you some slack. But don't overstep."

As Lilli walked with Hank to the foyer, she decided to test her interpretation of his words. "So as long as I report any leads about the investigation, I can pursue any stories I want. Am I right?"

"When in doubt, call me," Hank said calmly.

Lilli was certain they had forged a friendship, bristly and subject to change at any given moment, but a friendship nonetheless. She was convinced that he felt the same, but knew he would never admit it. That was just his way. When he left, Lilli leaned against the door and took a deep breath of satisfaction, then hurried back to Gram's kitchen.

"Okay, fellow secret agents," Lilli said to Gram and Bud. "Let's follow Hank's orders and hide our copies of everything, along with my photocopies of the student sketches." She tapped her finger against her chin. "Where would be a good hiding place?"

"That's easy as pie," Gram said.

"In your pie safe?" Bud nodded toward the antique cabinet in the corner and smiled.

Gram rolled her eyes. "Okay, forget the pie. I should have said 'it's a piece of cake.'" She peered over her glasses at Bud. "Don't even think about it," she said, sliding the tin cake-saver toward the back of the counter.

Bud threw up his hands. "So where are we hiding the stuff?"

Gram's eyes twinkled. "Stuff? It's a treasure. I'm thinking buried treasure."

"In the garden?" Lilli guessed.

"Of course not," Gram said. "Somebody might see us. Did either of you see the movie *Psycho?*"

"The cellar," Lilli and Bud said at the same time.

"Bud and I will take care of that, Lilli. You have your own work to do."

Lilli said goodnight to Gram and Bud and went upstairs to her room. She heard Gram say, "Come on, Bud. I'll race you to the root cellar. We'll plant all this beneath the green tomatoes." Lilli sighed. It had been a long day, but she was too excited to sleep. She opened her laptop and set it on the bed in front of her. She plumped up the stack of pillows behind her and made herself comfortable. Maybe more research would turn up new information.

She reviewed all the possible Web site information on Jefferson's wine and his trip home to America in 1789. Thinking about his second ship, she typed in the word *collier*. After countless clicks on the mouse, she came upon an entry about the British General Cornwallis.

Lilli read.

During the American Revolution when Cornwallis' troops were surrounded by enemy French and American troops in Norfolk, Virginia, Cornwallis scuttled twelve of his colliers. He hoped to create obstructions to prevent an attack by water. These vessels were long forgotten, until last year when faculty and students of the University of Virginia, using sonar, discovered one.

Lilli's jaw dropped. The University of Virginia? That sure was a coincidence. She plucked her press packet from her tote and ran her fingertip down the list of guest speakers at the conference. There it was. Dr. Elena Ellison graduated from UVA, the University of Virginia. Hmm. Thomas Jefferson had founded UVA. Had Dr. Ellison chosen that particular university to do special research on Jefferson? Her mind was really churning out theories now.

Lilli read the other notations about Dr. Ellison. Tomorrow, in addition to her seminar on diving techniques, Dr. Ellison would take Dr. Reed's place on the panel discussing ships of olden days. The other panelists would be Dr. Winfield and—Lilli's eyes narrowed— that show-off treasure-hunter Ronald Larson. He believed that since salvers took tremendous risks, they deserved whatever they found, regardless of its historic value. Sounded like the type of person who would salvage Jefferson's wine and sell it to the highest bidder. She definitely would attend that seminar.

Lilli flopped back onto the pile of pillows. Maybe Dr. Ellison had learned something about those colliers that led her to Jefferson's collier. And that brought her to Grayrocks. And maybe, just maybe, Silas' buddies got to talking about that hypothetical shipwrecked wine. If Dr. Ellison were a greedy person . . . If greed overcame her quest for scientific information . . . If . . . if . . . if. There were many ifs, many possibilities. But was Dr. Ellison capable of murder? Or capable of providing information to those who would commit murder? Tomorrow's conference might answer those questions.

Lilli's mind spun with more questions and then stuck on Beach Bum. Who was Beach Bum? Was Beach Bum a man or a woman? Did Beach Bum only know about the existence of a third fork or had he or she heard that Jefferson's wine was trapped there? There was only one way to find out. She decided to e-mail Beach Bum. In the morning? No. Now. Right now, before she lost her courage.

Leery about admitting her true identity and purpose, she created a new e-mail address. With a touch of whimsy, she baptized herself "Waterfront Writer," and claimed she was a college student writing a term paper about North Fork maritime history. She asked for Beach Bum's help, particularly his or her sources for the location of the third fork. Hoping to hear something about President Jefferson, she asked what Beach Bum knew about the role of the third fork, if any, in history. She asked Beach Bum to contact her. Rereading the e-mail, she felt nervous. It was as if she were opening a can of worms and unleashing the wriggling creatures. They would slither over her and sap her strength before she could force them back into the can. A tired mind struggling with reality, she told herself.

She drew a deep breath and hit SEND.

Chapter Nineteen

Early the next morning, Lilli found Gram in the backyard, lifting weights.

"Good morning," Gram called out, as she saw Lilli striding toward her. She set down the weights and wiped the perspiration from her brow.

Lilli opened her mouth to say "Good morning," but Gram said, "Cut to the chase. The expression on your face tells me you have news."

"You are so right," Lilli said. She quickly filled in Gram on her research about the colliers and Dr. Elena Ellison's possible involvement in searching for Jefferson's wine. "I'm pretty certain Dr. Ellison was waiting for Dr. Winfield in his car in your parking lot last night. I hope he didn't tell her anything. We know so little about her. Who knows what she might do with the information."

Gram squelched a laugh. "I see you're stepping aside and letting Dr. Winfield and Hank run the show."

"What can I say?" Lilli shrugged. "My mother was reading Sherlock Holmes when she went into labor. Sleuthing is in my blood. Seriously though, Hank and I have reached a nice working agreement. I know what he will and won't tolerate."

"Hank has his charming ways. I know that for a fact." Gram looked around as if to make sure no one was within hearing distance. "Since you've cast suspicion on Dr. Ellison, here's a tidbit for you. She arrived in Grayrocks early last week, days before the conference started. She wanted a room for two weeks. I couldn't accommodate her. She was disappointed. She said that other inns near mine were booked solid too. I made calls, found several places in Southold and Aquebogue, but she wanted only Grayrocks. This particular part of Grayrocks."

"That's strange," Lilli said. "At the conference, Dr. Winfield mentioned that she has close relatives in the area, whom she often visits. I wonder why she wouldn't stay with them. Did she say why she wanted this particular area?"

"Not that I remember, but at the time I wondered why she was so insistent. I hate to admit it, but there are ritzier inns with hot tubs, martini bars, and shuttles to the Islip Airport. Makes you wonder." She gulped some water. "Now after hearing what you've dug up, maybe I have a better theory."

"I'm all ears."

"She wants to be in Grayrocks close to the bay because, like Silas, she believes that Jefferson's wine is trapped in the third fork's zigzags. I doubt she's thinking finders keepers. I'd say she wants credit in the marine archaeology world for being the one to find it."

"We're on the same wavelength," Lilli said. "Well, we'll talk about all this later. You've got weights to lift, and I'm off to the conference."

Gram checked her watch. "What's your hurry? It's only seven o'clock."

"I have a few stops along the way."

"You're up to something. Detective work is my guess. Weren't you promising to cut back?" She chuckled. "Your promises are just like New Year's resolutions. Everybody makes them and, before long, they break them. Why should you be any different?"

"I knew you'd understand, Gram. We both like to know what's going on."

"That's right. We're not nosy. We're, uh, interested. I've got business interests to be concerned about. You've got a story to write."

"Well said, Gram. So I can come right out and say, I'm curious about what clues might turn up at the beach, especially the rugged area near the dugout caves. That's where Dr. Reed was murdered. That's where Doug found his wine bottle. And it could be the very place Dr. Ellison wanted to explore. Come to think of it, that's where I first met Dr. Winfield."

"You certainly have a lot on your plate today. I'd love to tag along,

maybe offer some local expertise, but I have hungry guests to feed."
Gram picked up her weights and water bottle and headed toward the
back porch. "Call me if you see or hear anything suspicious."

"I will," Lilli said with a smile, "if you'll save me some of that
blueberry cobbler on the kitchen counter."

Lilli descended the pedestrian walkway to Montauk Cove in the
early morning light. She had less than two hours before the conference began. No amateur at seaside sleuthing, she had packed her
tote for every possibility: recorder, notepad, binoculars, swimsuit,
snorkel gear, even Gram's gardening claw. And, of course, cameras.
Film cameras which added an organic quality, almost a three-
dimensional feel to pictures. Digital cameras for the convenience of
seeing immediate results and reshooting if necessary.

Lilli headed immediately to the area near the dugout caves. She
circled around the tents and waved to the campers. Several raised
their coffee mugs. They seemed friendly. Possibly they knew something that had eluded the police. Under pressure to solve two murders
that had occurred within maybe fifteen to thirty minutes of each other
and in close proximity—and to allay fears of a murder spree—the
officers had undoubtedly worked quickly, concentrating on big issues. With luck, she might pry loose pertinent information of a
smaller but no less important nature.

Minutes later, the campers were chatting with Lilli about the conference and their stay in Grayrocks. Here was her chance to find out
if they had seen anything suspicious during the time of the murders
or had found any bottles of wine. She wouldn't bombard them with
questions. Past experience as a professional photographer had taught
her that tourists, whether from idle curiosity or from time on their
hands, liked to ask their own questions while they watched people
work.

"It's time for me to get busy," Lilli said, and pulled her camera
from her tote. "I have a deadline to meet."

"You're a photographer?" asked a perky blond, her hair pulled
back into a ponytail.

"Yes," Lilli said, aiming her digital camera.

"What are you photographing?"

"I'm taking background shots to accompany the conference photos," Lilli said.

Click. Click. Lilli photographed the beach and the embankment.

"You just take pictures at random?" asked the bearded man who was passing around the coffeepot.

"I sure do." Lilli looked away from her camera. "You never know what might turn up"—she paused for dramatic effect—"under these tragic circumstances."

The man wearing an Islanders hockey cap spoke up. "You got that right."

Darn. No questions.

Click. Click. Lilli zoomed in on the gaping entrances to the five dugout caves. "Anything could turn up," she said, "considering all that's been happening around here."

Still no questions.

Click. Click. She focused on the fifth dugout, noticing its proximity to the beach, the bay, and the distinctive large gray rocks that lay strewn along the shore.

Not a single question. Okay, she needed to be more obvious.

She walked past the caves and headed toward the rugged area where Dr. Reed had been murdered. She stopped short. Her stomach tightened as she recalled horror stories about suspicious accidents and drownings at the site just around the bend. She plucked her recorder from her tote and spoke into it, "Only the most experienced campers, like Dr. Reed, would have set up their tents on such dangerous terrain. Local residents claim that the part of Montauk Cove up ahead, aptly named 'the Bad Side,' is jinxed."

The three campers followed in Lilli's footsteps, their faces etched with curiosity. Trying to pique their interest, Lilli walked around the bend and saw the Bad Side for the first time. She recorded loudly, "Here, on the Bad Side, we see the crime-scene tape, a ghastly reminder of the second murder in Grayrocks. Beyond, sandy areas appear randomly among the gray rocks and boulders that dominate this stark landscape and savage seascape."

With the three still trailing her, Lilli switched to her film camera.

Click. Click. She photographed the sprays that washed over the boulders and splashed into the swirling eddies. She recorded, "In the distance, the fortresslike tavern looms above the bay. It appears to belong to the Bad Side, like it had morphed itself out of the rocks, piling stones higher and higher until it finally culminated in a place of dominance." She remembered the article in which the architect described the dream that had inspired his controversial tavern. He'd said something about a creature with mammoth fists of granite that arose from the earth to protect the people from the fury of the storm. She would get the exact wording later.

"You there, ma'am," said an officer appearing from behind a boulder and startling Lilli. "No photos."

"But I'm a photojournalist," Lilli said, and flashed her press pass.

He frowned. "Come back when this is no longer a crime scene."

"Yes, sir," Lilli said, noticing the name Officer Lansing on his badge.

"You and your friends should be on your way," he said.

"Okay," Lilli said begrudgingly.

"Only someone with a death wish would hang around here," the bearded man said, and the other two campers nodded their agreement.

Lilli took one final look at the boulders and the tavern, and then turned back toward the way she'd come. The three campers followed on her heels.

"Just a minute," Lilli said, stopping abruptly, and they gathered behind her. "I need to write down my impressions before they evaporate." She held her pencil above her notepad for a few seconds, and then jotted a few quick notes.

The woman with the ponytail peered over Lilli's shoulder at the notepad. "You're here because of the murders, aren't you?" she asked.

Finally, thought Lilli. Before she could answer, the man wearing the Islanders cap asked, "Who do you think murdered Dr. Reed?"

As the campers followed Lilli back to the dugout caves, they fired more questions at her.

"I'm not a detective," Lilli said, returning her camera to her tote. "But I'd like to add something to my article about the murders. I wish I had some good theories."

"I've got a great theory," said the bearded man.

"Please. Let's hear it," Lilli said, and held out her recorder.

"People kill for money or sex," he said. "You want to find the murderer? Look at the victims' bank accounts and sex life."

"A crazy student angry at his teacher could have done this," said the Islanders fan.

"Nah. Campus competition is the key," said the blond. "I'd say the murderer is a jealous professor who wanted to replace Dr. Reed at the convention."

Lilli wondered if she had Dr. Winfield or Dr. Ellison in mind or just any professor.

"It could have been those nasty volunteers," the bearded man said.

Volunteers? That was the first Lilli had heard any mention of them. "What volunteers would that be?" she asked.

"Not the nice ones who give us maps and clean the area," he said.

"Right," chimed in the woman. "It's those two surly guys who registered us overnight campers, right here by these caves. Some nerve! They practically demanded our name, rank, and serial number."

The Islanders fan cut in, "They asked if we knew any of the speakers at the conference or any of the merchants on Bay Street. Said they were working on a survey to see how varied the campers were."

"A conference speaker and a Bay Street merchant," Lilli murmured, and a chill shot up her spine. Those words described Dr. Reed and Silas. That couldn't just be a coincidence. Those two volunteers were involved.

The woman flipped her ponytail with a wave of her hand. "They treated us like criminals!"

"How many volunteers were there and what did they look like?" Lilli asked, grabbing her notepad and pen.

"Two men, probably in their mid-thirties."

"One was almost bald."

"The other was scruffy and had curly hair."

Lilli sketched as the campers rattled off details and critiqued every stroke she made.

"A longer face."

"Good."

"A scowl that would frighten young children."

"Better."

"Eyes closer together."

"That's them. Dead-on!"

Lilli held the sketches at arm's length. Her eyes popped wide. She knew the men! Those terrible Bond brothers.

"Miss, do you recognize them?" the Islanders fan asked.

Lilli opened her mouth to answer.

"They could have murdered us!" exclaimed the blond.

"I'm not sleeping here again tonight," said the bearded man.

Lilli tried to calm everyone, but their nerves were raw. She passed out her business card. "Thanks for your help. I liked your ideas and descriptions," she said, "and I'd like to pump up my story. Please call me. I welcome your opinions."

As soon as Lilli was beyond their hearing, she called Hank at the police station. He couldn't come to the phone. She figured he was probably meeting with his supervisor about the correspondence. Not wishing to intrude, she left a message describing the campers' experience and asked if he was aware of any volunteers registering overnight campers in Montauk Cove. She closed her phone and headed back to the Bad Side.

"Helloooo, Officer Lansing," she called out.

Officer Lansing appeared from behind the same boulder as before. A pair of binoculars hung from his neck. "Yes? Did you forget something?" He huffed his impatience.

"Just one more question," Lilli said cheerily. "I haven't seen any volunteers. Aren't they scheduled to be here today?"

"They'll come later, about nine."

"Darn." Lilli bit her lip. "I wanted to speak to them about registering for overnight camping."

"That's handled at the town hall permits department, not here on the beach." He shook his head and mumbled, "Media. Demanding this, demanding that. Demands up the—"

"Thanks," Lilli cut in and headed back to the dugout caves. So, the Bond brothers had pretended to be volunteers. They must have been trying to find people who knew Dr. Reed and Silas. Hank would definitely welcome this information.

Doing a one hundred eighty-degree scan to make sure she was alone, Lilli entered the fifth cave. It was damp and musty. She hoped to find the murderer's weapon, reportedly a knife or other sharp object. The police hadn't discovered it, and TV reporters speculated that it might have been thrown into the bay. Lilli figured it could have been buried in one of the caves. If she could find it, and if it had fingerprints on it, she could help catch the murderer. Flicking on her flashlight, Lilli calculated that the cave was about eight feet high and wide, maybe twenty feet deep.

She directed the light close to the earthen walls and roof and the sandy floor. Then, starting at the rear of the cave, she shined the flashlight back and forth methodically, trying to cover every inch. Ten minutes passed, and she didn't see anything unusual.

Then, over there, dead center in the middle of the cave, something shiny reflected in the flashlight beam. She dropped to her hands and knees. A shard of green glass twinkled up at her. Could it be part of a wine bottle? Thomas Jefferson's wine bottle? Could it have been the murder weapon? Heart pounding, she nudged the shard aside with a tissue, so as not to disturb any possible fingerprints. Forcing herself to proceed in an orderly fashion, she raked the sandy floor this way and that with Gram's gardening claw. Nothing. Onward, she went, raking and sifting, raking and sifting.

Chink! The sound of metal striking glass.

Her heart beat faster.

There, right before her eyes, near the rear wall, lay bits of green glass. Forget orderly and slowly! She dug fast and furiously, unearthing more slivers. A piece of torn crinkled paper caught in her gardening claw. With tissues wrapped around her fingers, she carefully picked up the paper. She smoothed it, expecting a map or note, something somehow related to the murders.

She rocked back on her heels. A beer label! Heineken. It wasn't a wine bottle after all. That sure took the wind out of her sails. She quickly buried the pieces of glass deep in the sand in case barefoot kids explored the cave.

Coming out of the cave, Lilli set down her tote, stretched her cramped muscles, and checked her watch. 8:15. Before her, the bay sparkled like a cut-glass decanter. Could Jefferson's fifty bottles of wine be submerged somewhere out there? Well, maybe forty-eight if her bottle and Doug's were part of Jefferson's collection. Could the remaining two hundred fifty bottles salvaged from the shipwrecked *Victory* hundreds of years ago still exist and actually be hidden nearby? She tingled with excitement just thinking about it. If she could find one more bottle, she could determine, with the help of experts, if it really came from Jefferson's wine collection.

Shielding her eyes from the glare, Lilli studied each wave, half expecting a bottle of wine to roll ashore. And why not? It could happen again. She concentrated on the dilemma. There had to be a logical explanation for how the wine had surfaced after so many years of lying beneath the sea. Fishermen had probably been dragging their nets over the bottom of the bay for years, and yet they hadn't extricated any bottles. Maybe recent storms had dislodged the long-buried cases of wine and fierce currents had driven several loose bottles ashore. Or possibly during the past several days divers had brought the dislodged cases to the surface, and stray bottles had floated away. That wasn't such a remote possibility, given the number of divers in town for the convention.

Stop theorizing and get moving, she told herself. Before leaving, she wanted to climb Lookout Bluff for a panoramic view. The beach was nearly empty. Most campers had left for the conference. Someone might take advantage of this quiet time to dive into the bay, searching for President Jefferson's sunken wine bottles.

As she walked, she cast a wide and imaginary net and pulled in a boatload of suspects familiar with the sea: Doug from Doug's Diving School; those nasty divers, the Bond brothers; Silas' dock buddies; Beach Bum; Dr. Elena Ellison, an expert in marine archaeology; Ronald Larson, the show-off salvage expert; Miko Andropolis, the artist who worked with items he'd found at sea and on shore; and possibly Mia, his student, who had fashioned a third fork into her sketch.

Lilli had run into other suspicious people too: the man who had tried to burglarize her Bronco; the man in the janitor's closet who had stolen her wine bottle; Dr. Winfield, who may have revealed the presidential correspondence and Silas' notebook to Dr. Ellison; Walt, who was possibly a dirty cop; Walt's mystery accomplice, who had called him at Silas' shop; and the leathery old salts arguing about liquid gold, although they were most likely annoyed at the diving activity in "their" bay. There were so many possibilities.

She stopped walking and looked up. Lookout Bluff was directly ahead. She would follow her gut instinct and take advantage of the sweeping view from the bluff. That's where she had stood when she'd first seen Doug and his divers and his green wine bottle, like the one she'd found on the beach. Could something more be happening in the bay? Someone else diving there? More wine bottles tossed among the waves?

A series of long shots, but shots worth taking.

Onward and upward, she told herself, and strode to the base of Lookout Bluff.

Chapter Twenty

Lilli clutched her tote and began her climb to Lookout Bluff. The whistling wind whipped through the long grass that slapped against her ankles. Seagulls flapped their wings as they rose in the air and then glided before diving into the whitecaps. Lilli stopped and cupped her hand to her ear. What was that creaking noise she heard? It sounded like metal gears grinding against each other. She continued climbing, pressing her body close to the bluff. If someone was on top of the bluff, she wanted to see them before they saw her.

Creak! Creak! Came the sound, louder now. Then she heard a long low whistle.

"Well now, let's get one more look at that," a man muttered from somewhere above her.

Lilli's stomach churned. At least one man was definitely on top of the bluff. And he had seen something that surprised him. Was he spying on her or had he seen something else that startled him?

Carefully and quietly, Lilli approached the summit. Peering over the tufts of grass, she saw a wiry man turning a squeaky telescope, his back to her, his glasses perched on top of his head, his eyes pressed against the lens. She scrunched to the left for a better view. It was Mark Mastriano, that annoying wine entrepreneur who had pressured her to accompany him to the gala. She'd promised herself to stay clear of him, but right now she was too curious to leave. Was he somehow involved in the search for Jefferson's shipwrecked wine?

Could be. His field of expertise was buying and selling rare wine to rich clients. Could he have murdered Silas to get hold of the Jefferson-Washington correspondence? That question stuck in her mind as she watched where he directed the telescope. She strained to hear what he was mumbling to himself, but the gusting wind carried away his words. The sky was growing dark. The storm that had been predicted was definitely rolling in.

"Lilli Masters, don't be shy," Mark said loudly, startling her as he released the telescope and whirled toward her. His small white teeth glistened like polished pebbles. "Come on up," he said and extended his hand.

She nudged aside his hand and hauled herself up.

"I was hoping I'd see you again," he said, pushing his glasses down onto the bridge of his nose. "It's not every day I meet a pretty photographer who shares my interest in wine. Maybe we could have a picnic on the beach later. A loaf of crusty bread. A bottle of '42 Merlot. A nice Brie. What do you say?"

"I'd say it's quite a coincidence, our running into each other here," she said sharply. "Did you follow me?"

He shrugged. "It seems more likely you were the one following me. Even so, is pursuing a pretty woman a crime?"

She looked over the bluff, relieved to see several people still on the beach, although they appeared to be leaving, probably trying to beat the storm. She ran Hank's phone number through her mind, just in case.

"I apologize for my angry outburst yesterday," he said, leaning against the telescope, his eyes riveted on her. "I'm not very suave or clever around women. Dr. Winfield and Miko Andropolis have cornered that market. I saw how intrigued you were by them, so I thought I'd try."

At the mention of Miko's name, Lilli's eyes widened. At the gala, she and Dr. Winfield had spoken for quite a while in the main area and Mark could have easily seen them, but she and Miko had gone to a secluded table for a quiet drink. Could Mark have been spying on them? On her?

"The conference is keeping me busy," she said. "I don't have time to socialize."

"You make time for other men. Unworthy men." He narrowed his eyes. "Dr. Winfield is old enough to be your father, and Miko Andropolis is a phony. You could at least give me a chance."

He shot her a disappointed look. "You're brushing me off again, aren't you?"

"No," she said, wondering how to get rid of him. She wanted to use the telescope to see if any divers were in the bay.

"I'm glad to hear that," he said, "because you owe me the pleasure of your company. I covered for you when those pesky old fishermen wanted to know if anyone had been asking about President Jefferson and shipwrecked wine. I could have given them your name, but I kept quiet."

"I didn't ask you to," Lilli said.

"But you were watching us. You were up to something then and you're up to something now. I saw you a few minutes ago with those campers. You pretend you're working on an article for a magazine, but you're really involved in the murders. I saw you nosing around the crime scene by the caves not ten minutes ago. I can't vouch for those old fishermen asking about shipwrecked wine. I only spoke to them once, at my booth. But, if you think I'm involved, you're barking up the wrong tree."

"Why would I think that?" she asked.

"Because I believe Dr. Winfield and Miko Andropolis are feeding you information. Wrong information." He looked at the dark clouds rolling across the sky. "What do you say to that?"

"I'd say you have a very active imagination." He was really annoying her. Spying on her, judging her. Enough. She would provoke him just like he was provoking her. "You pass yourself off as a wine expert, but the way I see it, you spend most of your time trying to pick up women."

Ignoring his wounded look, she ploughed on. "I'm surprised you're not busy with your rich clients. Why waste your time with me? You really should leave."

He sucked in his breath. "I like a feisty woman," he said with a faint smile. "Especially one who plays hard to get."

Getting rid of him was going to be harder than she thought. "Don't you have to check on the tavern's wine list or wine cellar or something?" Lilli asked.

"All work and no play—"

"Speaking of work, I need to take a look at early morning activity on the beach." She cut him a frosty glance. "Believe it or not, for my magazine assignment." She turned abruptly, dropped coins into the telescope slot, and peered into the lens. Only a few row boats and small fishing boats had braved the choppy waters. None had divers aboard or in the surrounding water.

Mark kept his distance, but Lilli sensed that he was watching her every move. She steered the telescope to the east, catching sight of Shelter Island. Guiding the telescope slowly back to the center, she stopped and glanced away from the telescope directly at Mark. "I prefer to work alone. If you don't leave, I'll call the police. Go away," she said, nodding toward the edge of the bluff.

"I'm worried about you," he said. "Here you are traipsing around a murder scene, and you're not strong enough to defend yourself. You need protection."

"I can take care of myself," she said. The sky was nearly black now. She wouldn't have much time before the storm rolled in.

Mark moved closer to her, so close that his aftershave stung her nostrils. "In the wine business, I'm a big man." He raised himself up to his full height and pulled back his shoulders. "Everyone comes to me for advice. I'm well respected and I have connections. I could guarantee that no harm would come to you."

"Stay away from me," she said, grabbing her phone. If he didn't leave she would definitely call Hank.

"Okay," he said, backing away. "I can take a hint." He started down the bluff. "My offer stands," he called up to her, then hurried on his way, more agile than she would have imagined.

Lilli waited until she saw Mark below on the beach. She kept him in sight until he started up the pedestrian walkway toward Bay Street. Then, with a huge sigh, she returned to the telescope. Dropping in more coins, she scanned the beach again, this time studying everything from the midway point toward the Bad Side. Waves splashed over the rocks. Without the bright sunlight, the water appeared dark and murky. She slowed and inspected the area. Why had Mark lingered with the telescope in this very spot?

Were her eyes playing tricks? Something dark and rectangular lay at the bottom of the bay, near the Bad Side. She adjusted the telescope's focus, magnifying the object. Her breath caught in her throat.

Her nerves were frayed and her imagination was obsessed with death and dying, but she couldn't deny what she saw. The silhouette resembled a coffin. She shuddered.

The telescope didn't turn far enough to the right to allow her to see the entire area. Boulders blocked some of the view. Determined to push such macabre thoughts from her mind, she grabbed her tote and scrambled down the bluff. She hurried past the fifth dugout cave toward the water's edge, bypassing the DANGER NO SWIMMING sign. Dropping her sandals and tote, she struggled through the churning water.

Raindrops splattered on her face. Waves whipped past her legs. The sand sucked at her feet. She wobbled, trying to catch her balance. Another wave rolled in. Her arms flailed, and she fell. Struggling to her feet, trying to keep her balance, she spotted the dark object, just ahead. It was a scuttled boat, overturned on the bottom of the bay, just beyond the dropoff. A strong swimmer, she figured she could get close enough to see the name on the boat. But when she struggled forward, the sand beneath her feet slid away. The currents lifted her and pulled her into deeper waters. She tried to swim for shore, but which way was it? Her hair swirled across her face. Her eyes burned. She choked on sea water. Don't give up, she told herself, and fought the panic that tied her stomach in knots.

She pushed her hair out of her eyes just in time to see a wave cresting toward her. Turning her back to the wave, she was struck by its full force. It pulled her under. She felt the sand raking her body as the current dragged her across the stony bottom. Her lungs were screaming for air. She was tossed like a rag doll into the shallows. Seconds later, all four limbs touched soft sand. Gulping in air, Lilli fought to rise to her feet. Stumbling and trying to move forward, she struggled against the strong pull of the undertow of another wave.

"Get out of the water now!" Officer Lansing called out.

Through the spray of water, Lilli saw him drop from a boulder onto the sand. He was running toward her. She managed to swim several more strokes, got to her feet, and staggered out of the water. He stood a short distance away, arms crossed over his chest, a stern expression on his face. Lilli could read that expression. Ignoring her breathless trembling, he saw only a trespasser.

"I've been talking to Hank. He tells me you've been to Grayrocks several times," Officer Lansing said crustily, "but you sure are acting like a know-it-all first-time tourist. Didn't you see the no-swimming sign? Didn't you notice the waves? The approaching storm? I'm sure you've heard about the riptide here on the Bad Side. Everybody knows about that." He tossed her tote and sandals to her. On and on he went, his face growing redder with every reprimand.

Shivering, Lilli stood there like a little kid being chastised by an angry parent, not saying a word. She deserved it. He and every other member of the police department needed to concentrate on the investigation into the murders of Silas and Dr. Reed. She was wasting their precious time.

"I'm sorry," she said. "I'll leave and let you do your job."

"I just want to prevent another disaster," Officer Lansing said, softening a bit.

"Do you know anything about that boat?" she asked, as the words *another disaster* sank in. "I'm sure it wasn't here yesterday. I wonder whose boat it is."

"It belongs to Doug Carter. He owns Doug's Diving School."

"Is he okay?" Lilli asked, worried about him.

"Doug's a lucky man," Officer Lansing said. "He's shaken up, but he's going to be fine."

Officer Lansing sounded almost friendly. Lilli wondered how she could get him to open up more.

"What happened?" she asked, reaching for the towel in her tote.

"Early this morning, Doug was way out there in the bay. A diver, we think, sneaked up while Doug was out of his boat diving and cut the bottom of Doug's boat with a harpoon or something. It went down fast, but Doug managed to flip his boat and cling to it. He got it close to shore before it sank. The riptide nearly got him, but a rescue team pulled him out. That's about the time I arrived. He refused medical treatment and made a call. A friend picked him up."

"I know you pay attention to details," Lilli said, hoping to butter him up. "I wonder who that was. Do you remember what the friend looked like?" Images of the Bond brothers flashed in Lilli's mind. She struggled into her sandals, hopping on one foot, which was bleeding.

"Not that I noticed particularly—I'm married you know—but she was a curvy blond in a wet suit. She said she was Doug's cousin." He winked. "Uh-huh, sure thing."

Lilli felt like she was on a roll now. "Did you happen to see Mark Mastriano here on the beach around the time Doug's boat was attacked?"

"You mean that weirdo from the tavern?" Officer Lansing shook his head. "I can't say. Like I said, I'd just come on duty to relieve Walt and I got caught up in change of shift info."

Walt? Lilli shivered. Walt—always close at hand when trouble happened. Where was Walt when Silas and Dr. Reed were murdered?

Chapter Twenty-one

By the time Lilli arrived at the inn, she had decided to cut short her time at the conference so she could track down Doug. She wanted to hear from him about the attack on his boat—and possibly his life—at Montauk Cove. Staying clear of Gram, who would fret about why she looked like a drowned cat, Lilli changed clothes quickly and hurried to the conference.

As she approached the community center, she spotted Walt. His police cap was pulled uncharacteristically low over his eyes, as if he didn't wish to be recognized. What was he up to, she wondered. She pulled up behind a parked van, hoping she was out of Walt's sight. She peered out cautiously. Walt stopped in his lane in his patrol car.

Someone in a beat-up red VW Beetle came from the other direction and pulled alongside him. The person rolled down their window. Walt did the same. What Lilli wouldn't give to be a fly on the fender, hearing every word. This could be his accomplice! She tried to read the license plate, but several parked SUVs blocked her view. She couldn't see the driver either. A Honda Civic coming down the road beeped at Walt and his friend, whose cars were blocking traffic. Lilli saw Walt take off and the Civic roar by.

She telephoned Hank and described the car. Hank snorted his laughter. "That's Walt's girlfriend, Betty. He sees her on the sly and thinks nobody knows. Trust me, Miss Super Sleuth, everybody knows."

"Everybody except me," Lilli said. She saw the red Beetle pass by. The driver, a middle-aged brunet, dabbed at her eyes with a tissue.

"Walt and I had a good long talk. It was Betty, not anyone con-

134

nected to the investigation, he was talking to at Silas' when we found the correspondence."

"That's a relief," she said, but she still didn't trust Walt.

Hank sucked in a long breath. "Let's cut this short. I'm talking to Silas' buddies down at the docks. Go to the conference, write your story, and stay out of trouble. Okay?"

"Sure thing, Chief. No problem."

Looking over her shoulder before pulling into traffic, Lilli came face-to-face with Doug. He was banging on her window and mouthing the words "Open the door." Then he ran around to the passenger side.

"Get in," she said, startled by his sudden appearance and frightened expression. "I heard about the diver assaulting your boat. Are you okay?"

"I'm fine. Just drive," he said, plunking down next to her. He slumped way down in the seat, his shoulders pulled up to his ears.

She pulled away from the curb. "Where to?"

"Anywhere away from here. You're in serious trouble," he said. "We both are. There are people who want us dead. You should get out of Grayrocks while you can. I'm leaving in a few minutes."

"You're scaring me," she said. "Who wants us dead? What have we done?"

"We were seen with Thomas Jefferson's wine bottles."

"That's a reason to murder us?" she asked. More and more she believed that Silas and Dr. Reed were murdered because of something they knew about the wine.

She needed to concentrate on what he was saying. She pulled into an alley, came to a sudden stop, and gave him her full attention.

"You'd better start at the beginning," she said.

Doug nodded. He looked over one shoulder and then the other. "Last Thursday, at happy hour in the Clam Digger Bar in Cutchogue, I overheard the Bond brothers talking. Remember them?"

"Sure. Real bullies."

He nodded. "Right. They were drunk as skunks at the Clam Digger. I heard them mumble rumors that Jefferson's wine was going to be transported in the middle of the night, that very night I assumed, in Montauk Cove. So I left immediately. I brought my boat and some buddies down from Riverhead, and we kept watch at Montauk Cove. We didn't see any movement. When the sun came up, we began diving. It turned out you were watching us from shore. I found one bottle, and you found one."

"And the Bond brothers saw us?"

"They admitted they saw me. They must have heard you asking questions at the conference or maybe they saw you carrying your wine bottle. Then they saw the two of us together at the Terrace Café. They must have figured we were in this together." He squirmed in his seat. "Here's the scary part."

Lilli took a deep calming breath. "I'm listening."

"They think I know where a big supply of Jefferson's wine is. I wish I did, but I don't have a clue. They threatened to kill me if I didn't tell them. They asked me what you knew about the wine. 'Nothing,' I told them. I don't know if they believed me. They've been hounding me ever since. Maybe you know more about the wine than you let on. I don't know, and I don't plan on hanging around to find out. All I know is you need to take this seriously."

"Why are you looking out for me, Doug?" Lilli asked curtly. "We hardly know each other. For all I know, you're setting me up for something."

"Warning you wasn't my idea. Mia made me promise to talk to you."

Lilli's eyebrows shot up. "Mia, the art student?"

"Yeah. Mia's my friend. She said you bought her sketch and that you were nice to her. You tried to help her or something. You even returned her sketch when she asked you to. She's afraid that the Bond brothers are going to hurt you because of something she said or did. She'd have a hard time living with that, she said."

He jerked forward and rapped his fists on the dashboard. "This whole wine thing is getting out of hand. I dragged Mia into this. I don't want anything bad happening to her. I'm leaving town. You should too. I'm telling you this for your own good."

Lilli put two and two together. "Did Mia pick you up after your boat sank?"

"Yeah."

"She told Officer Lansing she was your cousin. Am I right?"

A wry smile tugged at Doug's mouth. He nodded. "So consider yourself warned."

"Thanks," Lilli said.

"You can let me out here." He looked warily at her.

"Is it safe for you to be walking around?"

"I won't be walking," he said.

A car pulled within view, and Lilli saw Mia clutching the steering wheel.

Doug smiled. "Mia won't let me out of her sight. She followed us."

"Good luck," Lilli said. "Watch your back."

"You too," he said.

Lilli pulled out into traffic. In the rearview mirror, she saw Mia make a U-turn and head in the opposite direction. Lilli felt a sudden pang of fear cut through her. She feared for Doug, for Mia, and for herself. All because of wine. Deadly, bloodred wine.

Chapter Twenty-two

It was almost noon when Lilli parked at the community center. What a difference a few miles and an hour made! At Montauk Cove, storm clouds had burst open and drenched everything. Here in the north end of town, a passing shower had barely dampened the grass. The sun now peeked from behind the clouds and a warm breeze was blowing. She leaned out the window to make sure she wasn't straddling two parking spaces, when who should she see approaching but Chuck Matthison. He strode toward her, hands in his pockets, his doubtful face checking the sky.

"Chuck?"

"I had just about given up on you, but then I saw your Bronco," he said. He leaned into her truck. "Just wanted to let you know I gave your gift to Gram some thought. After leaving here yesterday, I went through my stock and came up with eight matching pots, nothing fancy. They might do the trick. And I have lots of flowers and plants to pick from."

"Thanks. That was very thoughtful of you. I don't mean to seem ungrateful, but I can't take the time now. I'll come take a look later, okay?"

"There's no rush." His jaw clenched. "Anytime you want to talk."

Lilli again noticed a certain intensity about him, the clenched jaw, the way he had of locking eyes with her.

"Thanks again," Lilli said. "I hope it wasn't too much trouble."

He shook his head. "I owe you that much."

"For what?"

"For promising to keep rumors about my family out of your story."

"Wait. I never promised—"

138

But Chuck turned abruptly and melted into the crowd. Lilli felt uneasy about how he had misinterpreted their conversation from yesterday. And now she wondered if he was trying to bribe her silence for a handful of pots and plants. Was this how he treated all reporters?

She decided to pay a visit to Chuck and make it clear that she would write her story how she thought best, that she'd made no promises. But when she arrived at Chuck's nursery stand, he was nowhere in sight.

A helper, a teenager wearing a baseball cap with the brim turned to the side, saw her coming and leaned against his broom handle. "Help you?" he asked.

Lilli noticed he was sweeping up pottery shards. There was a row of seven matching pots lined up on the table. The eighth one lay shattered on the ground.

"Having a bad day?" she asked.

"Not me," he said with a shrug. "My boss. He is one stressed-out dude. He's heading for a heart attack."

Was the broken pot the result of an accident or bad temper? she wondered. "Tell him Lilli stopped by and will be back later."

"No problem," he said and started sweeping the shards into the trash.

As Lilli walked away, she tapped numbers into her cell phone. "Bud? Hi. It's Lilli. . . . Yes, I'm at the conference. . . . I would like a man's opinion on something."

He chuckled. "You've come to the right place."

"I'm trying to figure out Chuck Matthison." She filled him in about what Gram had said. "Do you know anything else about him?"

"Well, the barbershop guys say Chuck spent his time in Wyoming soul searching. He returned home, convinced it wasn't some weirdo curse that drove the Matthison men to an early grave. He figured it was evil people inspired by envy and greed."

"I'm surprised he returned."

"Well, he has property here."

"And maybe a special woman in his life?" Lilli asked.

"I heard most gals dropped him like a hot potato, but I never heard why. Silas told me Chuck bought a gift every now and then, obviously for a woman. A shark's tooth bracelet for one. Silas and Chuck chatted now and then, had a few beers."

"I'd be curious to know what Silas thought of him."

"Silas said Chuck was too serious, almost morose, and didn't seem to have any real friends. All Silas and Chuck had in common was their interest in local history."

Lilli thought about the smashed flowerpot. "This may be coming from left field, but did you ever hear that Chuck had done anything violent?"

"Quite the opposite," Bud said firmly. "He's a gentle soul. He appreciates Mother Nature's beauty. Spends more time with plants than people. According to Hank, he's never caused trouble. Never been in trouble either."

"Okay. I needed to hear that from a local."

"What do you think of him, Lilli?"

"There's a nice side to him. He's very protective of his family. He can be thoughtful, but there's a deep well of melancholy inside him that makes me feel sorry for him."

"Easy there, Lilli. Don't go trying to save him. Stick with Zack. He's the guy for you."

"You're sweet, Bud. And you've been a big help. See you later."

Lilli closed her phone. She felt foolish. Chuck hadn't gone off the deep end over a flowerpot. He had probably just dropped it. He was a perfectionist. He'd probably gone to find a replacement so that Gram would have eight matching pots on her patio.

Chapter Twenty-three

As Lilli headed toward the community center, music and the joyful noise of laughter and cheers greeted her. She tried to relax after the disturbing conversation with Chuck Matthison. Craning her neck, she saw that the food court was open for business and the first lunchtime entertainment, a grape-stomping event, was about to begin. Exhibitions from Grayrocks High School's athletic teams would follow. Crowds of people rushed about, enjoying the outdoors and the break from the seminars. Lilli didn't blame them. All those facts, figures, and films could be overwhelming.

Here was her chance to capture the lively spirit of the North Fork residents who sure knew how to enjoy themselves. *Viewpoint* readers would love all this small-town fun-time activity. Her editor might even consider a separate article coming out of this. Convinced that good photos would assure a go-ahead from her editor, she photographed everything.

She zoomed in to capture vendors selling lemonade, iced tea, and soda. What a brisk business they enjoyed in booths circling the entertainment area!

She zoomed in again. This time she caught the grape-stomping contestants gathered around a huge wooden vat. They were warming up with jumping jacks.

How could she resist the adorable children? Drawn like magnets to the face-painting booth and games of horseshoes and ring toss, they whooped it up.

She was on a roll now. Unable to resist the pungent aromas wafting through the air, Lilli followed the crowds to the row of cooking stations. She chatted with the chefs. As she complimented one chef on the veggie kabobs, her cell phone rang.

"I'm watching you, Lilli Masters," a man's raspy voice growled. "You stick your nose where it don't belong one more time, and you'll be sorry." The line went dead.

Lilli froze on the spot. What did he mean by "one more time"? What had she already done that irritated this man? Something in Silas' shop? At Montauk Cove? Here? But what? She scanned the crowds, but didn't see anyone watching her.

The threat from the mystery caller had shaken her. Forget about him, she told herself, but she couldn't. She called Hank and explained what had happened. She heard the fear in her own voice.

"Let me finish one quick detail," Hank said, his voice filled with concern, "and I'll come over there. Stay calm. Don't take any crazy chances. Don't go anywhere with anyone. Got that?"

"Yes, Chief," she said, looking left then right with frightened eyes.

Get to work, she reminded herself, *and the time will pass quickly. Hank will be here soon.* Exhaling slowly, she aimed her camera.

Click! Chefs, wearing white bib aprons, peered from beneath the tall white toques perched on their heads. They bantered with customers as they grilled fish fillets.

Click! A soup chef demonstrated how to make Manhattan clam chowder, laced with juicy tomatoes. "Go figure why they call it 'Manhattan chowder,' " he said into his microphone. "Last I heard, Manhattan was in New York City. We grow the vegetables and harvest the clams right here on the North Fork."

Lilli smiled nervously and moved along.

Click! Chefs tossed salads brimming with the North Fork's famous produce that filled roadside stands.

A ruddy-faced chef carving vegetables caught Lilli's eye. *Click!* He had sculpted a huge squash to look like an Indian chief wearing a feathered headdress.

"That's Chief Wyandanch, the chief sachem of the Montauk tribe," the chef said.

"Two handsome fellows, a chief and a chef," Lilli exclaimed and snapped their picture. Everything was so pleasant, so picture-perfect.

She began to question whether she had actually received a threatening phone call.

Reaching into her tote for pen and paper to record the word *sachem,* she discovered a Post-it note stuck to the cover on her notepad. Written in bloodred block letters, the words nearly jumped off the page: GOOD RIDDANCE, SILAS AND DR. REED. YOU COULD BE NEXT, LILLI MASTERS!

Lilli's heart beat like a trip hammer. With trembling fingers, she fumbled for her phone. She called Hank again and told him about this latest threat.

"Hang on, Lilli. We're only ten minutes away. Don't let anyone get close to you. Don't leave the conference area. Are you with me on this?"

"Yes, Chief," she said and heard his phone click off.

She jammed her phone into her tote. She was angry at the note writer and angry at herself for letting down her guard. Someone had gotten close enough to reach into her tote. He could just as easily have stabbed her. She grasped the cruel note, eager to show it to Hank. Sweat beaded her forehead.

She studied the sea of faces that surrounded her. About fifteen feet away, standing by a maple tree, one of the Bond brothers snarled and the other brother cut his cold, hard eyes at her. *Come on, Hank,* she said to herself. *Hurry. Please hurry.*

Frightened, she hoped and prayed the Bond brothers wouldn't dare harm her here with so many witnesses. She wanted to run, but they would follow. She thought about screaming for help, but what proof, besides an unsigned note, confirmed that she was being harassed?

A man's deep voice boomed from the loudspeaker, startling Lilli. "The grape-stomping event will begin in five minutes." When she looked again at the maple tree, the Bond brothers had vanished.

Unnerved, Lilli moved with the crowd back to the entertainment area. *Get to work or you won't have enough information and photos for the* Viewpoint *article,* she told herself, *but keep a sharp eye out for trouble.*

She still didn't hear a police siren. Hank must have run into trouble on the way. Where was he?

Click! She captured the huge wooden vat, filled knee-high with grapes.

Click! Click! She photographed the mayor and several council members rolling up their pant legs and climbing the ladder into the vat.

Click! Click! Click! Click! She caught every moment as they jumped and stomped . . . crashed into each other, tottering, tumbling . . . rolled around in the grapes . . . staggered to their feet, splattered with purple juice. She would have laughed along with the rest of the audience if she weren't such a nervous wreck. Where was Hank? What was taking him so long? *Zack, how I wish you were here.*

The loud speaker squawked and a man's melodious voice called out, "Come join us for our next exhibition, starring Grayrocks' talented athletic teams."

The blare of trumpets burst forth.

Lilli rushed toward the sound of the trumpets, staying in the safety of the crowd. Everywhere she looked, she saw a sea of purple-and-gold uniforms. The marching band, cheerleaders, majorettes, pompom girls, and flag twirlers crowded the area. The athletic teams rushed forward as the crowds of parents, friends, and classmates cheered them on.

Eager to cheer Gram's helper, Skeet, the varsity team's number two wrestler, she headed toward the wrestling area in the side parking lot. She saw the team stretching on blue rubber mats, marked with an inner and outer circle, surrounded by safety mats.

Click! She photographed Coach Velasquez, who addressed the crowd, "We don't slam bodies, crunch necks, or stomp on kneecaps. This is a mental challenge, the real deal."

She photographed Skeet and his teammate-opponent and the other pairs of wrestlers, wearing headgear and singlets on their toned bodies. She was about to zoom in for a reverse body lock when Carl, the clean-shaven Bond brother, stepped in her path, leering at her. He ran his index finger across his throat as if he were slicing it with a knife. Then he pushed past her and slithered into the crowd. She watched him sprint toward the deserted area beyond the crowd, mouthing off information into his cell phone. The knot of anxiety in her stomach tightened.

"Lilli Masters," a gruff voice said from behind her.

She swirled around. Frank Bond's face was inches from hers.

"Final warning," he snarled. "Mind your own business, or someone will get hurt . . . or worse. Someone you care about."

Before Lilli could say a word, Frank Bond rushed off.

Someone she cared about! Her parents? Zack? Gram? Bud? Friends here in Grayrocks? Her mind spun with possibilities. Hands trembling, she called Hank. He answered on the first ring. "Where are you?" she asked, practically in tears. "You promised you would come here."

"Gosh-dang traffic snarl-ups. It's a mess, but we're on our way. The community center is coming up as we speak."

"Hurry," she said and heard the police siren wail in the distance. She couldn't risk someone she loved being harmed. No way. She decided to pack up her cameras and make a beeline for the parking lot where Hank was headed.

"First up, our best juniors," Coach Velasquez announced. An uneasy feeling nagged Lilli. Those two guys were supposed to wrestle after Skeet and his teammate. Why were they going first? Where was Skeet?

Her phone rang. It must be Hank, letting her know that he was in the parking lot! She flipped open her phone.

"Lilli," the raspy voice said. "You didn't listen. Now Skeet will pay for your stupidity."

The line went dead.

Frantic, Lilli called Hank again. Thankfully, he was just minutes away. "Please, come straight to the wrestling area right now," she said.

"Two minutes and we'll be there."

Lilli tossed her tote over her shoulder and hurried over to Coach Velasquez. "Where's Skeet?" she asked.

"He got a call. Some kind of emergency. He rushed off to the locker room."

An image of Carl Bond racing toward the locker room flashed through Lilli's mind. "Coach, Skeet's in danger. Someone might try to kill him. Help him! Please help him!" Lilli pleaded. *The police will be here soon, but maybe not soon enough,* she said to herself and hurried away to find Skeet.

Minutes later, she saw both Bond brothers outside the locker room. They were pushing and shoving Skeet up against the wall. Lilli watched in horror as they knocked him to the ground. Carl Bond raised his foot, ready to kick Skeet in the gut, but Skeet rolled away. He picked up a handful of gravel and tossed it in the face of one of the Bond brothers. He tossed another handful in the other brother's face. They yelped in pain, shook their heads like mad dogs, and brushed grit from their eyes.

Skeet took off running.

The brothers chased after him.

Lilli followed, shouting, "Help!"

She couldn't believe it. The few people around must have thought this chase was some kind of crazy entertainment.

"This is for real. Stop those men!" Lilli shouted.

Skeet turned at the sound of her voice.

"Get help, Lilli!" Skeet called.

Sirens blasted from close by. "Hank's on the way!" she called out.

The sirens were really screaming now. Skeet stopped running and turned to face the enemy. Extending his arms in front of himself, he stood his ground, almost inviting them to invade his territory, his circle.

Lilli tripped, then scrambled up. She saw Skeet, a steely glint in his eyes, as the Bond brothers bore down on him.

Skeet tackled Frank Bond, the taller brother. *Bam!* He had him in a hammerlock.

Carl Bond jumped in and began pummeling Skeet.

Lilli kicked Carl, but he continued his attack on Skeet. She swung her bag and clipped him on the side of the head. She lost her balance and fell.

A whistle blasted again and again.

Lilli looked up and saw Coach Velasquez, arms and legs pumping, coming over the crest of a hill. The entire wrestling team, led by Skeet's opponent-partner, followed behind Coach.

The team scrambled down the incline and locked arms in a circle around the Bond brothers.

Coach Velasquez helped Lilli to her feet.

"Get your camera ready," Skeet said to Lilli. Then he turned to his teammates and swiped the saliva from his mouth with the back of his hand. "Stand back, guys. Give me room to finish off these creeps."

Skeet's partner tugged tight his headgear straps. "Be a sport, Skeet. Let me even the odds. I'll take the ugly one."

"Okay," Skeet said, sounding resigned. "I'll take the uglier one."

Their teammates egged them on with cheers and advice.

Lilli felt proud as Skeet and his teammate tackled the Bond brothers and pinned them to the ground. The wrestlers seemed to make a game of it, loosening their grip and letting the brutes squirm away, only to tackle them again.

Finally Coach Velasquez said with a lopsided grin, "Guys, what's taking you so long? We need to get back to finish our matches with some real competition."

In three seconds flat, the Bond brothers were sprawled on their stomachs, begging for mercy. Their stunned expressions seemed to say, "How did two high school kids humiliate us like this?"

Sirens screamed.

Patrol cars roared into the parking lot next to the locker room.

People rushed in from all directions to see what was happening. Hank pushed himself out of his patrol car and shouted through his bullhorn, "Nobody move until I sort this out!"

Hank's sidekick, Walt, snickered. "That could take a while," Lilli heard him mumble under his breath.

Hank slowly and dramatically surveyed the scene. He pulled off his sunglasses. "Don't worry, Lilli," he said, "we've got this under control."

He snapped his fingers in the general direction of his officers and pointed at the Bond brothers, who were staggering to their feet. Two officers shoved the brothers against a patrol car and handcuffed them.

"This is all a big mistake," Frank Bond said.

Carl Bond growled, "Police brutality. You'll pay for this."

"Stuff a sock in it," Hank said. "I'll take your statement at the station."

Maggie and the girls' track and field team pushed through the crowd. Maggie ran toward Skeet, but Hank held up his hand, signaling her to stay back.

Hank turned to Skeet and draped his arm across Skeet's shoulder. "Now, son, suppose you tell me what this was all about."

Skeet shrugged. "I never saw those guys before in my life."

"If your memory improves, call me. Here's my number," Hank said and palmed a card into Skeet's hand.

"Chief, you have a business card?" Skeet asked, opening his eyes wide in feigned surprise and winking at his teammates.

"Yeah," Hank said sheepishly. "That's how the cops do it on TV. People expect them now."

Maggie came to Skeet's side. She pressed a tissue against a nasty cut over his eye. Lilli could see that Skeet was enjoying every minute of Maggie's attention.

Putting on his official face, Hank snapped his fingers and nodded at his officers. They nudged the Bond brothers into one of the patrol cars.

Hank stuffed himself back in his car. "Glad you called for help, Lilli. You were in over your head."

"And you threw the life preserver to me," she said.

Hank roared the engine and, with a wave of his hand out the car window, signaled his officers to follow him. He left, leading the patrol cars in a flurry of flying leaves, sand, and grit that had everyone shielding their eyes from the fallout.

Playing leader of the pack, Hank was putting on a show for the crowd, Lilli thought. Once the show was over, the crowds broke up and headed back to the entertainment. The athletes raced past them, ready to continue their demonstration matches before the afternoon seminars began.

Lilli walked over to Skeet and whispered, "I think you know more than you're telling."

"Give us a minute, Maggie," Skeet said.

"Sure thing, hero," Maggie said, smiling at Skeet. She waited a short distance away.

"Frank and Carl Bond—that's the brothers' names," Skeet began.

"I know," Lilli said. "I've had the pleasure of their company."

"They wanted me to tell them what I knew about wine coming and going at Baywatch Inn. I told them wine deliveries were made first and third Thursday of the month. They said, 'Not that kind of wine, kid, special wine. Do you get our meaning?' I told them no, I didn't. I guess they didn't believe me. Those guys have vicious tempers. They wanted to know about your connection to the Baywatch Inn. I said you were a guest." He gave a sly smile. "Nobody special."

"Thanks, Skeet." She returned his sly smile. "I appreciate that."

"There was a good side to this fight," Skeet admitted.

"I saw," Lilli said. "You melted Maggie's heart. Are you sure you're okay?"

"I'm fine," Skeet said. "Any trouble, my teammates will handle it. They are sick and tired of football players getting all the media attention."

Lilli headed back to catch a few seminars. She felt somewhat relieved knowing that the Bond brothers wouldn't be around for a while to cause trouble, but she still wondered why they had threatened her. They thought she knew something about the wine, but what? What did they have to do with all of this? They were rough and nasty, but she wasn't convinced they were clever enough to plan the murders of Silas and Dr. Reed. Someone more experienced and less obvious was responsible, she was sure of it. For now at least, the Bond brothers were temporarily out of the picture.

Chapter Twenty-four

Lilli ducked into Gram's apartment. "Have a fun evening," she said to Gram and Bud, who were sitting on the couch shuffling through a stack of DVDs.

"We're going to watch a movie," Bud said, "but first we need to make a decision."

"I like excitement, adventure, with spies running around," Gram said as she held up a fistful of DVDs. "Bud prefers comedies."

"A good belly laugh clears a muddled mind." Bud pulled Gram close. "Let's compromise. How about a comedy tonight and spies tomorrow night?"

"Be a good sport," Gram said, "and start with the spies tonight."

"Okay." Bud's eyes twinkled with mischief. "But no wheedling tomorrow night for another tale of intrigue."

Smiling at their good-natured bantering, Lilli checked herself in the mirror. She tucked her yellow silk top into her black linen slacks and dabbed on some lipstick. "See you later," she said, tossing her black sweater over her shoulders.

Gram slipped a DVD into the slot. "Enjoy your evening with Miko," she said.

"Will your evening be an adventure or a comedy, Lilli?" Bud asked with a wink.

"Or an evening of intrigue and spying?" Gram added.

"That remains to be seen," Lilli said and breezed out of the room, her stylish black sandals clattering on the wooden floor.

Soon Lilli was driving west on Main Road toward Mattituck. Her tote, holding the sketches by two of Miko's art students, occupied the passenger seat. She didn't know what to make of the enigmatic artist. Did he know anything about the deaths of Silas and Dr. Reed? Thomas Jefferson's wine? Could be he was only interested in spending a pleasant evening with her. She couldn't wait to hear him interpret the student sketches about the North Fork. She wondered if he would avoid the third fork. Would she dare bring it up? Possibly Miko might reveal something that she, Gram, Bud, and Hank hadn't noticed, something related to the murders. There was only one way to find out. She floored the gas pedal.

A few minutes before 8:00, Lilli turned onto the narrow lane that wound down to the bay. In the beam of her headlights, she caught sight of a small green shingled cottage with a fieldstone chimney. The only home on the road, it emanated a golden glow from the windows and screened front door. She rolled to a stop and opened the door of her Bronco. What a peaceful, storybook setting. A cottage in the moonlight, nestled among blue pines and white birches, with the soft lapping of waves in the distance.

Stepping away from her Bronco, Lilli allowed herself several moments to soak up the atmosphere. She was rewarded with the fragrance of fresh-brewed coffee, the salty taste of the sea air on her lips, and the sounds of joyful Greek music coming from Miko's cottage.

Through the screen door she could see the well-lit living room, dining alcove, and kitchen. She felt as if she were peeking into an artist's studio, not a home. Canvases were stacked against the walls. Mobiles with metal objects dangling from fish hooks and barbed wire hung from the ceilings. Pieces of driftwood scattered among random chunks of metal and wood filled the living room. How on earth could he move around or find anything? Nuts and bolts, junk metal, shards of colored glass, and hood ornaments and other car remnants lay scattered on every table. Paint brushes poked from the kitchen sink. Paint drips splattered the newspaper pages that covered the kitchen table.

Her eyes could hardly take in all the contents of Miko's studio. His finished creations, large ominous metal conglomerations, hovered in the corners of the room like boxers waiting for the bell to ring so they could burst forth and attack their opponents. She was glad the lights were on, because his bulky works made her feel un-easy, threatened. Miko had admitted that his creations seemed in-spired more by a mechanic than an artist, and Lilli agreed. She thought they were a reflection of the man himself: macho, mascu-line, muscular.

Her glance darted back to the colored glass. Was any of it green, like she'd seen in the dugout cave? Yes, she could see a few green shards mixed among the blue and brown. But this green was a lighter shade than the slivers she'd found in the cave. She wondered if Miko was a beer drinker. Did he like Heineken? One quick peek in his refrigerator and she'd know for certain.

Foolish woman, she chided herself. Thousands of people drink Heineken. A bottle of Heineken in his refrigerator wouldn't prove a thing. But her women's intuition wouldn't quit. A peek here, a bit of exploration there, a clue somewhere else. Why, she might turn up something that could help with the investigation. *Research, it's a wonderful thing,* she told herself.

"Hello!" Lilli called out, but there was no answer. The Greek music drowned out her voice. She tested the door, but it was latched. Sus-pended from a beam next to the door was a huge three-dimensional copper fish, about the size of her microwave. On a table next to the fish was a large padded hammer. A message scrawled on a paper plate with a red neon marker read KNOCK YOURSELF OUT! Another read LET ME HEAR FROM YOU!

So, Miko had a sense of humor. She grabbed the hammer and took a swing at the fish.

Claaangg!

Claaaangggg!!

Claaaaaaanggggggg!!!

"Be right there," came Miko's sultry voice from somewhere at the rear of the cottage. He appeared at the door wearing black jeans and T-shirt, his appearance as rugged and exotic as she'd remembered. He held a glue gun in one hand and a chisel in the other. Energy seemed to emanate from every pore of his body.

He looked as if he'd been dragged from his work. The scowl on his face suggested he wasn't too happy about that. Had he forgotten all about inviting her to dinner?

"Sorry. I'm running late," Miko said. "Inspiration struck and I struck back. Did I mention that you look beautiful? Come on in." A broad smile replaced his frown. Still holding the glue gun and chisel, he leaned his arm against the doorframe and propped the screen door open with the heel of his sandal.

She resisted the urge to admit to herself how handsome he looked or how involved he appeared to be in his work. She found that sexy in a man. But right now she was on a mission—to find out what he knew about the murders. Distractions would defeat her plans, especially if the distraction was a man who had charmed her when they'd first met and continued to impress her now. Zack, heroic and a real heartthrob, had her distracted enough.

"You have a great place here," Lilli said as she ducked beneath his arm and stepped over the threshold.

"My decorator has done wonders with the place," he said, and they both laughed.

She glanced into his bedroom, the only room she hadn't seen from the porch. She gawked at the massive work in progress that dominated the floor space. Part metal and part wood, possibly a mythological sea creature, the work crouched amid a pile of rocks attached to the metal base. The primitive creature had a certain familiarity, but she couldn't place where she'd ever seen anything like it.

"Do you like the *Briny Brute*?" he asked, pointing at the sculpture. "He's my latest, so he's been getting all my attention."

"A spoiled brat?" she asked.

"A spoiled beast," he replied. "He's a commissioned work. As soon as he's finished, he'll go to his new home."

"Where?"

"The tavern."

"A perfect fit," Lilli said. Now she knew why the creature seemed familiar. He had the same primitive, unleashed power that permeated the tavern.

"Congratulations," she said.

"Thanks."

Lilli couldn't resist getting Miko's opinion. "What was it like working with Chuck Matthison?"

Miko cocked his head to one side. "It's like he's two different people. As someone who appreciates art, he was great to work with. He thought *Briny Brute* fit the tavern's style and mood. He said his ancestors would have approved, especially his grandfather, the architect."

"But—"

"But, he's difficult to get together with. He won't go inside the tavern. He's busy all the time with his landscaping business. We've worked out details for next week. He gets *Briny* delivered and installed. I get a check." He crossed his fingers. "Let's hope he shows up."

Lilli quickly scanned the room. A copier, printer, and computer occupied most of the desk. The customized screensaver—cubes of black, brown, and gray tumbling across the screen—swirled before her eyes. If only she could spend a few minutes with that computer. What secrets would it reveal? The room was as topsy-turvy as the rest of the place, with papers scattered everywhere. On the enclosed patio off the bedroom, Miko's finished creations—a tangle of geometric metal shapes—seemed right at home on the gritty concrete floor in the dim light sliding in from the bedroom and kitchen.

"How about a glass of wine?" Miko asked, heading into the dining alcove, where half the table was set for two with black glossy china and black-stemmed wine glasses. Candles glimmered, reflecting off the black bowl where pinecones sat nestled among polished stones. A crusty French baguette sat on a sleek silver bread dish. The other half of the table held hammers, chisels, and pumice sticks. "As I remember, you like red, but we're having grilled fish. Maybe you'd prefer white? I have Chablis and Sauterne."

"Chablis would be great," Lilli said.

He plucked the wineglasses from the table and took them to the kitchen. He chose a bottle of Chablis from the refrigerator, uncorked it, and filled both glasses.

"Cheers!" she said, her slim fingers gripping the glass.

"Opa!" he said.

Leaning against the kitchen counter, they clinked the rims of their glasses and sipped the wine.

"This is wonderful," she said and took another sip.

"I didn't fix any hors d'oeuvres," he said. "I'm an entrée kind of guy. How about you?"

"I'm a dessert kind of gal."

"Glad to hear it," he said. "The local bakery makes a mean blueberry cheesecake, and I just happen to have two slices." He glanced out the kitchen door, which led to the side yard where a grill was set up. "The coals look just right." He grabbed a platter from the counter. "I'll get the fish."

"I'll help."

His cell phone jangled. He dropped the platter and it clattered across the tile floor. He hurriedly picked up the platter and set it on the counter. Fumbling his cell phone out of his pocket, he checked the caller's name. The blood drained from his face. "I'd better take this," he said, his voice suddenly gruff. He turned his back to her and began pacing back and forth.

Why did he seem so jittery? His expression was grim as he continued pacing and listening to the caller. "We're on the same page," he finally said. He snapped his phone shut and thrust it deep into his pocket. When he turned back to Lilli, he was checking his watch.

"You must be starving. I know I am. Let's get that fish on the grill. Everything else is ready," he said, once again the gracious host.

He opened the refrigerator, and Lilli saw a bowl of salad and husked ears of corn on the top shelf, next to two slices of the famous blueberry cheesecake. The bottom shelf was crammed with bottled water, soda, and beer. Was there a Heineken among the assortment? She peered over his shoulder, but he blocked her view. He reached down to the crisper drawer for the fish filets, and she inched closer for a better view. Just then, he stood up, slapped his hand to his forehead, and shut the refrigerator door with a bang. "I forgot to buy lemons," he said.

"We can do without them," Lilli said, hoping he'd open the refrigerator again.

"Fish without lemons? My grandmother would chase me around the kitchen with a wooden spoon if she found out."

He plucked his car keys from a hook by the front door. "I'll be back from the store in a flash. It's just a few minutes away."

Lilli didn't remember passing a store. *Must be in the other direction,* she figured.

"Make yourself comfortable while I'm gone." He looked at the crowded rooms, shook his head, and then pushed everything from an overstuffed living room chair onto the floor. "There," he said. "How about choosing some music for us? My CD collection is over there." He pointed to a cabinet with a TV perched on top. "And in case you're wondering, I didn't forget about my students' sketches. I saw them in your tote. We'll talk about them when I get back," he said, and closed the door behind him.

She latched the door. What a difficult man to figure out. At first he seemed eager to move the evening along as quickly as possible. Now he couldn't live without lemons.

As soon as she heard his Lexus SUV's tires crunch the driveway, she hurried to the kitchen. She had to make every minute count. He'd be back soon. She quickly opened his refrigerator and looked through the bottles. Not a single Heineken. But three lemons were shoved behind the mustard and ketchup bottles. Did he forget they were there? Or could he be rushing out to meet someone? Maybe the caller?

She dashed into Miko's bedroom and went straight to the computer. Holding her breath, she gripped the mouse. In a flash, the screensaver disappeared. An Internet browser was open, and Miko was logged into his webmail. She clicked ADDRESS BOOK and saw a long list of names and addresses, including her own, "Waterfront Writer." How did Miko get that? She'd used it only once, for Beach Bum. Was he Beach Bum? Maybe he'd hacked into Beach Bum's site. But why would he do that?

She heard a noise at the window. She froze and shifted her eyes toward the window. What was that darting into the trees? A person? Miko could be out there spying on her. But she hadn't heard his Lexus return. It must be someone else. Oh God, it could be the Bond brothers. Had they been released from jail? The hair on the back of her neck rose.

She looked frantically for a weapon. None in the bedroom. Where? Where? The dining alcove.

She rushed back to the dining table and grabbed two hammers. Clutching one in each hand, she killed the lights with her elbow and waited in the dark, listening to her heart beat wildly. Then she heard another sound, louder than her heart. Someone was pounding on the screen door.

"Lilli?" Miko's voice. "Unlock the door."

She flicked on the lights and rushed to open the door.

"What's wrong?" he asked, stepping inside and staring at the hammer. "Have you taken a dislike to my work?"

"Somebody's out there. A man was at the window."

"Don't be frightened. I'll check it out." He turned on all the outdoor lights. "Stay here," he said.

Two minutes later he returned. "Whoever it was is gone."

Two minutes! He'd hardly checked.

"Could it have been your imagination?" Miko asked.

"No," Lilli said. "I saw someone."

"Shadows lurk everywhere. I can see why you might think someone was there. Let's forget it for now—you're safe. We should enjoy the evening together. The first of many, I hope."

"I didn't hear your Lexus," Lilli said, trying to control her runaway suspicions.

"It's been temperamental lately," Miko said. "It stalled halfway down the drive and I left it there. A few minutes' rest and it will be good as new." He strode to the refrigerator. "Turns out I didn't need to go buy lemons after all. I remembered where I'd put them." He opened the refrigerator and pulled out two lemons.

Lilli didn't believe him. She figured he was the one out there, spying on her. He didn't seem overly concerned or even surprised that someone was on his property. She should leave. She'd be crazy not to. But if she stayed, she could possibly find out what he knew about the murders. He seemed like her best lead yet. She promised herself to be very cautious.

"I need to make a phone call," Lilli said, and punched in the numbers. *Come on, Gram, please be home.* "Gram? Hi, it's Lilli," she said loudly so that Miko could hear every word. "I'm at Miko Andropolis' place in Mattituck."

"I already know that," Gram said. "Why are you shouting?"

"Okay, Gram, if you say so, I'll call before I leave."

"Lilli." Gram dropped her voice to a near-whisper. "Are you in trouble?"

"Maybe," said Lilli.

"Do you want Bud and me to come there?"

"That would be great."

"Should we storm the place or stay in the shadows?"

"Definitely the second," Lilli said.

"Dark clothes?"

"Absolutely."

"We'd better alert Hank."

"Yes. That's a good idea."

"Okay."

"Okay." Lilli hung up, relieved that Gram and Bud would soon be close by. And so would Hank.

"Sounds like Gram watches over you. Grandmothers are famous for caring," Miko commented, leveling his gaze at her.

Did he know of Gram Jenkins, or did he assume she was speaking to her grandmother? Lily wondered.

"Does she always worry like this?" Miko went on. "Or is it because you're with me? I'm afraid I may have earned a reputation as a ladies' man. An undeserved reputation trumped up by . . . well, I'll drop that subject and get cooking before the coals die out."

Miko took the fish from the refrigerator, and Lilli followed him to the side yard, carrying the corn and butter. At a redwood work table, Miko set each filet on a strip of aluminum foil, squirted lemon over the fish, sprinkled them with salt, pepper, and fresh parsley, then secured the foil around the fish.

Working next to Miko, Lilli set each ear of corn on a sheet of aluminum foil, dotted them with butter, and sprinkled them with salt. She tried to stay calm and imagined Gram, Bud, and Hank speeding through the night. As Lilli crimped the foil tightly around each cob, she sensed that Miko was studying her.

"You have an artist's touch," he said. "But I'm not surprised. Photographers and artists share the same goal."

"What would that be?"

He thought for a moment, and she sensed that he was choosing his words. "We try to strip away the veneer and arrive at the essence of our subject, animate or inanimate." The glow from the coals captured a melancholy expression on his face. "But sometimes the essence can be painful. It can hold secrets. And if we explore those secrets, the truths we find can turn out to be more than we bargained for. Especially when we're talking about people we love. We can end up with a sense of betrayal."

Lilli had the feeling that Miko wasn't spouting vague generalities. He mentioned secrets. He could be trying to turn the conversation around to Silas and Silas' secrets—the correspondence and notebook. The more she thought about it, the more certain she became. Good. Here was her chance to go on a fishing expedition.

"I think I know what you mean," she said. "And sometimes those secrets set off a chain reaction and trouble shoots at us from all angles."

"You have a very active imagination," Miko said, "and I am being a terrible host, depriving you of your dinner."

Miko knew something about Silas' murder, Lilli was sure of it. She would have to be very subtle, or he might clam up. "You are right about secrets," she said. "Just the other day, Silas and I—"

His cell phone jangled. "Now what?" Miko asked angrily. He checked the caller ID. "I have to take this call too," he said. "Sorry." Flicking open his phone, he blurted, "I'm at my place. What happened?"

Lilli could see from Miko's troubled expression that the caller had to be describing a problem or an emergency.

"Lilli, I'm afraid it's not good news," Miko said, snapping the phone shut. "I have to leave right away." He turned off the grill and hurriedly returned the fish and corn to the refrigerator.

"I'm usually more hospitable," he said. "And I'd like to get to know you better. Can we pick this up another time?"

"Of course," Lilli said. "I understand." Something important must be happening. She needed to stay close to Miko.

Moving quickly, Miko grabbed a bulging gym bag from the hall closet and rushed her out the door. "I don't have time to explain," he said, locking the door and pocketing the key, "but you must not follow me."

"Why?" She grabbed her tote and quickly checked the contents. The students' sketches were still rolled up, just as she had left them.

"It could be dangerous," he said, rushing her down the path. "Take a different road. Pass me. Whatever."

"Are you sure your Lexus is going to work? Maybe we should go in my Bronco."

"Right now you need to get as far away from me as possible," he said. He waited until she was in her truck. Only then did he jog toward his Lexus.

Lilli immediately called the police station. "This is Lilli and this is an emergency. I must speak to Chief Borden."

"That's not possible. He's busy."

"But he wanted to hear from me if I had a lead about the case."

"I'll let him know you called, and he'll get back to you ASAP."
Click.

Lilli called Gram's cell. "Did you get in touch with Hank?"

"No. Hank isn't taking any calls, even from me. Must be a big emergency."

"Darn. I was hoping to get straight through to him. There's a change of plans," she said. "Miko's driving off in a hurry. He's in some kind of trouble or danger and doesn't want me to follow him. Of course I will, but not close enough for him to notice. I'll call back as soon as I see which way he's going, and I'll keep trying Hank."

"This is a real-life spy movie," Gram said. "We'll join the chase."

"I think we're about to find out who murdered Silas Jones and Dr. Reed," Lilli said. "I can just feel it in my bones."

Chapter Twenty-five

Lilli gripped the steering wheel of her Bronco and followed Miko along the private drive, away from his bungalow. When he came to Main Road, he turned right and sped away. Fighting the urge to chase after him, she kept her distance and immediately called Gram.

"Miko turned east," Lilli said, her eyes riveted on the road ahead. "He's coming your way on Main Road, in a black Lexus SUV. If I stay on his tail, he might lead me on a wild goose chase. If I give him too much leeway, he could turn onto a side road and I'll lose him."

"Don't worry," Gram said. "We'll figure a way to turn the tables and cook his goose."

Gram clucked her tongue several times. Lilli had heard that clucking before, when Gram had been busily concocting a special recipe, surrounded by pots, pans, and casserole dishes. She knew it meant Gram's imagination was cooking on all four burners.

Gram gave a very pronounced double-cluck. "Tell you what, Lilli. Don't give yourself away by crowding Miko. We're barreling toward you on Main Road. Bud will park at the 24/7 store in Cutchogue, same side of the road as you and Miko. Pull in, park, and ride with us. Miko won't spot Bud's VW, so we can follow close. Hoo-hah! We'll see what Miko's up to, and he'll never suspect a thing. This is a dilly of a plan!"

"You and Bud are the best," Lilli said and roared into the dark night.

The light rain that had misted the windshield now turned to a drizzle. Soon the road became slick and slippery. Slivers of pale moonlight pierced through the branches of pine trees that towered over vineyards and farms on either side of the road. This was Lilli's first time to drive along this part of the North Fork at night, and nothing looked familiar. The area was so dark and desolate, it gave her the creeps. Every now and then she caught sight of fiery red tail-lights breaking through the fog and hoped they were from Miko's Lexus.

Ten minutes later, Lilli saw the orange neon sign of the 24/7 flashing FINE DASHBOARD DINING. She zipped into the parking lot, parked, and hopped into the back seat of Bud's VW Beetle. "Did you see Miko?" she asked breathlessly, leaning into the front seat between Bud and Gram.

"He roared by like a rocket ship," Gram said.

"Catch up to him," Lilli pleaded.

"Prepare for blastoff," Bud said. "This souped-up engine is raring to break the sound barrier." He zoomed out of the parking lot, brakes screeching, onto Main Road.

"Come on, slowpoke," Gram urged from the passenger seat. "A slice of blueberry pie is yours if you can catch Miko."

Bud swerved right on the road, slick with rain. "With a scoop of vanilla ice cream?"

"Bud, please don't haggle at a time like this."

"You started it."

"Did not."

Bud veered left. "Did so. Ice cream?"

"Okay, you win," Gram said, and Bud floored the gas pedal.

"I'll try Hank again," Lilli said.

"Save your breath," Gram said, clutching the sides of her seat. "I tried his private number. First time ever, I got his voice mail. Hank is getting too big for his britches."

"Nothing new there," Bud interjected.

Gram chuckled. "I asked him to call you and me. There's nothing more we can do."

On and on they sped, through Cutchogue, Peconic, and then entered Southold. Lilli wondered where Miko would stop.

"I'll try Hank one last time," Lilli said. She made the call and spoke to the officer on duty. "Same answer as before," she told Gram and Bud.

Soon they approached the outskirts of Grayrocks.

"We're back where we started," Bud said. "Is Miko pulling a fast one?"

Lilli pointed ahead. "Miko's right signal just flashed."

"He's going to the tavern," Gram said.

"Miko told me Chuck Matthison, the tavern owner, bought one of his sculptures. They were supposed to finalize everything next week. Besides, Chuck won't set foot in the place, so that's not who he's meeting." Lilli gritted her teeth. "I sure hope this isn't just a business meeting with the manager. We've got to catch a break soon."

Miko turned into the tavern parking lot.

"Duck down, Lilli," Bud said and passed right by the tavern.

"What are you doing?" Lilli cried. "Follow him."

"He'll see us. We'll spook him." Bud killed his lights. He continued to the crest of an incline and turned his car into a clearing alongside the road. "We've got a good view overlooking the parking lot. Let's see what he's up to before we go charging in and scare him off."

"I'm going down there," Lilli said and gripped the door handle.

"That's too dangerous," Bud said. "Just take my night binoculars and see what Miko's up to." He pulled them from the glove box and passed them to her. "I've seen some mighty fine night creatures in my time with those binoculars."

Gram nudged Bud. "Is that hussy, Little Miss Hot-to-Trot, pestering you again?"

Bud guffawed.

Lilli peered into the lens. She saw the bay, the tavern, and then Miko running toward a grove of pine trees. "Hold on. Miko's got company. Someone just stepped away from the pines."

"Who is it?" Gram asked.

"A woman."

"That hussy, Little Miss Hot-to-Trot?" Bud quipped.

"They know each other," Lilli said. "They just embraced." The moon slid from beneath a cloud, and Lilli caught a glimpse of long dark hair. "It's Dr. Elena Ellison. Miko and Elena. Childhood friends, but maybe more."

"What's she doing?" Gram asked.

"She's carrying something like a toolbox. She and Miko are running hand in hand toward the back door." Lilli focused the binoculars. "The service entrance. Hey, there's more. A line of figures in dark clothes, moving along the shrubs toward the service entrance. Who on earth are they? They could be stalking Miko and Elena. Something big is happening."

Lilli opened the car door. "Call the police again and convince the officer on duty this is an emergency. Please run by him where we are. And promise me you'll stay here where it's safe until help arrives. I'm going down there." She knew Hank wouldn't approve, and she was frightened, but she had to do what she thought was best. That meant following Miko and Elena before they disappeared from sight. And possibly finding out what their connection was to the murders.

"Don't do it, Lilli," Gram pleaded, but Lilli was already out the door, buttoning her black sweater so her bright yellow blouse wouldn't give her away. She scrambled down the grassy incline to the tavern's parking lot.

Lilli hurried toward the service entrance. Heart pounding, she quickly and quietly cracked open the door. Not a sound came from inside. The nightlight just inside the doorway glimmered faintly and the pale moonlight barely came through the one small window above her head. She removed her sandals and gripped them in her hand. Stepping inside and flattening herself against the wall, Lilli got her bearings. She was at the top of a long wooden staircase.

She peered into the dim light just in time to see Miko and Elena hurry through the doorway at the bottom of the staircase, into whatever lay beyond, and close the door silently behind them. She thanked her lucky stars they never looked back. Where were the people who had been creeping through the shrubs? They must have preceded Miko and Elena through the door. Or had they doubled back and were now following her?

Lilli gripped the banister and began her descent toward the door. A step creaked. Then another. And another. Each creak resounded in

Lilli's ears like gunshots. The *drip-drip-drip* of water came from somewhere beneath the stairs. Above her, spooky sounds. Was someone creeping up on her? She looked up. The spooky sounds grew louder. Her heart pounded. Then she saw a ceiling fan wobbling, its blades moving slowly and awkwardly. Whew! It wasn't a person after all.

Easing herself down the steps, Lilli glanced to her right and gasped. An elongated shadow was slithering down the wall. It stopped when she stopped. It moved when she moved. She stopped again and realized it was her own shadow she stared at. Her heart still pounded as she continued down. Her imagination kicked into overtime. Unknown assailants. Murderers. Knives. Guns. She was scared out of her wits with every step she took, with every creak and squeak she heard, with every shadow that skulked down the staircase. Finally, she arrived at the bottom and took a deep breath.

Now or never, she told herself.

She cracked open the door. Cool air hit her.

Total blackness faced her. A wine cellar? She hesitated, terrified of stepping into an abyss.

Her hands in front of her, a sandal gripped in each fist, she blinked several times, hoping her eyes would adjust to the dark.

One step.

Mmphh! A hand clamped her mouth shut. A strong arm flattened her arms against her waist and lifted her off the floor.

She struggled in the darkness. Kicked her feet. Tried to scream. Couldn't scream.

"Lilli, it's me, Miko. If you promise not to scream, I'll release my hand. And then you must do exactly what I say. Okay?"

Lilli nodded fiercely.

He released his grip and spun her around to face him.

"I asked you not to follow me. Prying into my Beach Bum Web site was one thing. I get it—you have your suspicions about me— but coming here was reckless. Extremely dangerous too, and not just for you."

"I'm sorry, Miko. I got carried away."

A flashlight beam circled the cool, woodsy-smelling room. From the shadows Elena Ellison emerged, moving toward Lilli and holding a flashlight at shoulder level. The light flashed across hundreds of bottles of wine that lined wooden racks from floor to ceiling.

"This might sound melodramatic, but we're here to preserve America's past," Elena said and quickly closed the door that Lilli had come through. "I've heard that you mean well, but you shouldn't be here."

"Dr. Ellison—"

"Please call me Elena. Do you understand there's a murderer—"

The floor creaking from somewhere above them cut into Elena's words. Lilli looked up. She feared that someone might be unlocking and opening the door from the restaurant to the wine cellar. They were trapped down here with only one escape, back the way they'd come, up that creaking staircase. They'd never get away! Never.

"Sshhh! Miko, I think they're coming," Elena whispered. "Let's go."

Miko pulled Lilli toward the far wall. He ran his fingers beneath one of the shelves.

Lilli couldn't see exactly what he did, but she heard a soft click. Her eyes widened as one section of the wall turned on its axis. Miko drew Lilli to the opening right behind Elena into some kind of hidden vault. The door began its slide back to its original position. Lilli raised her arms, a reflexive defense against the unknown. Her sandals flew from her hands.

"My sandal," Lilli whispered. It had landed outside their hiding place.

"That sandal will be a dead give-away," Miko hissed. "These guys play for keeps. You could get us killed."

Lilli dropped to her knees, reached back into the wine cellar, and groped the floor. She felt the opening, only inches wide now. "Got it," she whispered, clutching her sandal and jerking her arm back.

A second later, the camouflaged door snapped shut. Lilli felt sealed in a tomb.

"That was close," Elena said in a trembling voice and shone her flashlight around the room.

Lilli noted that the space was about the size of Gram's smallest guest room.

Several men emerged from the shadows. Lilli covered her mouth with her hand to squelch her scream. Amazed relief followed. She recognized Dr. Winfield, Hank, and Officer Lansing, along with two other officers she hadn't seen before. So that was who she'd seen creeping through the shrubs—four of Grayrocks' finest in their navy blue uniforms and Dr. Winfield in a black warm-up suit. They hadn't been stalking Miko and Elena after all.

Hank turned toward Lilli. "I thought we had an agreement. Like any good citizen, you would let me know if you had any information about the investigation." She had never seen him so angry. "You came here after-hours through a deserted parking lot into an unlit building. All for a story. You reporters, you drive me crazy!" His eyes flashed daggers. "Suddenly I've got to worry about crowd control and keeping an uninvited civilian—that's you—out of harm's way. That's a mighty big job, with a clock ticking away like a time bomb. And furthermore—"

"I'm sorry," Lilli said, "but—"

"Sorry doesn't cut the mustard," Hank growled.

"But this wasn't for a story," Lilli said. "This was to help with the case. I've been trying to get in touch with you. When that didn't work, I—"

"You're here. Too late to boot you out, so help, don't hinder." His voice softened. "Got it?"

"Got it," Lilli said, and she meant it. This was serious business. Hank and his officers had their Glocks out of their holsters. Fierce determination etched each face.

Dr. Winfield held Lilli fast with his eyes. "Promise me you'll be careful. Gram will never forgive me if anything happens to you. To her, you're family."

"Sshhh! Keep your voices down," Hank said. "I want to surprise these creeps."

Lilli wondered exactly who Hank meant by "these creeps," but she figured this wasn't a good time to ask.

Miko pointed at the far wall. "Let's make sure the wine is still here."

"Good idea," Hank said, and Lilli was relieved that her arrival hadn't completely stalled the investigation.

Miko walked across the floor, a patchwork pattern of craggy stones outlined with dark grout, to the rear of the secret vault. He stopped in front of the largest stone, a greenish-black beauty, picked it up effortlessly, and moved it several feet away. Lilli saw that it was lightweight, actually a thin sliver of slate that looked like all the thick heavy stones around it. In the opening left by the sliver, a large metal ring was affixed to a metal sheet.

She watched in awe as Miko tugged on the metal ring and, after several tries, it budged. A large rectangle of the floor lifted up. Lilli noticed that all the stones on top of this trap door were thin slivers of stone, a dummy set of stones cemented to the metal sheet. Whoever designed that was a master of camouflage. And deception.

Everyone crowded around the opening. Dozens of bottles of wine were stacked in neat rows in wooden racks. Lilli's eyes widened. The green bottles looked just like the ones that she and Doug had found at Montauk Cove. Hers in the water. His in a dugout cave.

A tingle shot through Lilli. These had to be Thomas Jefferson's wine bottles.

"The wine is still here," Miko said, and relief showed on everyone's face. "Nothing looks changed. I won't take the time to count, but I'm quite sure it's close to two hundred fifty bottles."

"How on earth did you know about all this?" Lilli asked. "The trap door, the—"

Hank shushed Lilli. "Dr. Ellison," he whispered, as he signaled his men to step toward the revolving panel. "Show me that peephole."

She directed him to what appeared to be a knothole in the wood paneling on the back of the revolving panel. "Douse your lights," Hank said and peered into the peephole.

Lilli wondered if Silas had installed it. Quite a coincidence—there was a knothole in the workbench at his shop to camouflage a lever, and now a knothole here to camouflage a peephole.

"Okay, Miko, go ahead and fill Lilli in, but keep your voice down," Hank said.

"Sure thing," Miko said and turned to Lilli. "I came to the tavern several weeks ago to talk to Chuck Matthison. Mr. Vincennes manages the place, but Chuck makes many decisions, especially artistic ones, to preserve his grandfather's ideals. So, meeting on the patio, I talked to him about the delivery of *Briny Brute*. He wanted to place it near the dining room above the wine cellar. I came down the stairs to check the structural beams to make sure they could support the weight of my sculpture. Guess who was working here in the wine cellar?"

"Mark Mastriano, the wine expert."

Miko nodded. "Mark was so wrapped up in his own mischief that he didn't notice me. Next thing I knew, the wall revolved like a door, and Mark slipped inside the secret vault. He left the door open. I hid in the deeper shadows and watched. I saw him open this trap door. When he returned to the restaurant, I opened the vault and the trap door and saw all those bottles of wine. I took a quick count and told Elena what I'd seen."

"Okay, civilians," Hank said, "now that we got that out of the way, let's get organized. I'd like you to stand in the corner, away from my officers."

Only as Lilli edged toward the corner did she notice the black tarpaulins, covering something bulky, along both side walls. She peeked under a tarpaulin and caught sight of crates of wine. Judging from the sand and bits of seaweed that dotted the crates and the puddles on the floor, they had been submerged until very recently. She'd bet a week's wages the crates had been trapped in the mucky holes of the third fork, just like Silas had predicted. The bottles of wine beneath the trap door were dry and had probably been stored there for awhile. So all the bottles could be accounted for, those stored since Jefferson's *Victory* sank and those salvaged in the past week.

Lilli's heart raced. The investigation was coming to a head. Soon she would know who was behind the theft and possibly the murders of Silas and Dr. Reed. But then regret quickly set in, and the excitement of the moment faded. She had jeopardized the lives of Dr. Elena Ellison, Dr. Winfield, Miko, Hank, and his officers. Her nosiness had slowed down their plan. She would be responsible if something terrible happened to them. Guilt weighed heavily upon her, bringing tears to her eyes.

Hank whispered, "Someone just turned on a light." He pointed at Dr. Ellison. "Turn off your flashlight."

"Right," she whispered, and the room turned pitch-black.

"Can you see anyone out there in the wine cellar?" an officer whispered.

"Not yet," Hank said, and Lilli heard a hint of fear.

Lilli listened hard, but all she heard was her own ragged breathing. Finally noises came from beyond the secret room. Scraping sounds, like metal on metal. Footsteps on the stairs, then *thud-thud-thud!* Like heavy items dropped on the floor. Men's muffled voices.

Lilli pictured Hank flattened against the wall, his eye glued to the peephole. She wanted desperately to see whatever he was seeing right now. A scrap of a childhood taunt echoed through her: Curiosity killed the cat!

"It's going down," Hank whispered. "Civilians, stay back. Men, be ready for anything."

"How do we open the revolving door?" an officer whispered.

"Okay, I didn't think of everything," Hank hissed. "Miko, get up here and show me that gizmo."

Miko brushed past Lilli.

"Ready," Hank whispered.

Click went the door hinge.

"Set," Hank whispered.

The door swung open.

"Go!" Hank shouted, and Lilli froze with fear.

Chapter Twenty-six

F orcing herself forward, Lilli peeked out just in time to see Hank and his men jump through the secret vault opening and charge into the wine cellar, guns waving.

Four men, dripping wet and wearing ski masks and dark clothes, were huddled over three large trunks.

Startled by Grayrocks' finest leaping into the room, the intruders dropped their tool bags. Hammers, saws, and chisels clattered across the cement. They raced to the stairs, tripping over each other in a frantic attempt to escape.

"Stop right there! Don't make me shoot!" Hank shouted, leading his officers.

The intruders stopped short and reached for the ceiling. Heated accusations and excuses flew between them.

The officers handcuffed the men and whipped off their ski masks while Hank rattled off their rights.

Lilli wasn't surprised when she saw their faces. The Bond brothers had been vicious on several occasions. Mark Mastriano, the wine entrepreneur, had given her the creeps from the moment she'd met him. Ron Larson, the show-off treasure hunter, with a finder's-keeper's mentality, would do anything for money. But were any of them capable of murder? she wondered.

Hank rubbed his hands together briskly. "Everything under control, men?" he asked.

His officers responded in unison with clipped syllables, "Everything under control, Chief!"

"Here are my three basic rules," Hank snarled at their prisoners as his officers glared at them. "One—" Thumbs hooked in his belt loops, Hank strutted past the three trunks. "Don't question me or my officers. Two—" He stepped over the ropes, pulleys, and boards the intruders had used to slide the trunks down the stairs to the wine cellar. "Don't sass us. And last, but not least . . . three. Don't tick us off, or you'll regret it." The hint of a smile replaced Hank's trademark scowl.

Lilli knew that smile. It signaled relief. In this case, because he and his men had captured all four men without anyone getting hurt. She could read relief on the faces of Dr. Winfield, Elena, and Miko too.

As the handcuffed men fumed, Hank plowed on. "We're leaving here in an orderly fashion and stopping at the Grayrocks jail. The first one of you who mouths off—" He swirled around and brandished his stun gun. "Don't make me spell it out."

The intruders glanced back and forth at one another. Beads of sweat glinted on their foreheads.

"Okay, men, listen up," Hank said, facing his officers. "These two tough guys"—he nodded toward the Bond brothers—"are downright nasty. Watch out. They might spit or curse. They might even try to kick you or jab you with an elbow. You know how to deal with bullies, right?"

"Right, Chief," the taller officer said and punched his fist into his open hand several times, wincing, Lilli thought, in pain. She hoped the thugs thought it menacing.

"Now this guy"—Hank nodded at Mark Mastriano—"he thinks he's a slick operator. But he's just a low-down two-bit go-between. You know how to handle him, right?"

"Right, Chief," the shorter officer said and whacked his nightstick on the banister.

"Now, this guy here with that annoying grin on his face?" Hank said. "His name's Ron Larson. He's not just a diver. He's the mastermind behind this steal-stack-store-and-sell salvage operation. He likes to call the shots." Hank cocked an eyebrow. "You know how to deal with that, right?"

"Right," Officer Lansing said, slapping his holster.

Lilli followed everything Hank said. Something struck her as odd.

Hank hadn't mentioned murder or accused any of the four of being murderers. His over-the-top performance and his team's theatrical reactions wouldn't scare a hardened criminal. Certainly not a murderer. No. Hank had captured thieves, not the murderer, and he knew it. Lilli was convinced of it. Did Hank know who the murderer was? Had he laid a trap to catch him?

Lilli peered at the men's hands. She didn't see a gold ring with a crossed-swords design like the one worn by the man who had stolen her bottle of wine and nearly strangled her in the supply closet. How lucky she was. She could have been a hairbreadth away from being murdered. Whoever he was, he was still at large. She shuddered. He could kill again.

"Come here, please," Hank said, motioning Dr. Winfield, Elena, and Miko to his side. "My men and I will be leaving now. You'll be busy here with the wine and trunks and all, but keep your eyes open for more trouble. My two officers who guarded the parking lot will stay on duty. Right now they are with Gram and Bud, reassuring them that everything down here is under control. They'll stop anyone who comes looking for trouble. Speaking of trouble," he cranked his thumb toward Lilli. "It's your call if she stays or goes." He touched his fingers to his hat and saluted. "Good luck," he said and headed for the stairway.

As soon as Hank left, Elena, Miko, and Dr. Winfield huddled at a distance from Lilli. They talked fast, all at the same time. Finally, Dr. Winfield looked Lilli in the eye. "To be fair, you're the one who found Silas' notebook and the Jefferson-Washington correspondence. So, we agree you can stay and help, but—"

"Thank you," Lilli cut in, thrilled to be included. "You won't regret this. I'm sorry for the trouble I've caused."

Miko shrugged. "Trouble, but with good intentions."

"We're used to trouble," Elena said, and her expressive lips revealed a half-smile. "It comes with our line of work. We'll forgive you if you promise not to break this story until we've finished our work here and inspected the dive site. Is—"

Dr. Winfield cut in. "There could be more treasures. We want to make sure that all artifacts go to museums."

"Of course," Lilli said, relieved there were no hard feelings. "Like you, I'm all for preserving America's history, not selling it off to the highest bidder."

"That's what I like to hear," Dr. Winfield said. "Now, what are we waiting for? Let's see what's in those trunks."

Lilli could hardly stand the suspense. History was about to happen right in front of her. She knew it. From everyone's excited expressions, she figured they knew it too.

Chapter Twenty-seven

As soon as Hank and his officers hustled the thieves out of the wine cellar, Dr. Ellison and Dr. Winfield sprang to action. They snapped open their tools-of-the-trade kits and whipped out latex gloves and high-beam flashlights. With Lilli and Miko assisting, they measured and photographed the three identical trunks. They checked air temperature and other matters and inspected the trunk locks and wood grain with magnifying glasses. Several times they searched for information on their laptops. Moving from one task to the next, they recorded their observations into a small device. Throughout all this, Lilli and Miko spoke only in whispers to make sure they didn't interfere with the recording. They patched up their differences and misunderstandings with a handshake, and agreed to be friends.

"What a day this has been!" Elena Ellison exclaimed, as she placed all her tools in her kit. She radiated happiness. "If those guys hadn't been stopped, they would have hauled these trunks into the secret vault too. The treasures would have remained hidden from the world until they struck a deal with some cutthroat buyer who doesn't care one iota about history."

She fanned her flawless face with her hands. "Sorry about that outburst. I just couldn't resist. I need to verify one last thing," she said. Her slender fingers tapped across her laptop keyboard.

She turned to Dr. Winfield and her dark exotic eyes flashed with excitement. "It's just as we thought," she said. "These trunks haven't been submerged for centuries. Judging by their fine condition, I would say they've been on dry land a long time, possibly since salvers pulled them from the bay in 1789. Apparently, the trunks were only recently dragged through water. The contents could be"—she squeezed her

175

eyes shut and crossed her fingers—"an archaeologist and historian's dream come true."

"We'd better get down to business and open the trunks," Dr. Winfield said. "It could take a while."

"I can speed things up"—Dr. Ellison's eyes twinkled—"in a very unscientific way." She plucked a set of skeleton keys from her bag.

"She moonlights as a cat burglar," Miko teased, and Elena laughed as if he were the cleverest man in the world. Lilli noticed Dr. Winfield's scowl and wondered if jealousy could be the reason.

With a whispered prayer, Dr. Ellison knelt before the trunk nearest the wall of wine and carefully slipped the key into the lock. As she turned it, everyone held their breath. In the silence, the tiny click of the lock roared like a cannon.

"Yeah, baby!" She made a fist and pumped her arm, like an athlete celebrating a win.

Under Dr. Winfield's direction, the others tugged open the metal fasteners, then gripped the lid and struggled to push it open. With squeaks and a loud groan, the lid gave way. Dr. Ellison photographed the quilt that covered the contents.

"The quilt is dry," she said cheerfully. "So the trunk definitely wasn't in water for very long." She carefully peeled the quilt back, exposing the treasure wrapped in its folds. Everyone gasped at the exquisite copper bell before them.

"It looks like a miniature of the Liberty Bell," Lilli whispered.

"I'd guess about a third the size, but just as dramatic," Miko said. "And without a crack."

"A beauty perfectly preserved." Lilli sighed.

Dr. Winfield rotated the bell slightly. Everyone leaned closer. Like magic, letters and words appeared.

"Wow!" Lilli exclaimed.

"Liberté," Dr. Winfield said. "Inscribed right across the top of the bell. What a beautiful sight. Come on, team, let's see what the rest says."

Lilli thought he was as excited as a kid about to open presents on Christmas morning. As an inscription came into view, she studied the French words: *Commissioné par le Marquis de Lafayette pour le peuple des Etats-Unis, avec gratitude au grand homme d'Etat, Monsieur Thomas Jefferson.*

At the same time, Dr. Ellison translated the French into English: "Commissioned by the Marquis de Lafayette for the people of the United States, with gratitude to the great statesman, Mr. Thomas Jefferson."

Lilli peered at the bells. "What are those inscriptions on the lower part?"

Dr. Winfield squinted at the words. "That would be the last names of the two founders who cast the bell, Dufrène and Dubois." He looked up and his eyes glinted. "The rest tells us the name of the foundry, Fonderie Blanchard, and its location, Paris, France, and—"

"The date 1789 in Roman numerals," Miko cut in. "Even I can figure that out."

"Well, bully for you," Dr. Winfield said sarcastically. "Let's move on, shall we? It's time to open the other trunks."

Minutes passed as they struggled with the key, the latches, and the lids. Dr. Ellison photographed the quilts and commented on their unique delicate designs that resembled embroidery.

"I wonder if they could be the work of Thomas Jefferson's wife, Martha, who was known for her needlework," she said, and gingerly rolled back the quilts.

Lilli wondered too about the quilts and their value, both sentimental and historic. Had Martha sent them with her husband to keep him warm? To remind him of their life together? Lilli knew she was getting ahead of herself, but there might be another story in those quilts.

The two lids finally gave way and Lilli blurted out, "Two more bells!"

Dr. Ellison's eyes widened. "These bells have been well cared for." She studied one with a magnifying glass. "We'd need an expert opinion, but I'd say the bells haven't been touched with scouring powders or steel wool or any of those home remedy salt-flour-lemon solutions that leave tiny scratches. Whoever has been taking care of the bells fell under their charm. Forensics might find some helpful fingerprints."

"These two bells are identical to the first," Lilli said.

"Except that *Egalité* is inscribed on the second bell," Dr. Winfield said, his voice filled with awe.

"*Fraternité* is on the third," Dr. Ellison murmured.

"Liberté, Egalité, Fraternité," Lilli whispered.

"The motto of the French Revolution," Miko said.

"No need to state the obvious," Dr. Winfield said, his voice dripping with sarcasm.

"Of course there is," Dr. Ellison said, practically reprimanding Dr. Winfield and bringing a smile to Miko's face. "In this complex world of ours, it's so nice to see the basic principles of liberty, equality, and fraternity—the qualities of a civilized society—spelled out."

"Just to be safe, let's lock the bells up," Dr. Winfield said. "We need to guard them until they are moved to a safe location."

"I'm a step ahead of you," Dr. Ellison said. "I already called the museum security services that have done previous work for me. They are bringing along an archaeological forensics team. They should all be here soon." She gazed upon the bells. "They are spectacular. Worth everything we've gone through."

Her fingers flew across her laptop keys. "Just one more detail and I'll be done." Several minutes later, she looked up and said, "Philadelphia's Liberty Bell is seventy percent copper, twenty-five percent tin with trace amounts of lead, zinc, arsenic, gold, and silver." She crossed her arms over her chest. "I'm guessing that these three bells—I'm going to christen them the Jeffersonian Bells—are similar in composition. No wonder they shine so brilliantly."

The feeling of exhilaration and awe filled the room as everyone stood side by side in silence admiring the bells. The only sound came from water dripping off the trunks and trickling into the drainage grate in the concrete floor. Lilli thought she heard muffled sounds, like metal clanking and water splashing, coming from the drainage grate.

"Did anyone else hear that?" Lilli whispered.

"Yes," came their whispered replies.

"What's beneath this old wine cellar?" Miko asked.

Lilli crept to the round drainage grate, about the size of a manhole cover, and dropped to her hands and knees. She peered into the darkness below while everyone gathered around her.

The noise stopped as suddenly as it had begun.

"Is anything down there?" Miko asked.

"It was nothing, I guess," Lilli said and peered at the grate again, "but it sure spooked me."

Miko stepped back to the far wall and waved everyone over. "We should investigate," he said, lowering his voice. "The tavern rises out of rocks in an area near the Montauks' dugout caves. There could be tunnels connected to the tavern, escape routes the Montauks used when enemy tribes attacked."

"I doubt that," Dr. Winfield said, shaking his head. "I've been digging in those caves long before you ever came to Grayrocks. There are no tunnels."

Lilli's eyebrow shot up. Dr. Winfield's statement surprised her. She thought from something Gram had said that he had dug in only one or two of the caves, but not all five. Was Gram wrong, or could Dr. Winfield be purposely misleading everyone? Or did Dr. Winfield try to minimize anything Miko said? That could be it, since Dr. Winfield seemed to resent the special friendship between Miko and Dr. Ellison.

"This old tavern is truly filled with mystery and intrigue," Dr. Winfield said. "A hidden vault. A trap door. Centuries-old salvaged wine. Who knows what else. Why, there could—"

"Ssshhhh!" Miko said, cutting off Dr. Winfield and pointing at the grate.

In the tense silence, they heard water gurgling and splashing sounds from beneath the grate.

"I could be going out on a limb here," Lilli whispered, "but maybe there's someone down there listening to us."

"Lilli could be right. I'm going to call Hank," Dr. Ellison whispered and snapped open her cell phone.

As she finished speaking to Hank, Officer Lansing rushed down the stairs, his Glock and flashlight raised in front of him. "Is everyone okay?" he asked, his breath coming in short gasps.

"We're fine," Dr. Ellison said. "What's—"

"A guy, maybe five foot nine, five ten, in a wet suit . . . We couldn't make out his face in the dark. . . . He came running from the rock formations near the tavern. . . . He was carrying snorkel gear. . . . Water was dripping off him. I shouted 'Stop!' but he hit the beach at full speed and dove into the bay. Did you see him? I thought maybe he'd been hiding down here somewhere. Another secret vault or something."

"He might have been down there," Miko said and pointed to the drainage grate. "But he sure didn't come out this way."

"I think he was listening to us," Lilli added. "And trying to find out about Jefferson's treasures."

Officer Lansing peered into the misty blackness beneath the grate. "There could be a way in from the beach. I've never seen an underwater entry, but then I never had any reason to look for one." He pulled on the grate. It came up easily. "The screws are missing, and I don't think they just happened to fly away." He set the grate back in place. "Hank will want to know about this."

"Whoever was down there could be involved with the four creeps Hank led out of here in handcuffs," Dr. Ellison said. "Or—"

"He could be working alone," Officer Lansing said, then lowered his voice. "Or he could have a partner who's still down there. I need to run all this by Hank."

"I just spoke to him. He's on his way," Dr. Ellison said.

Officer Lansing's eyes nearly popped out of his head at the sight of the three bells. "Keep on with whatever you were doing," he said. "Don't worry. We'll get this snorkel guy and any partners he might have too." He hurried back up the stairs and left as quickly as he had arrived.

"I'm wondering if this snorkel guy is the last missing piece to the puzzle," Dr. Ellison said.

"I wish the three of you would tell me what you know," Lilli said. "I'm used to working with facts, noticing details, and drawing conclusions. I know my imagination sometimes runs wild, and I don't have any background in archaeology, but maybe I could bring fresh insights to what you've discovered."

Dead silence.

Lilli continued more passionately. "We all want the same thing, to help solve this case. How about giving me a chance?"

"Sounds good to me," Miko said. "I think we can use all the help we can get."

Dr. Ellison and Dr. Winfield locked eyes and nodded.

Dr. Ellison motioned Lilli to sit down beside her on the steps. "Let me start at the beginning," she said. "Two weeks ago, my cousin who lives nearby called me. She said rumors were circulating around the beach bars about a dive site in Grayrocks Bay that might involve sunken treasures owned by President Jefferson. She knew I'd want to track that down. I came a week early and investigated.

"My colleague"—she smiled at Dr. Winfield—"and my oldest and dearest friend"—she reached out and touched Miko's hand— "offered to help me. The pivotal piece of the puzzle was the treasure hunter, Ron Larson. I found out about him from Silas' buddies, a tight-knit group of old-time divers and fishermen who hang out at the docks. I fished with them, got to know them. We seemed to bond because of our shared love of the sea and because as a child I swam and fished and collected shells in Grayrocks Bay. I mentioned the rumors I'd heard and asked them who they thought was capable of stealing American treasures."

"Who did they suspect?" Lilli asked.

"Their unanimous opinion? Money-hungry Ron Larson, and probably his low-life friends the Bond brothers too. Miko and I visited local bars. Sure enough, it turned out that the Bond brothers had been bragging that they were being paid big bucks to squelch curiosity and keep people away from the dive site."

Lilli remembered that the artist Mia's friend, Doug, had overheard rumors in a beach bar. He had named the Bond brothers too. She wondered how many people had heard about the treasures by now. Quite a few, she figured, since news seemed to travel along the docks and through the fish camps as fast as hungry fish gobbled chum. She looked apprehensively at the drainage grate. How many of those people would come looking for the treasures and how?

Dr. Ellison interrupted Lilli's thoughts. "Next piece of the puzzle fell into place when I saw Ron Larson talking to Mark Mastriano, the wine expert. Obviously, Mark was valuable because he could verify the authenticity of Jefferson's wine. The final missing piece was where they planned to hide the treasures. Mark again. He had knowledge of the tavern's every nook and cranny. Thanks to Miko, we discovered that Mark planned to hide the wine and salvaged goods in the secret vault until he could make arrangements. He planned to act as a middle man between agents and buyers on the black market, no questions asked. That's how the wine would be disposed of."

She gently tucked a quilt around the first bell. "I had the dock guys keep their eyes on Ron, Mark, and the Bond brothers. They called me when those four creeps made a move, I called Miko and, well, you can figure the rest. That brings you up to date, except for the snorkel guy. I don't know how he fits into the puzzle."

"Well done," Dr. Winfield piped up. "Now while we're waiting for security, let's document everything we can about the bells."

"Good idea," Dr. Ellison said, and began rewrapping the second bell in its quilt.

The door at the top of the stairs slammed open. Hank charged onto the landing and hooted, "The perps are now cooling their heels in jail." Holding onto the banister, he huffed and puffed his way down, but stopped midway when he saw the bells. "What have you got there?" he said, his eyes wide with curiosity as he continued to the bottom step.

Dr. Ellison quickly explained.

"Old Tom Jefferson would jump for joy if he knew his bells were safe in Grayrocks after all these years! Yes, sir." Hank whistled through his teeth. "Anybody want to hear what happened when we booked those thieves into our cozy little jail?" Without waiting for an answer, he plowed on, "They ratted out each other, hoping for a deal."

"What did you find out?" Lilli asked.

"Lots of good stuff." Hank chuckled. "Frank Bond was the guy who tried to break into your Bronco in Gram's parking lot. Larson admitted he told the Bond brothers that the treasure was hidden in Silas' shop, and that probably the best place to begin their search was inside the figureheads, Silas' favorite items. That's why the brothers took the three figureheads to Big Creek Woods and smashed them open. They were certain they'd find the treasure, whatever it was, but hoo-boy!" Hank slapped his knee. "They were wrong."

"I'm guessing Larson scuttled Doug's boat and tried to kill him," Lilli said.

"Right," Hank said. "But Larson said he only wanted to scare him off. I believe him. If he were a cold-blooded murderer, he would have killed Doug outright." Hank tapped his watch. "The jailbirds are catching their second wind while I come here and see about this grate that Officer Lansing mentioned."

He strode to the center of the floor, shone his flashlight at the grate, and peered into the opening. "Officer Lansing's our expert swimmer and he's a certified diver. A real snorkeling nut. We always use him in cases like this. He's getting his gear. He'll be here soon."

Hank killed his flashlight beam. "I've got a team looking for the snorkel guy and how he got in there, if that's where he was hiding. They're looking for any other divers that might have been working with him. The rest of my men are staying put until these bells and the wine and anything else that turns up is taken to a safe place."

Officer Lansing, wearing a diving suit and carrying snorkel equipment, hurried down the stairs, followed by another officer Lilli didn't know by name. Officer Lansing had a knife strapped to his thigh. "Chief," he exclaimed, "We found an opening near the base of the tavern, hidden behind a bunch of rocks. Water rushes in at high tide." He tugged on his swim fins. "The opening is large enough for a person to swim through. A strong swimmer could swim the channel that leads to the area beneath the wine cellar. Right here." He tapped his fin on the concrete floor. "I'm going to find out for sure. The rest of our team is at the other end by the rocks, with flashlights and lanterns."

The other officer hooked a line on Lansing. "Okay," he said. "You're good to go."

Officer Lansing pulled the grate aside. "I'm going down."

"Don't let the sharks take a bite out of your skinny butt," Hank teased.

Lilli heard the catch in his throat. She figured he was worried about Lansing.

"Geronimo!" Lansing shouted and jumped in.

"Geronimo was Apache, not Montauk," Hank called after Lansing.

A funnel of water shot up and splashed onto Hank's shoes.

"Lansing's a good man. He'll be fine," Hank said, stepping away from the puddle, and Lilli thought he was reassuring himself as much as everyone else.

Hank turned to Lilli. "Bud and Gram are waiting to take you back to your car. Get some sleep. Tomorrow's another day."

Lilli almost detected a bit of affection from Hank. Maybe the fatigue that had been building up all day had finally hit her. All she wanted to do was fall into bed and forget about murders and theft. Nothing would stop her from doing that.

Chapter Twenty-eight

Hank switched on his flashlight and gripped his Glock. As he walked Lilli toward Bud's VW in the tavern parking lot, he looked left, right, and over both shoulders, his beady eyes peering into the darkness beyond the beam of light. Ahead, beneath low tree branches, headlights flashed. Gram opened the car door, thrust out her arms, and hugged Lilli. "Thank God you're safe," she said and patted Lilli's back. "You sure have a way of frazzling our nerves."

"Come on, Margaret," Bud said with a chuckle. "You and I frazzled each other's nerves long before Lilli came to town."

"The three of you better go straight to Baywatch Inn," Hank said as Lilli ducked into the back seat. "Whoever is running around here in a wet suit might have seen your car. Your license plate too. Southold is loaning me several officers to keep an eye on all of you who were here at the tavern. Lilli"—he poked his head into the back seat—"take pity on my poor heart and don't leave the inn until all the bad guys are rounded up."

He touched two fingers to the brim of his hat and raised them toward Bud and Gram. "I've got to see what's happening with my officers. And then it's back to the jail for me. I'm hoping my quartet of canaries will sing a second verse."

Bud backed his VW away from Hank.

"We didn't learn anything from the police radio," Gram said and jerked forward as Bud roared out of the parking lot. "Give us the scoop. What happened in there? And can you please tell me why Hank doesn't just say the thieves talked? Why is he using fancy talk about canaries singing?"

"Hank's just being cagey," Bud said and laughed at his own little joke.

"He really is for the birds," Gram said, and they all laughed.

Lilli knew they were releasing tension that had been building for hours. She leaned into the front seat and told them everything, playing up the drama for their enjoyment. Bud and Gram hung on her every word.

"We should hear soon who the diver is," Lilli said, holding on tightly as Bud took a corner. "And if he's in cahoots with the thieves or anyone else. I'm wondering if it's someone we know or a complete stranger."

"Here we are, back at the inn," Bud said. He pulled into his special parking spot next to Gram's. Both were marked with matching plaques that portrayed lovebirds. "Two of my buddies already picked up the keys to your Bronco, Lilli. They'll drive it here."

"Thanks, Bud," Lilli said, relieved that she didn't have to drive anywhere. She was so tired she could hardly hold her head up. There would be no shower tonight. No writing in her journal. No laptop entries. She would just roll into bed and sleep until the sun came up.

"We've got company," Bud whispered, as he stepped out of his VW. "Looks like Southold officers Mary and Marty hiding in the hedges, keeping the inn under surveillance."

"Good evening," Bud said, keeping his voice low. "Thanks for being here. We'll do our part inside, taking turns keeping watch."

"Just go inside and let us do our job," hissed a female voice.

"Yes, ma'am, Officer Mary," Bud whispered back.

A section of the hedge stirred. "And don't go checking the back door," Mary continued. "Two of Southold's finest have that covered."

"I'm just trying to do my civic duty," Bud whispered.

"Don't make me come out there and drag you inside," a male voice growled and another section of the hedge stirred.

"Got it, Officer Marty," Bud whispered, ushering Gram and Lilli toward the front door. "Guess I won't be winning any civic award," he whispered and stepped inside.

*   *   *

Alone in her room, Lilli made sure the window was locked and no one was hiding under the bed or in the closet. Finally, she slid beneath the crisp, cool sheets. She hoped and prayed that Hank and his officers had already captured the diver and that every danger had passed. She was thankful that Bud was sitting outside her door and that Gram was patrolling the hallway. Poor Gram. What a tightrope she walked. She tried not to scare guests with talk of a murderer on the loose in Grayrocks. But, concerned about her guests' safety, she warned them to stay put for the night and lock their windows.

Lilli rolled onto her side. Her eyelids drooped as she peered at the window and caught glimpses of moonlight flickering between the leafy branches of a maple tree. Her eyelids grew heavier. She didn't even realize she'd fallen asleep until muffled sounds that seemed to come from far away awakened her.

In the dim moonlight, she didn't see anything suspicious. She clenched her teeth and sealed her lips so she wouldn't scream if a branch brushed against the window or a neighbor's dog barked. She didn't want to scare Gram and Bud with a false-alarm cry for help.

What was that? She thought something moved at the window. Could that be a man's hand at the window? No, not here on the second floor. She blinked and looked again. She must be seeing things.

Her eyelids grew heavy.

She fell into a deep sleep.

A noise, close to her, jolted her awake. A presence hovered over her. The stale smell of brine stung her nostrils. She heard a sharp inhaling breath. Before she could scream, a man's hand squeezed her mouth shut. His other hand pushed her down on the bed.

Quickly he pinned her arms, torso, and legs to the bed with his body. She looked into the cold vacant eyes of Chuck Matthison. His face was smeared with black polish. His dark ski cap and warm-ups served as camouflage.

"You couldn't let things be," he hissed, and his warm breath slithered across her face. "People like you took my grandfather and father away from me. You won't take the treasures they left me."

Lilli saw the glint of a knife blade in his hand.

She tried to struggle free and call for help, but his hand covered her mouth and nose.

He flashed his knife before her eyes. "See what I have in store for you, Lilli Masters?"

Lilli's eyes filled with terror. Her lungs burned. She twisted her head to the right. He jerked it back and pressed down harder. He brought his face closer. His mouth formed a tight grim line.

"I've got a busy night ahead of me," he snarled. "You're the first of the troublemakers, stealing my treasures."

His voice began to fade. A wave of darkness passed over Lilli. She couldn't breathe. A few more seconds and she would black out. She saw the blade of the knife glisten as he lifted it high, ready to strike.

What could she do? *Think. Think.*

Raising the knife even higher, Chuck rolled partly off her. That split second gave Lilli the chance to act. She rammed her elbow into Chuck's gut. He fell back, letting out a cry of pain and surprise. His hand slid away from her mouth.

"Help!" Lilli screamed, jumping out of bed and backing away from Chuck Matthison. "Bud, Gram, help me!"

Lilli's door banged open.

"He's got a knife," Lilli cried.

Officers Mary and Marty, guns drawn and flashlights flashing, brushed past Gram and burst into the room. Gram and Bud peeked over the officers' shoulders.

Chuck Matthison bolted toward the window.

"Stop or die right here!" shouted Officer Mary.

"Drop the knife!" shouted Officer Marty. "On your knees, scumbag. Hands on your head."

"Forget the back door," Officer Mary commanded into the phone attached to her shirt collar. "Get up here to room 210, ASAP." She looked at Lilli. "You okay?"

"I will be," Lilli said, still trembling.

Chuck crouched low and jabbed the knife at Officer Marty. This way, that way, again and again, the knife flashed. Officer Marty dodged left, then right, left and right, then knocked the knife to the floor and yanked Chuck's arm behind his back. In a few brief seconds, the officers had handcuffed Chuck and were accompanying him out of the room. Bud and Gram hovered protectively near Lilli in the hallway.

As Chuck was led past, he stopped and glared at Lilli. "They say my grandfather died of a heart attack." He spat the words. "They're wrong. People prying, humiliating him. That's what killed him. People like you."

The officers dragged Chuck away. Only then did Lilli realize that he was wearing a gold ring with crossed swords.

He called over his shoulder, "They killed him as sure as if they'd shoved a knife into his heart. You're just like them. You're taking what's mine."

"Save it for the trial," Officer Marty said. He and Officer Mary helped hustle Chuck down the stairs.

Lilli heard the patrol car start up. Shaking, she stumbled to her room and looked at the window that Chuck had somehow managed to open. The maple branches danced lightly in the breeze as though they'd never felt the weight of a man only minutes before. She leaned against the window sill and watched Chuck Matthison in the backseat of the patrol car on his way to jail. He looked up toward her room. The moonlight glinted off his handcuffs.

It's finally over, Lilli thought. She turned toward Bud and Gram and collapsed into their arms, exhaling her fear. Sobbing, she welcomed the warmth of their sheltering embrace.

"That was close," Lilli said between sobs, remembering the knife, mere inches from her body, ready to plunge into her.

"Too close," Gram said, drawing Lilli to her side. "Come on, a cup of hot cocoa is just what you need."

If only cocoa would erase the sorrow caused by Chuck's murders, the terror brought on by his crazed sense of justice, Lilli thought. *If only . . .* She couldn't even finish her thought. She just wanted to sleep. Glorious, heavenly sleep.

Chapter Twenty-nine

Lilli awoke with a start and sat bolt upright in bed. She remembered Chuck holding a knife over her, ready to strike. In this room. In this very bed.

Sobbing and blinking at the bright sunshine that streamed into the room, Lilli stumbled to the bathroom and splashed water on her face. Glancing at the mirror, she saw red swollen eyes, blotchy skin, and damp curls matted to her neck. She tried to relax, to return to the normal life she had once enjoyed before a murderer hunted her down and tried to kill her. But she couldn't defuse her terror or stop her tears from flowing. She was suddenly afraid to be alone.

A soft knock came at the door. "Lilli, it's Gram. Come on out. Bud and I are having brunch in my kitchen. I've got blueberry muffins, fresh fruit, and your favorite chamomile tea."

Lilli opened the door. "That sounds wonderful," she said between sniffles.

"The muffins won't last long," Bud called from the kitchen. "Margaret is devouring them!"

"Am not," Gram said, steering Lilli toward the kitchen.

"Don't believe her," Bud called out.

"Lilli, Hank asked me to call him when you were up and about. Let's use my kitchen phone, and you can get comfortable at the table."

"Good morning, sleepyhead," Hank began as if this were an ordinary morning following an uneventful night. "This place is hopping. Whoo-ee! People tripping over each other. Silas' correspondence and the Matthison family documents spread everywhere. Laptops, cell phones, iPods, a total tech world. We know you're curious, but we don't want you down here, adding to the confusion. Dr. Ellison is happy as a clam with some newfangled maritime theories. Dr. Winfield plans to send along the highlights of a preliminary report that this bunch of eggheads is writing. *Preliminary* to them means 'detailed.' Stay close to Gram's fax machine and don't let it go into overload."

Hank sure was cheerful, thought Lilli. But when he signed off with "Good-bye, rest easy, Chuck had no accomplices," she heard the fatigue in his voice.

As Gram and Lilli helped themselves to seconds, Bud settled back in his chair. "Lilli, would you like me to share Dr. Ellison's information?"

"That would be nice," Lilli said, squeezing a lemon slice into her tea.

Bud shifted to the edge his chair. "You already know Jefferson's *Victory* sank near Montauk Point in 1789 and salvers brought most of the cargo to shore. Here's the new stuff. Deals were struck. Money exchanged hands. A wealthy shipbuilder from Grayrocks scooped up most of the salvaged goods. Guess what was included?"

"My guess," Lilli said with a wan smile, "would be the Jeffersonian Bells and Jefferson's French wine."

"Right. Two hundred fifty of the three hundred bottles. The bells and wine—Dr. Ellison is calling that combo the Jeffersonian Treasures—passed down through the salver's family. When the economy tanked in the early twentieth century, the family sold the treasures. Guess who bought them?"

"Would that happen to be Samuel Matthison, the tavern architect?" Lilli asked coyly.

"Right again," Bud said. "It was all done hush-hush. The treasures passed down through the family and ended up with Chuck."

At the mention of Chuck's name, Lilli cringed.

"On a happier note," Gram said, "Dr. Ellison and Dr. Winfield believe the Jefferson-Washington correspondence will be entrusted to them and eventually placed in a museum. They want Silas credited with finding and preserving the correspondence. They want you, Lilli, and Hank thanked for seeing that it got into the right hands."

Lilli dropped the muffin she was holding. "Wow!" was all she managed to say.

Gram set another muffin on Lilli's plate. "Hank and his officers found Silas' folders in Chuck's home."

Lilli's curiosity revved up. "What was in those folders?"

"What you might expect. Lots of details about Jefferson's ships, manifest, and routes." Gram nudged the country fresh butter toward Lilli. "But Dr. Ellison was thrilled with Silas' maritime maps of the North Fork dating from the late 1700s up to the present. She's jumping for joy. She's going to make sure Silas is recognized for finding the maps."

Gram's eyes twinkled. "Those maps tell how Jefferson's wine remained undetected for centuries."

Lilli set down her mug of tea. "I can't wait to hear this."

"You, curious?" Gram patted Lilli's hand. "First off, Dr. Ellison reminded me that Grayrocks once was famous for its wharves. It was a port of call for ships loaded with goods from the Caribbean. Then she took me back to the days when Grayrocks was a hub of shipbuilding activity, especially whaling ships. And she had lots of facts from both world wars about the hundreds of ships built and launched in Grayrocks. Dr. Ellison's a sweetie, but she does go on. Anyway, her point was that Grayocks' harbor was much deeper in the old days, deep enough to accommodate such big ships."

"Gram, I'm not sure where this is going."

"Why, the third fork, of course. Jefferson's crates of wine that didn't get salvaged? As Silas figured, they sank, got caught in the third fork's nooks and crannies, and broke free. Dr. Ellison is convinced the crates dropped deeper and deeper as they tumbled into Grayrocks Harbor and finally got covered over in layers and layers of muck. There the wine sat, weighed down, hidden—"

Bud cut in, "Grayrockers have been fishing and swimming, even snorkeling, over that wine and never knew it was there."

"Thank you, Bud," Gram said. "Dr. Ellison figures that over the years the docks were repaired and replaced, and new ones were built nearby. Dr. Ellison plans to investigate possibilities—construction, hurricanes, drilling, newfangled diving equipment, what have you— to explain what eventually dislodged the wine."

Lilli was still digesting all that information when Bud jumped in. "Some more information about Silas has come to light. Hank said fingerprints and footprints place Chuck outside Silas' shop, probably when you and Silas were inside discussing the figureheads, and the important folders were on Silas' counter."

"Am I right?" Lilli asked. "Chuck had already murdered Dr. Reed and was coming after Silas and he was going to murder anyone he assumed had read Silas' folders?"

Gram began clearing away the dishes. "That's what Hank believes. He says the evidence will eventually prove it. Chuck lawyered up. He'll be convicted. You wait and see."

Bud gulped the last of his coffee. "Hank has pieced together lots of stuff, much of it very clever guesswork. It goes like this. After Chuck murdered both men, he went home and read the contents of Silas' folders. He became curious about the figureheads, probably expecting more folders, something. When he returned to Silas' shop to investigate, the figureheads were gone. The Bond brothers have confessed to stealing them."

He gulped his coffee and continued. "There's more. Mark Mastriano, that creepy wine expert, built the secret vault in the tavern's wine cellar in case he ever struck it rich and needed a hiding place. On a sad note, the idea for the vault's secret knothole-peephole came from Silas himself. He often described the hidden joys of woodworking to tourists and locals in his shop." Bud's voice cracked. "Word spread. Ideas took wing."

Morning turned into afternoon. Lilli tried to stay calm by keeping herself busy. She jotted down notes for her magazine articles while she waited for the written report to arrive via fax. She had already spoken to Miko, Elena, and Dr. Whitfield. They were concerned about her. They said they had worked through the night with a criminal psychiatrist, Grayrocks and Southold officers, the forensics team, and their own colleagues, who stood by on conference calls.

Lilli willed herself to write first drafts for her articles, but kept her eye on the fax machine. Finally, it buzzed. She picked up the page and read Dr. Winfield's first words. *Lilli, this should fill in some of the missing pieces for you. The first part is from the thieves' confessions.* Lilli lowered herself to the floor and sat cross-legged as she read.

*Several weeks before the history conference began, Chuck re-
turned home from a business trip, discovered his Dobermans
asleep and the Jeffersonian Treasures gone. Ron, the diver and
his sidekick, Mark Mastriano, the tavern's wine expert, confessed that they had put sleeping pills in the Dobermans' food
and, with the Bond brothers' help, had stolen the wine. They
were curious about the other items in the locked room, especially the three trunks that held the Jeffersonian Bells. Pressed
for time, they didn't open the trunks, but guessed from the
weight that they might contain gold. They temporarily transported the wine and trunks to a rundown warehouse near the
docks. They planned to move everything to the tavern by boat
under the cover of darkness as soon as Mark gave the go-
ahead.*

The next page landed in the tray and Lilli read on.

*Lilli, this next part is speculative, based on Chuck's frenzied
ranting. He did not report the theft, probably because in his
twisted mind this was Matthison family business, not a police
matter. A secondary reason: He didn't want the theft publi-
cized because he didn't want hoards of people rushing to
Grayrocks to search for his treasures. While the treasures sat in
the warehouse, Chuck desperately ran down every lead imagi-
nable.*

*He heard the rumors circulating along the docks, unwisely
let slip by Silas' buddies that wine lay somewhere in the bay between Montauk and Grayrocks and that Silas and Dr. Reed
were going to investigate. They blabbed that Silas had put his
nautical observations in folders. Chuck, probably losing touch
with reality, became convinced that Silas and Dr. Reed had
masterminded the theft of his treasures. If so, then it's proba-
ble that Chuck confronted his so-called enemies, murdered
them without discovering where his treasures were, and stole
the folders to see what they might reveal. He vowed to hunt
down whoever stole from him. Fortunately, the police stopped
him before he took another innocent life.*

"Poor Silas," Bud said. "And poor Grayrocks. We lost our unofficial historian."

"And my favorite armchair adventurer," Gram said, wiping away her tears.

The enormity of the murders overwhelmed Bud, Gram, and Lilli. They sat in silence. Gram finally stood up. "If Silas were here, he would say 'Get to work and put a smile on your face.' And that's what I intend to do. Come on, Bud. Help me with my inventory."

After Gram and Bud went downstairs, Lilli sat back, letting the information wash over her like the waves at Montauk Cove. She felt sad for Chuck's victims, Dr. Reed and Silas Jones, and lucky to be alive.

Downstairs, the front door slammed. Gram and Bud's voices traveled up the stairs.

"Lilli," hooted Gram. "There's someone here to see you."

Who could that be, Lilli wondered.

"Love is in the air," Gram sang out.

"What else is new?" Bud said and Gram giggled.

"Lilli?" Zack Faraday called out.

Zack? At the sound of Zack's husky voice, Lilli's knees nearly buckled. *Play hard to get,* she told herself.

Hurried footsteps came up the stairs.

Lilli knew her overactive imagination had convinced her that Zack and Isabella were in love. She knew in her heart that Zack loved her, not Isabella, but she needed to hear that from him.

Lilli took one look at Zack and dashed into his arms. His kisses were so thrilling, his embrace so strong, the electricity that always flashed between them so powerful. And that lopsided grin was so endearing. He was just plain irresistible. She loved him with all her heart. But—

Lilli pulled away. "About Isabella—"

"I can explain if you'd give me half a chance," Zack said.

"I'm listening." How could she deny or doubt him after such a greeting? His eyes were so appealing, so sincere.

"Okay," Zack said. "You know that Isabella's brother is my partner."

Lilli nodded.

"We were on a stakeout. He got out of the car to grab us some coffee. Shots were fired. He took a bullet to the shoulder. I pulled him into the car and managed to get away. Isabella insisted I saved her brother's life. When you saw us, Isabella was thanking me. That's all. Isabella has her own guy, and I have . . . you." He shifted to his other foot. "I wish I had you. I love you, Lilli."

Lilli frowned. "So when I saw the two of you together, Isabella was surprising you with those kisses."

"Yes."

"You did nothing to encourage her."

"Nothing." His eyes were so imploring. "Lilli, I wish we'd had this conversation sooner."

"Me too."

He swept her into her arms, kissed her long and tenderly, and this time she didn't pull away.

Lilli looked at Zack with love in her eyes. "How about a walk on the beach? I have so much to tell you."

Author's Note

When a contemporary novel delves into historical events, readers often wish to know which parts are factual and which are fictional. *The Treasures of Montauk Cove* is loosely based on the fact that when the French Revolution erupted, Thomas Jefferson, then ambassador to France, returned to America on board the ship *Clermont*. Among his belongings were approximately three hundred bottles of fine wine, chosen for his extensive wine cellar at home. He arrived safely. So did the wine.

From additional research, this amazing bit of information, possibly legend, caught my eye: When Thomas Jefferson visited Suffolk County, he went horseback riding near the eastern tip of Long Island. Amazing because that was close to where I had placed the fictional seaside resort town of Grayrocks—famous for its beaches and vineyards—in two of my previous mysteries.

My imagination soared. What if Thomas Jefferson had a second ship, also loaded with wine, sailing later that same day? What if that ship blew off course and sank in the rugged open waters near Montauk Point, Long Island? What if some of the sunken cargo surfaced many years later in Grayrocks Bay?

The plot began to take shape at a wine lecture I attended, where a sommelier referred to certain bottles of rare old wine as "liquid gold." She estimated that a crate of wine salvaged from a sunken ship could be worth more than a pirate's chest overflowing with gold coins. She added that a single bottle of rare wine often brings thousands of dollars at auction houses and on the black market. She stated that the most sought-after wines are those connected to a famous person, such as Thomas Jefferson, or a famous event, such as the sinking of the *Titanic*.

I immediately envisioned my story developing around modern-day pirates. They would pop up in Grayrocks Bay right along with the wine bottles. Money-hungry scoundrels, they would sell wine salvaged from a shipwreck to the highest bidder, with no concern for any historical artifacts on board.

However, an unanswered question remained: What could have trapped the wine in Grayrocks Bay for more than two hundred years without detection? From the mountains of research materials, Long Island's Third Fork emerged. According to speculation on a Web site, such a fork, most likely a glacial deposit, existed near Montauk thousands of years ago until it broke up and sank to the ocean floor, where it eroded. With a few strokes of the computer keys, I reassembled the theoretical fork, moved it away from Montauk toward Grayrocks, and propelled it forward in time.

Other liberties with history were also taken. The correspondence between Jefferson and Washington came from my imagination. However, correspondence between the two men does exist. The originals guided my choice of words and style. The Jefferson Bells are also an invention. They do not exist. I wish they did. I've grown quite fond of them.

In many instances there was no need to alter the facts because they were so helpful in shaping the story. This is especially true regarding the information about wine, sunken ships, and salvaging efforts.

The Treasures of Montauk Cove is a work of fiction that blends facts, legends, imaginative what-ifs, and speculative theories. My hope is that the blend resulted in a satisfying story.